The Ravenwood Conspiracy

MICHAEL SIVERLING

2024, TWB Press
https://www.twbpress.com

The Ravenwood Conspiracy
Copyright © 2024 by Michael Siverling

Edited by Terry Wright

Cover Art by Terry Wright

ISBN: 978-1-959768-51-7

Chapter One:

I'd just stepped into the lobby of the Fulton Theater at intermission. I was there to watch a play drawn from Bram Stoker's works with a Hungarian actor playing the part of the vampire when I heard a pageboy shout out, "Call for Stephen Locke." I traded a tip for a note that held those three little words I loathed to read: 'Telephone at once'.

Miss Nadia Ravenwood was about to spoil my evening.

Mind you, it's my job. I'd worked for her father, Nicholas Ravenwood, ever since he brought me back from Russia, where I'd been a young and thoroughly disillusioned volunteer with the American Expeditionary Force, and he a freelance spy who plied his trade all over the world. He took me with him to New York City where he established himself as an effective and discreet problem solver for rich and influential people who happen to get themselves into a spot of trouble. Our arrangement worked well and prosperously until a couple of years ago when Nicholas disappeared and was suddenly replaced by his daughter, Nadia. I was quickly convinced she had the skills and dangerous abilities to take over the family business. In other words, she terrified me.

I found a telephone booth and placed a call to her West Side Brownstone residence. When the operator connected us, Nadia said, "Where are you now?"

"Broadway theater district."

"I'll pick you up in front of the Algonquin." And with

that, she rang off.

I made a brisk walk along the avenues under the shifting, neon-lit signage, wondering if I'd make the short distance before Miss Ravenwood came roaring up in her automobile, hoping traffic would keep her speed down to something less than a runaway locomotive. She didn't keep me waiting long; I spied her gold and black Rickenbacker coupe charging down the street. I was barely aboard before Miss Ravenwood engaged her one hundred motorized horses and thrust us into Times Square like a Roman chariot race. "Where are we off for tonight?"

"Chinatown," she said, not taking her eyes off the street. "We have a runaway heir to collect."

I stole a look at her face in profile. It's a nice view: Midnight black, bobbed hair that matches the ebony feather affixed to her scarlet cloche cap and fur-trimmed coat. She had bold but beautifully balanced features and large dark eyes that could flash fire with a single glance. This I knew from regrettable experience. Her voice, while melodic, carried a slight, unidentifiable accent when she spoke, the result of growing up abroad in various countries. Like myself, she was born roughly at the same time as this new Century. "Which lost lamb are we after tonight?"

"Richard Bowen."

I was sorry to hear that. Richard fought in the War, as I did, only he left part of his leg behind. He wasn't made an invalid in battle, mind you, but by an infection caused by the filthy, rat infested trenches we were forced to live in. I counted him as honorably wounded as any who took a bullet or bayonet, but others didn't quite see it that way, including himself. This wasn't the first time Nadia Ravenwood and I were called to find and fetch him from whatever speakeasy, boudoir or backroom gambling hall he found himself.

I was thrown over to my left as Nadia swerved to pass a vehicle who dared go the speed limit. "Chinatown, eh? Is it too much to hope that he's just out for some chop suey?"

"Word from his brother is he'll be after opium again."

And so we were off for a late night excursion to Chinatown. By and large, the place was pretty tame now, and all the lurid tales of white slavers and Tong wars were just that, except during tourist season, when the locals made a bit of coin engaging in theatrical reenactments for the suckers who came for the tours of the exotic fleshpots. Though events like the Chinese Theater Massacre were well over two decades behind us, there was still plenty of actual danger to be avoided.

We eventually made it to Mott Street, the main thoroughfare of Chinatown, marked by its horizontal Chinese lettered signs, red paper lanterns, and lovely temples that the ignorant refer to as *Joss Houses*. We proceeded to the intersecting corner of Pell Street, the so called *Bloody Angle* that'd seen its share of the Tong battles. Here, Miss Ravenwood brought her mechanical beast to a stop. "From what I hear, we're close. Time to move on foot."

The only trouble I expected as I set out this evening was perhaps some difficulty getting a cab after the show, and had therefore left my revolver at home. After we exited the Rickenbacker, I went to the tapered trunk and retrieved the small black-leather valise we refer to as the 'bag of trouble'. Among the burglary tools we kept for our less than legal forays was a slim Belgium Browning .32 automatic that once belonged to Nadia's father. I checked it over and found it ready for use.

"Bring a flashlight," Nadia added.

We walked a short distance past men, some who wore traditional Chinese attire with their hair in a queue and others who embraced more traditional Western dress, until we came upon a diminutive woman in a plain wool overcoat and wide-brimmed hat at the corner of Doyers Street.

Nadia made a formal bow with the woman, after which they exchanged a warm handclasp. "Thank you for coming out tonight, Doctor."

"I am glad to help." The woman's English was flawless. "From what the congregation tells me, your wayward tourists should be upstairs over the shop next door. You're supposed to say, "John from Shanghai" sent you."

"Thank you, Doctor Lee."

The woman looked me over. "You two be careful. You're interfering in some dangerous people's business."

We waited as the woman made her way out of sight past the glow of the streetlamps. Nadia had expanded on her father's secret army of eyes and ears, from servants who wanted to make some extra money, to respected professionals who needed us to keep their embarrassing secrets under wraps, to people who simply wanted to help others. This lady was new to me, but she appeared to fall into the last category. "Who, may I ask, is the charming Doctor Lee?"

"Mabel Ping Hua Lee is a brilliant woman who received her doctorate from Columbia. She works toward achieving legal rights for women, even though in this country, she's not even considered a citizen." Nadia, with her ire now stoked over the thought of the unfairness of her friend's situation, abruptly turned and marched down the darkened street.

I quickly followed, wondering who might wind up the recipient of her recently ignited anger.

Chapter Two:

The shop on the narrow street was small and crowded with exotic porcelain figurines and brass furnishings. An imperious picture of Chinese Royalty embossed on a silkscreen loomed from the back wall amidst the aroma of jasmine incense. Seated on low stools were a pair of gentlemen: one dressed traditionally with a long braid of hair trailing from under a skullcap while the other wore a black tunic, loose trousers, and a western-style hat. As we entered the shop, Nadia Ravenwood took my hand and swayed, as if unsteady on her feet as she approached them with a lopsided smile on her face. "Uh, hi. John? From Shanghai? Is that right?"

The man in black shook his head slightly as he rose from the stool, holding out both hands with fingers spread. "Ten."

I decided to jump into the act. "Ten? American dollars? Really?"

"Just pay the man," Nadia said with a touch of impatience.

I groused as I handed over the money, then the other Chinese gentleman got off his stool and gestured for us to follow him to the back. There he spread a curtain, revealing a sharply slanted set of stairs. As we passed, the man called up a phrase I didn't understand.

When we reached the halfway point, Nadia whispered, "I don't think he liked the look of you. I heard him use the Cantonese phrase for *trouble*."

"For that, see if I leave a tip," I whispered back. I

wasn't surprised Nadia understood the man. Her father spoke seven languages, and I've personally heard her curse in at least that many. But my banter was cover for my tightening nerves as I felt the reassuring weight of the pistol in my overcoat pocket. As we climbed, the smell of the incense was soon overpowered by the sickly stench of burnt opium, and as we reached the top, a creaking door swung open, revealing a tableau of drug-addled debauchery.

This was no glamorous, exotic *Den of Iniquity*; this was a sad, tawdry sprawl of people lying about on a frayed carpet and threadbare pillows amidst crates that held candles that shed a paltry light over the scene, where a pair of watchfully alert men stayed in the background as a woman in a shabby robe slowly gathered up the opium pipes and gear used to smoke the poisonous stuff.

There were three bodies strung out on the floor, two men and a woman, all dressed in evening clothes. One man was stretched out as if sunning himself, while the other was a light-haired gentleman with wire-rimmed glasses, wrapped in the arms of the woman, who whispered into his ear as he stared off dreamily. That one was our man.

Nadia called out sharply, "Richard!"

It was the woman who roused. She had large dark-rimmed eyes and wore a gold-leaf adorned turban that gave her a faux Eastern look. Her face twisted in annoyance. "What do you want?"

I fired the beam of the flashlight, and she recoiled as if I'd slapped her. In the glare, I saw her eyes were a deep emerald green. "It's time for Richard to come home."

The other man leapt up from the floor, showing no trace of drug impairment. He wore a white eye patch across a face flushed with anger. "He's not going anywhere."

His mistake was trying to move past Miss Ravenwood

to get to me, thinking I was the threat. A mistake he was made to painfully regret. Nadia spun her arm in a fast wheel that ended with her fist colliding with the man's stomach, causing him to blow out all his air, and he staggered backwards, tripping over Richard to crash to the floor. In the beam of my flashlight I saw that Nadia had donned a memento of her misspent youth, one of a pair she'd dubbed her 'little sisters', an ornately engraved knuckleduster.

Her action triggered a response from the lurking guards, who leapt out of their corners, shouting at the top of their lungs as they brandished weapons: a club and wickedly carved knife.

I showed off the gun in my other hand, and for the moment, the three of us silently agreed that bullets trumped knives and clubs in this particular game.

As I played Horatio at the Bridge, holding off the menacing hoard of two, Nadia was busy with Richard Bowen. I was just starting to wonder how we were going to get his supine body away when she simply grabbed his hands and dragged him toward the stairway, where she then allowed the steep incline to move him along. Judging from the thumping sounds his descent made, the poor soul was taking a beating that he'd feel later.

I eased my way down after them as the blonde, kneeling on the floor next to her fallen comrade, wailed like a banshee. I kept the pistol aimed toward the threat behind us, trusting Nadia to handle what would lie ahead. Knowing her, I wasn't worried. As I made my way past the curtains, I saw Nadia employing the other of her 'little sisters' to wave back the two gentlemen in the shop: her wickedly sharp, bone-handled push dagger.

She was shouting at the men in their own language, most likely with a string of curses, knowing her. Whether it was the threat of the knife blade or the fact that they were shocked at her linguistic ability, they gave ground, allowing me to get Richard Bowen lifted up in a clumsy fireman's carry. Thus Miss Ravenwood and I made our escape.

Soon, we had Bowen sprawled in the small back seat of the Rickenbacker and were speeding north out of Chinatown.

Chapter Three:

I had a lazy awakening in the bed of my room at Nadia Ravenwood's Brownstone. I keep my own apartment on Lexington Avenue, but last night ran late, as we had to deliver Mr. Richard Bowen to the somewhat loving arms of his family who lived over on Park Avenue. I found my robe and wandered out to the parlor to find Miss Ravenwood on her accustomed throne.

This parlor was like a museum in miniature, with exotic furnishings from all over the world: Chinese porcelain, Persian rugs, French chairs of exquisite craftsmanship, Indian silver tea service, Japanese silkscreen paintings, all and more were gathered together as a kind of Universal Exposition in one setting. Presiding over all was Nadia Ravenwood in her imperious high-backed chair under the portrait of her father, Nicholas Ravenwood. The artist truly caught his fierce, eagle-like face, and his coal black eyes that even now followed one around the room.

Nadia herself was sitting comfortably sideways, dressed in a Japanese kimono and Persian slippers as she finished off two of her pet weaknesses: Swiss chocolates and Turkish coffee. "Would you care for one?" She raised her demitasse in greeting.

"It's quicker than arsenic, I'm sure, but I think I'll stick with tea and toast for a start, if I may. Any word on our client from last night?"

Nadia rang a silver bell.

Miss Murphy, the maid, appeared. "Morning, Miss Nadia."

"Breakfast fit for your granny for Mr. Locke, please."
Then she turned back to me. "I thought we'd drop by the
Bowen mansion later. Did you notice anything odd about
our rescue mission last night?"

"Other than the fact the last two times we retrieved
Richard Bowen, he was with companions who literally left
him in the gutter? His playmates last night seemed fiercely
attached to him."

"And strangely sober."

"What are you suggesting?"

"That we see how Richard is doing, and maybe
discover why we had more trouble than usual last night."

"Prying into Henry's affairs might put us out of
business."

"Richard's brother..." She raised a delicate eyebrow.
"His goose eggs aren't that golden. If he doesn't like
questions, he can always hire those clumsy thugs at
Pinkerton's."

When Miss Ravenwood was on the move, one could
only get out of her way or try to keep up. When I joined her
before setting out, I thought she must have dressed in a
hurry indeed; she forgot to affix her signature black feather
to the tight-brimmed ivory cloche hat she wore. Quicker
than I liked, she was driving us down to the mansions of
the rich and influential under a cloudy October sky. We
found our particular address: the cream colored manor
among an array of mansions, neatly arranged together like
ornate children's blocks and sized for a Greek God. We
proceeded to the front door, where Miss Ravenwood
presented her card to the butler. Ere long we heard the
voice of Henry Bowen, older brother of Richard, call out.
"Well, for God's sake, don't leave them outside where
anyone can see them."

Nadia and I applied our best poker playing

expressions as we were admitted in time to see Henry Bowen, darker of hair than his younger brother and with a face built for scowling, rush down the winding stairs. "What brings you by this morning? Didn't my man see to your payment?"

"Yes," Nadia replied. "We were concerned about your brother. How is Richard today?"

Henry Bowen stopped short, confusion stamped on his face. "How is Richard? He's an embarrassment, as usual. One that I pay you to keep under wraps."

"May we see him?"

Confusion was replaced by suspicion. "Why?"

"Because if we can discover what drives him to seek these, shall we say, diversions, then perhaps he'll cease them on his own."

Henry shook his head. "Ridiculous. He's a common hop head. Has been ever since he got back from that ridiculous war. It's his own damn fault."

"You're telling me that your own family physician won't prescribe pain medicine? Of any kind?"

It was an open secret, to those in the know, that rich people could get any kind of drugs they wanted, all with the blessings of a doctor with more concern for his lofty position as a physician to the wealthy and powerful than the actual wellbeing of his patients.

Henry looked away, perhaps a tad guilty. "Richard knows I'll give him whatever he needs. Why he chooses to drag his worthless carcass out of the house and humiliate himself is beyond me."

"Let me speak with him," Nadia said softly. "What harm can it do?"

Henry looked at her then nodded in resignation. "I'll have Oscar take you in. Let me know if you can see a way out of this mess."

Oscar, the butler, and a lady's maid arrived to assist us with our coats, hats, and Miss Ravenwood's handbag. When she removed her scarlet overcoat, I was surprised to see her attired in a simple long-sleeved day dress of cream-white and wearing a small ruby-red cross at her throat. Then it hit me: in her dress and hat she looked like a modern, idealized version of the nurses who tended to the wounded during the Great War.

Oscar, with measured tread, escorted us back through the house. "Mr. Richard keeps a room here on the ground floor." Eventually we reached a door off a wood-paneled library where Oscar knocked.

"Go away," Richard shouted.

Nadia reached out and opened the door, entered with me close at her heels, then she turned to the butler. "Thank you, Oscar, that will be all." And shut the door in his face.

The room was more of a chamber, with rich wood paneling like the library and a number of books strewn about. There was a tall window with the heavy drapes drawn shut, allowing in only a sliver of light and a slice of a view of an enclosed garden with a fountain. The air was stale with the aroma of too many cigarettes smoked in too small a place for too long a time. On the bed, where a set of crutches were close to hand, lay Richard Bowen, sprawled amongst pillows and clad in blue silk pajamas. The missing half of his right leg was quite in evidence as his pajamas were neatly tailored to enclose what remained.

He stared at us through his round eyeglass lenses. "Unless you're here to help me kill myself, then I'm afraid I'll have to ask you to leave." His voice came out flat and calm, as if he really meant it.

Chapter Four:

Nadia Ravenwood marched straight to the window covers and threw them aside, flooding the gloomy room with hazy, pearl-shaded light.

Richard Bowen winced.

She put on a stern face. "No more nonsense, please. We have business to discuss."

He coughed up a bitter laugh. "Business? You'll want my brother. I'm the useless one in the family."

Nadia sat on his bed, right next to the place where his leg would have been, and casually examined an open book lying there. "Norse Mythology," she muttered. "Interesting." She set it aside. "You've been making my associate and I a fair amount of money with your tantrums, but this game of hide and seek is getting tiresome, even at the rate we charge for your return."

Richard squinted at Nadia, then up at me. "You," he said slowly. "You're the ones who keep dragging me back here. Very well. How much for you to go away and leave me alone?"

"Nothing at all. All you have to do is quit acting like a petulant child."

He grunted, twisted about, and grabbed a cigarette from his nightstand. He winced a bit as he moved, probably a reaction to the drubbing he got when Nadia dragged him down the stairs like a sack of laundry.

I assisted him with a light as Nadia opened a window, allowing a wave of cold air to wash through the room.

"Hey. Close that up," he barked.

In the harsh light of day, Richard's hair was less the blond of a youth and more like the gray of a man aged beyond his years.

Nadia allowed the air to get a changeover before she obliged. "Suffocation is a slow way to go about the suicide business, and it's rude to try and take others along for the ride. You're no Egyptian Pharaoh, you know."

With ill mannered grace, he snuffed out his cigarette. "And you're no Angel of Mercy. Listen, if it's money you want, my brother controls all the family purse strings, so it does no good to waste time on me."

"I'm trying to save your life. What were you thinking when you went roving through Chinatown last night?"

He crossed his arms. "It was a bit of a celebration, if you must know."

"Celebration? What was the occasion?"

"Private matter." Richard turned his gaze on me. "You're not much for conversation." He tilted his head at Nadia. "This one not let you get a word in?"

"I can when one's needed. By the by, I hear you were *Over There*."

Richard's eyes narrowed. "26th Infantry, 2nd Brigade under Bullard. Made it as far as Saint Mihiel."

"Dagger Brigade, eh? I was sent to North Russia with the Polar Bears."

"Damn." Richard breathed then quickly looked to Nadia. "My pardon, Miss."

"Would you boys care to reminisce?"

Richard frowned bitterly. "We would not. But I have to ask you, sir...how did you feel when you first got back home?"

"Lost. But I was fortunate. I met a man who took me under his wing, gave me something to do."

"Something to do? I was completely adrift when I got

back, or what was left of me. And I was having a hard time of it." He looked away, weighing out his words, until he turned back to us. "But I've found my new path now."

Miss Ravenwood narrowed her dark eyes. "So your talk of suicide in lieu of saying hello to us was, what exactly, a ruse?"

"Forgive me. A reflex left over from a long, bad time. Frankly, I just said that to get rid of you."

"I see...and your newfound path, as you call it?"

He uncrossed his arms. "A private matter, as I said, but I can promise you there'll be no cause for you both to hound me further."

Miss Ravenwood and I exchanged looks, but before making our departure, Richard said, "By the way, you didn't happen to see where my walking stick wound up last night, did you?"

"Your walking stick?" I couldn't recall seeing one.

"Yes. Black lacquer wood, brass fittings...a raised lion's head on the finial? No?"

"Sorry," Nadia replied. "Perhaps your friends have it. If you let me know who they are, I could ask them."

A look of fear flickered across his face, an expression quickly shut down like the slamming of a window. "No. I'm certain it will turn up. Thank you and goodbye."

Nadia and I made our way forward until Oscar the butler found us. "Mr. Henry Bowen will see you now." We followed him upstairs to a lavishly appointed study with a massive mahogany desk.

Henry Bowen remained seated with his eyes on a letter in his hand. "What have you to report?" he asked without looking up.

Nadia quickly answered, "The job is done, for now. But I am quite certain you will call upon us again, for despite your brother's latest affirmations, I don't believe anything has really changed."

Henry shook his head and raised his eyes. "Actually, Miss Ravenwood, I shall be pursuing other remedies for my brother's condition, and as such shall no longer require your services."

If Nadia was surprised at the news, her face didn't show it. "Have it your way." She turned to me. "Come on, Stephen. Seems all our efforts are not appreciated around here."

We were stopped by a knock on the door and Oscar's entrance. He stood in the doorway with a stupefied look on his face.

Henry Bowen bristled. "Oscar? What is it now?"

"S-sir...eh..." Oscar stuttered and finally uttered the words: "The police are here."

Chapter Five:

T he announcement led to a frozen tableau: Henry Bowen's eyes opened wide in shock, as Nadia Ravenwood and I did our best to remain stock still, although the expression on Bowen's face threatened to tickle a burst of laughter out of me.

"What in God's name are the police doing here?"

"I had them come in the servant's entrance," Oscar added.

Nadia turned to Henry. "Well, you have problems to deal with I see, and as I am no longer employed by you, I'll leave you to deal with them."

Henry's eyes took on the look of a hunted beast. "Wait," he cried. "Miss Ravenwood, before you leave, would you be willing to assist me with the police?"

"Why would you want me to do that? We don't work for you any longer."

Henry waved his arms, flustered. "I have no experience with the police. I can only imagine Richard must have really done something awful this time. It seems I've been too hasty in dismissing you. Please. For his sake?"

Nadia let him dangle for a few moments, then: "Very well. Oscar, would you be so kind as to bring me my handbag?"

"Yes, ma'am."

"Thank you. Now, Henry, I suggest we meet your visitors and find out why they're here, shall we?"

Henry Bowen swallowed and nodded, hustled into his

suit jacket, and then led us to the stairs. As we wound our way down, I had a chance to get a look at the officers of the Law awaiting us in the foyer. One was a young dark-haired man in uniform, holding his cap smartly under one arm, while his partner, with wintery cold eyes, watched us descend. His hair and mustache were frosty white, and he wore a baggy brown suit. Once we reached the main floor, he took charge. "Good afternoon." His voice was rough and deceivingly pleasant. "I'm Detective McDonough from the 5th Precinct. We are here to see Mr. Richard Bowen."

The 5th Precinct handled the Chinatown beat, a fact I was certain wasn't lost on Nadia. Henry cast a sharp look back at her, and then addressed the detective. "I'm Henry Bowen, Richard's brother. May I ask what this is about?"

The Detective gave a smile that didn't touch his eyes. "It's a matter I must take up with him. Is he here?"

"Why don't we all gather somewhere more comfortable," Nadia said. "There's a nice library down the hall."

Detective McDonough glared at her. "And who may you be?"

"Nadia Ravenwood, and this is my associate, Mr. Stephen Locke."

McDonough looked more amused than annoyed. "What is your relationship to Richard Bowen?"

Nadia held up a finger as she received her handbag from Oscar then produced a silver card case, embossed with a Chinese Dragon.

I braced myself for what I knew would come next: shock and anger.

She handed Detective McDonough a card, and after a glance, he looked up, frowning. "So?"

Nadia smiled sweetly. "Turn it over, please."

I watched the detective's face droop as he read the

words aloud. "Please extend to the bearer all courtesy. It's signed by Joseph A. Warren, the Commissioner of Police." His hard expression didn't crack a bit as he handed the card back to her. "What do you want?"

"I suggest that my associate and I stay with Mr. Richard Bowen while you question him. That lovely library should do just fine. Oscar? Please assist Richard in joining us there."

She turned to Henry. "See that we aren't disturbed." Then she walked away, silently dismissing him and leaving him with a mouth agape in shock.

Detective McDonough ducked his head to muffle a growl, then followed after her, leaving the young officer and me to bring up the rear.

Detective McDonough took a stroll about the library, seeing everything and saying nothing. His young officer stood at the door. It wasn't long before Richard entered on crutches, wearing a royal blue robe. Displaying better manners than his brother, Richard indicated a chair for Miss Ravenwood to be seated, then he settled into his own while Detective McDonough and I shared a buttery-soft leather couch long enough to accommodate a couple more of us.

Richard Bowen lit a cigarette and blew smoke. "What can I do for you boys?"

"For the record, you are Richard Bowen, correct?"

"Yes."

The detective got straight to the point. "Do you know a young woman by the name of May Scott?"

Richard hesitated to answer, a bad sign when speaking with police. "Why do you ask?"

"Answer the question, sir."

"Yes. I know Miss May Scott."

"Who is she to you?"

"We've been friends since childhood. What's it to you?"

"When did you last see her?"

Richard took a long draw from his cigarette, contemplated the glowing ash, then: "Last night."

"Where?"

"I don't know. I was a bit inebriated. It's all a blur. Is she all right?"

"You tell us."

"I don't understand..." Richard stood on his only leg. "Is she in some kind of trouble?"

Detective McDonough's face turned coldly impassive. "You could say that. She's dead."

Chapter Six:

The silence was absolute.

All eyes were on Richard Bowen as he sat down, hand stopped midway to his lips with a cigarette that shook like a hovering insect. Finally, he uttered one word. "Dead?"

Detective McDonough pressed harder. "When, exactly, were you with her?"

"I...don't know, really. Last night, of course, but as to the time, it's all...lost to me."

I kept my eyes on Nadia, wondering if she was going to reveal the fact that we had custody of the unconscious Richard Bowen between the hours of 11:30 and half past midnight. The burning question was, who was May Scott, and was she the green-eyed vixen from the opium den? If so, I could attest to the fact she was quite vocal and very much alive when we left.

Nadia Ravenwood addressed Detective McDonough. "For the benefit of the rest of us, what did Miss May Scott looked like?"

McDonough nodded to Richard. "Care to do the honors?"

He took a final draw off his cigarette, burning it close to his fingers, and quickly stubbed it out. "She's about, oh, five foot two. Light brown hair that she keeps neat. Slender. Blue eyes."

I shrugged. *So much for the vixen...*

"What was she wearing when you saw her last?"

"Peach... It was a peach-colored gown."

"And where was she?"

"Where?"

Detective McDonough took a short breath, as if that would quell his impatience. "Where did you see her wearing the peach-colored gown?"

"We had dinner...at Henri's."

I knew that place was close by and many miles north of Chinatown. So far, so good.

"What time was dinner?"

"Roughly eight o'clock. We had a disagreement, didn't stay through the whole meal." Suddenly, he frowned, as if he just figured out where the detective was going with his questions. "Wait. You don't think I—"

"Did you?"

Richard sunk his face in his hands. "I last saw her at the restaurant. She was very much alive."

"When did you leave her?"

He looked up. "After the argument."

"What was it over?"

"She was worried about me, thought I hadn't been taking care of myself. I told her she was being ridiculous."

"So you killed her."

"No. Never!"

I about choked. The detective went for broke with that accusation.

"Then what *did* you do?"

"Nothing. She ran out. I paid the bill and saw her catch a taxi. She was mad, but she was fine, I swear. And I was pretty upset when I left."

"What time was that?"

"It must have been before nine."

"Where did you go?"

Richard ventured a look toward Miss Ravenwood. "Chinatown. It's all a bit hazy after that."

"Where in Chinatown?"

Richard shrugged.

I knew the answer...where we found him, but chose to remain mute. Miss Ravenwood seemed to be on the same page. Waiting.

Detective McDonough sighed. "So you have no idea why May Scott's body was found in Columbus Park?"

That was bad. I knew Columbus Park was right on the border of Chinatown, putting Richard in close proximity to the crime scene.

Richard Bowen's eyes were frozen wide open, his mouth was slack and made no sound, until he sighed and collapsed into himself, dropping his chin to his chest. "I don't understand." He quietly moaned.

"Mr. Bowen, do you have anything to add, anything you've left out of your statement?"

It took Richard a moment to raise his head. "No. Nothing. I didn't see her...not since she left the restaurant. I'm sure of it."

I caught Detective McDonough's arched eyebrows, as if there was something odd about Richard's last sentence. Could be the police knew more than the detective was letting on. He rose from the couch. "Mr. Bowen, I may have more questions for you...later, downtown. I would advise you not to leave Manhattan unless you clear it with me. Am I understood?"

Richard made a vague nod, then the Detective and his young officer took their leave.

The moment Oscar shut the door, Nadia turned to Richard, "What did you leave out?"

"What? Nothing."

Nadia knelt down to eye level with him. "What was your argument with May Scott really about?"

"She wanted me to stop seeing my new friends."

"The ones from the opium parlor last night?"

Richard shook as if suddenly doused with cold water. "No, wait. Look, it doesn't matter. I didn't kill May. I couldn't. I've got nothing to be afraid of."

Nadia Ravenwood stood up and stared down at him. "We can't help you if you won't be truthful with us. Now, just who were those people you were with last night?"

Richard looked up, face straining with defiance. "None of your business. Now, I would ask you to leave. I told you, I'm on a new path, so you two won't have to hound me anymore."

Nadia Ravenwood spun about and marched out of the library. I rose and caught Richard's eye. "I hope you're not being an idiot."

He coldly returned my stare, so I left, caught up with Nadia in the foyer where she was engaged in a heated conversation with Henry. "Your brother is determined to keep secrets."

I also caught sight of a small, hunched figure at the top of the winding staircase. Her hair was a cascade of light brown that tumbled to the shoulders of a blue and white ensemble fashioned like a sailor's uniform, complete with a matching bow in her hair. I thought she was middle ground of her teenage years. As she saw me notice her, she quickly put a finger to her lips, and I conspiratorially winked in return.

"Secrets may be his undoing," Nadia went on. "What do you know about his new friends?"

"Nothing." Henry shook his head. "I assumed he was with the usual gang of hangers-on, you know, the type who attach themselves to get a free ride. He's had more than his share of those *so-called* friends."

"Who is May Scott?"

"His girl. Or, she wants to be. God knows why she

keeps after him. I've told her my brother is a complete waste of time."

"Well, now she's dead."

There came a loud gasp from above, and as we all looked up, the girl at the top of the stairs stood with her fists to her mouth, turned and ran away.

"Mary," Henry called. Then, to us, "Damn it all. My sister didn't need to hear that. But, my God...not May? She telephoned me last night to tell me that Richard had gone off to Chinatown. They had a fight...at dinner. She felt terrible about walking out on him. Dear, God, what did she get herself into?"

"So, you think she followed him?"

Henry Bowen's eyes clouded with sadness. "Of course she would," he muttered. "The silly girl thought she could save him from himself."

Chapter Seven:

Nadia Ravenwood and I sat in her roadster. Before she engaged the engine, she exhaled. "Did you see how fast Henry came crawling back to us?"

I scoffed. "Our shortest unemployment ever."

"It seems to me that Richard's problem with his *new friends* is going to ignite into a raging fire under Henry. The question is, should we get a head start before he comes crying?"

"I'm in. What do you suggest?"

"You go to the Medical Examiner's Office and get the information on the deceased. As a reward, I'll buy you lunch at the Waldorf."

"Done. Should I take a taxi?"

"Nonsense, I'll drive you there."

The way Nadia drove, I was certain to wind up at my destination dead. However, I was slightly surprised to be among the living upon my arrival.

I was no stranger to the antiseptic air and tiled hallways in the underbelly of the Medical Examiner's Office, and some of the staff knew me and my wallet quite well. As usual, I'd exchanged money for the doctor's autopsy notes. This time, I was informed, with a smirk from an intern, that I could get a glimpse of May Scott's body, as well.

I declined, somewhat forcefully.

The notes were all I needed, as there was no mystery to May Scott's death. Translating the medical jargon revealed she'd been stabbed through the heart by a weapon that left a wound inflicted by a *thin double-edged blade with a central reinforcing spine* that exited out her back. It was an act of horror distilled down into cold, clinical words.

I made my way out of the bowels of the building and caught a taxi to the Waldorf Astoria, which was actually two hotels, built by competing members of a family so rich they could afford to construct these God-sized dollhouses. The red sandstone of the ornate exterior graduated upward until it looked like an enormous cherry wedding cake, crowned with domes and turrets. The lobby's archways were large enough to accommodate Barnum and Bailey's troop of elephants and led to the Empire Room, but as we weren't dressed for that venue, I met Miss Ravenwood at the first-floor café.

As I was seated, I noted Nadia had a book on the table, with a green cloth cover and an embossed gold figure of a bearded man seated while holding a spear with a wolf on either side of him. "Well, hello, there," I said to the tome on the table. "Is that Wotan I see before me?"

Nadia smiled. "Careful, your education is showing."

In truth, my life took a drastic turn away from my planned future in academics when I opted to enlist for duty in the War. And after Nicholas Ravenwood chose to pluck me out of the trenches, my life went on a different path altogether. "So, what's with the book?"

"I got this from the public library up the street from here."

She must have meant the enormous Grecian Temple-like structure guarded by that pair of marble lions.

"It's the same book that Richard Bowen had lying open on his bed."

I took up the book and saw it contained a collection of Norse Mythology, written by a professor named Anderson and published in my old hometown of Chicago. "So what does this tell us?"

"It may apply to whatever is going on in that scrambled-egg mind of his. I caught a glimpse of the chapter he was reading."

I thought back on some of the stories I knew. "Well, like all myths everywhere, they're tales of love, hate, betrayal and revenge. Especially of revenge. The Greek tale of Artemis turning a peeping tom into a stag to be chased down and killed by his own hunting dogs always reminded me of something you'd do."

"Don't be ridiculous. I'd never use dogs for something I could do myself. Now, what did you discover at the morgue?"

"You want to know before we eat?"

"What difference would that make?"

No question, the woman had ice water in her veins. "I read the doctor's notes. Death came quickly, at least, from a single stab wound to the heart."

"Front or back?"

"Oh, front and out the back."

"So she saw it coming?"

"Unless she was surprised and turned around fast."

"Anything in particular about the wound?"

I took a belated moment to look around at the other diners. It was early enough that we were allowed considerable space between occupied tables so I doubted people could hear us. "Long thin blade, double edged."

"Like a sword?"

The penny, as they say, dropped, as if from a great height. "Damn," I whispered. "You want to make a bet that walking stick that Richard Bowen is so concerned with finding has a sharp little surprise inside?"

Nadia arched an eyebrow. "No takers. Could that man

dig himself into any worse trouble?"

"I would bet on *Yes*...a whole dollar."

Nadia looked me straight in the eye. "You think he could have done it...killed the girl?"

"I don't know. He couldn't have buttoned his own pants at the time we found him. Those playmates if his, however, seem a lot more suspicious on the face of it."

"Agreed. Let's not keep our waiter hovering any longer. When we've finished, I think it's worth at least a telephone call to see how everyone in the Bowen house is doing. Better yet, we should just drop in uninvited."

A bisque of oysters and a hot-house lamb with French peas were later followed by a visit to the Turkish Smoking Room that looked like a page out of the *Thousand and One Nights*. The hotel appeared Old World, but they were very modern as to allow women the run of the place, even to the point that if a man wanted to attend an Afternoon Tea, he had to be escorted by a woman. And after that refreshment, we were off.

This time as we approached the Bowen mansion, we were more circumspect, parking down the street and strolling our way to the delivery entrance around by the kitchen. Our knocking finally drew Oscar the butler to the door. "How's the household faring, Oscar?"

His face was a scowl. "I believe Mr. Richard told you he didn't want you hounding him any longer.

Just then, a youthful, breathless voice called out, "Who's there? Is it them?"

Bounding into view behind Oscar was the girl, Mary Bowen. "I watched you drive up. I'm so glad you're here."

Nadia frowned. "Why's that, young lady?"

Mary's face became defiant. "Because I know who's out to get Richard."

Chapter Eight:

It was quite the standoff: Oscar holding his ground as Miss Mary Bowen invited us in.

"I cannot allow you entrance," Oscar proclaimed.

Miss Mary was having none of it. Her long, ribbon-adorned hair and sailor smock were becoming to a younger girl, but she was certainly learning the use of her voice in an adult manner. "Oscar. This is my house too. And when Henry and Richard are away, I am mistress here."

"Oscar..." Nadia Ravenwood interposed. "Mr. Henry Bowen begged my associate and me to help when the police arrived today."

I thought back and could not recall any specific offer of payment, but I kept quiet as Nadia pressed on.

"Perhaps if you simply let us use the library to speak with Miss Mary, I promise we'll be on our way quickly."

Oscar glanced at the petulantly glaring Mary. "Very well. If you are indeed here on Mr. Henry Bowen's request, although he said nothing to me about it."

With that, he turned and led us through the kitchen and past the cooks and servants who kept their heads down so as not to be caught laughing at pretentious Oscar's defeat. I caught the eye of one young girl and winked, and she snorted out a laugh.

As we arrived in the library, Miss Bowen said to Oscar, "That will be all." She waited until he closed the door behind himself, then she rushed up to us. "You're really here to help Richard?"

"If we can," Nadia replied. "Whether he wants us to

or not."

I took the opportunity to quietly move to the door Oscar exited through, only to open it and reveal the butler still present. At least he wasn't crouched by the keyhole. We exchanged glares, and he gathered up his dignity and slowly departed. I waited until he was out of sight before closing the door.

Mary dropped herself on the couch. "He's always sneaking around."

"And that wasn't you upstairs behind the banister as we were leaving today?"

"Hey. I'm only trying to figure out what's been going on with Richard. I'm worried."

"As am I."

Mary scowled. "Are you really a detective?"

Nothing quite so legal, I thought.

"Mr. Locke and I simply help people when they've fallen into trouble. People like your brother, Richard. What can you tell us that will help him?"

Mary looked down. "Well, he's got a problem with his medicine. He's been in so much pain since he got back from the War. It's hard for him." She brought her head up, eyes shining. "Is it true...May's dead?"

Nadia sat close to Mary and took her hand. "I'm so sorry for your loss."

"How did it happen?"

"I'm not sure what I can tell you."

Mary's eyes glared in defiance. "I'm not a child. I'm going to be sixteen."

I translated that into the fact that she'd probably just turned fifteen.

Nadia squeezed her hand gently. "It's not that I'm keeping anything from you, Mary. The police are still investigating."

"Oh." Mary sighed. "All right."

"Getting back to Richard?"

"Right. So, Richard and Henry are from my dad's first marriage, but their mother died, and then he married my mother, then I came along. That's why I'm so much younger than my brothers. When I was small, my parents took a voyage to England. They were on the Lusitania."

That was a shock. Two years before the United States entered the War, a German U-Boat sank the passenger ship with a number of Americans onboard. The attack was quite the patriotic 'Cause Celebre' to induce young men to sign up and fight. Myself included.

Mary's eyes got teary. "Father died, and mother never recovered. She passed away within a year. I barely remember her. Richard went off to fight, but Henry stayed home. Even now he'll say that war had already taken enough from the family. But when Richard came home, he was so badly injured. Growing up, I saw a lot of May. She always tried to help him, but lately, he said he didn't want to see her anymore."

I ran the numbers. "They must have started dating at least ten years ago."

Mary nodded. "Yes. And Richard's been in and out of hospitals and drinking and shouting and arguing ever since, all my life. I'm not supposed to know this, but I found out he tried to kill himself, just a couple months ago. He went away for a while, and when he came back, he had these new friends."

Mary said the word *friends* the way some people say the word *snakes* or *spiders*. "You didn't approve of these people?"

Mary's jaw tightened. "No. They were, well, sneaky. They'd never stay here, they always came by to take Richard out somewhere. And when he got back, he was always drunk. I'm sure they have something to do with Richard's problems." Mary looked up to me. "Like the other night when I saw you bring him home. That was the first time I saw you. I was waiting at the top of the stairs when I was supposed to be asleep, and you came in with Richard over your shoulder. I heard Henry getting mad and telling you to bring him in around the back next time. But I remember you were gentle with him."

I believe I was the recipient of Miss Mary's kind shading of memory. All I recall doing was making an effort to not bash his head against too many walls as I lugged him through the house. I then thought back to the man at the opium parlor. "Mary? Did one of Richard's new friends wear an eye patch?"

"Yes. I've seen a man like that, but it was only once when it was late and I wasn't supposed to be out of bed."

Nadia asked, "What else can you tell us about these new friends of Richard's?"

She looked grim. "They were all soldiers, like him. Not in uniform or anything, but they were still like him."

"How so?"

"All of them were wounded in some way. I remember one making a remark about how they were all *broken toy soldiers*."

Chapter Nine:

Nadia asked Mary, "Did you ever see a woman among your brother's new friends?"

"Richard chased off all the women who knew him. Except May. She stuck with him no matter how hard he pushed her away."

Nadia Ravenwood took out her silver card case and handed one to Mary. "Listen, I think you've shown great promise in your ability to look after your family. I'd like to you take my card, memorize my telephone number, then get rid of the card."

"I see. You want me to spy on my family."

"For their own good. I believe you're doing that already."

Mary, to her credit, didn't even blush.

"Now, I want you to let us look around Richard's room for clues we can use to help him. Is this all right with you?"

Mary rose regally, as if feeling the weight of importance fall on her. "Yes. Let's do it now, before he gets home."

We followed her to Richard's room and discovered he had locked his door. I was about to inquire if I should go out to the Rickenbacker and retrieve our burglary tools when Nadia turned to Mary. "I bet a clever girl like you knows where the passkey is kept, right?"

With a smirk, she reached down the front of her blouse and came up with a key attached to a strip of ribbon. "Like this one?"

"If I ever retire..." Nadia took the key, "I may just leave my business to you."

After the three of us entered and Nadia went to work, Mary assisted with the hunt for clues. It took no time at all to find nothing beyond a wealthy man's attire and accouterments within the confines of a room fit for a cloistered monk.

As we left, Nadia handed the key back to a disappointed Mary. She locked the door. "Now what?"

"Looks like Mr. Locke and I will have to follow other avenues. You be vigilant and telephone if you find out anything helpful."

All at once, Mary rushed over to give Nadia Ravenwood a hug, and just as quickly disengaged, blushing. "I'm sorry. It's just that I've felt so helpless. Thank you for being here."

And with that, she turned and quickly stepped down the hallway.

Nadia sighed. "That poor girl."

As we walked back to the kitchen, I held out a hand, indicating the richness around us. "I see nothing *poor* about this place."

Nadia caught my meaning but had her own take on it. "Money doesn't compensate for the lack of a mother and father."

That pretty much shut me up.

We retreated through the aromatic kitchen to the street, and soon we were motoring away down Park Avenue. After a couple of quick turns, Miss Ravenwood drove up to the entryway to the Waldorf Astoria.

"Bit early for dinner," I said.

"I intend to get a couple of rooms here. My house is miles away, and your apartment isn't much closer. This way, if Mary calls, we can reach the Bowen residence within minutes."

"So we're committed?"

"I'm committed to seeing that no more trouble falls on the Bowen family, especially Mary Bowen, if we can help it. Now, go fetch your bag and meet me back here. We'll discuss strategy over dinner. Black tie."

I had one of the decorative doormen flag me a taxi and proceeded to my apartment on Lexington. I didn't linger, as my rooms were cold since the radiator had been off in my absence. I didn't need much in the way of time because I always kept a bag packed for a couple of day's worth of traveling. I was most happy about finally being reunited with my .38 caliber Smith and Wesson revolver. The thought of someone intruding a thin length of sharp, cold steel into my person left me queasy, and I was glad to have a ready answer to that problem, should it arise.

I dressed in my evening clothes and called down for a cab, happy to see it wasn't raining as of yet. Upon arriving at the hotel, I distributed gratuity all about until I was free to make my way to my room, a comfortable little place on the Astoria side of the hotel with its own full-sized bathtub and unfortunately, its own telephone, as well. I let the bellhop deposit my bag and gave him something extra to ensure the delivery of a bottle of Ballentine's. At least here I was certain it'd be the genuine article and not something distilled in someone's basement.

I then took the elevators to stroll through the opulence of this modern-day castle to find my companion in the majestic Empire Room, a place so impressive I found myself looking for the likes of a modern Marie Antoinette eating a whole cake by herself amidst the ornate columns and murals on the ceilings, as a stringed quartet played music fit for angels.

I'd heard it said that the Waldorf Astoria is the bastion

of American Royalty. If so, then Miss Nadia Ravenwood was one of their premier princesses. Her gown was draped black satin with Egyptian Hieroglyphics worked in gold beads all about, while her gold-wrought tiara brought to mind a Grecian goddess.

"Attempting to capture all the attention in the room?" I inquired. "Because judging by the catty glances from the women and the expectant leers from the local old goat society, you've succeeded quite handily."

She smiled, her lips red as polished rubies. "Hardly. I just wanted to remind myself that we can go to places less tawdry than a walk-up opium den."

"So, is it too much to ask if we are taking the rest of the night off?"

She delivered a secretive grin. "Tell me what you know about the Norse god Tyr."

Chapter Ten:

After we were seated, I said. "Tyr, Norse God of War. He had something to do with the Fenris Wolf, as I recall."

Nadia rolled her dark, lovely eyes. "Skipped out on class early that day, did you? Yes, Tyr was the God of War, and also Justice. He was called 'bravest of the gods'. And judging by the creases on the book Richard Bowen was reading, this was his favorite chapter."

"I liked Robin Hood. Also James Fenimore Cooper's Hawkeye."

"People who live out in the woods. That may explain much about you. Regardless, Richard liked this character. It was written that the Norse gods grew fearful of the Fenris Wolf, because he'd become so large and dangerous. They tried to trick the Wolf into letting them bind him, telling him it was just a game, a test of his strength. The Wolf agreed to be bound, but only if one of the gods placed his hand inside the Wolf's mouth, as a sign of trust. Only Tyr was brave enough to do that."

"And then lost his hand, as I recall."

Nadia Ravenwood tilted her head. "Think on it, a man who loses a limb in war would certainly have sympathy with a story of a man who loses a limb in an act of sacrifice."

"Certainly. So how does this apply to Richard's current antics?"

"I don't know, but I think it shows what's been going on in his mind, at least."

We turned our attention to the menu, and I was vacillating between fried oyster crabs and breast of Scotch grouse in a port wine sauce when a waiter glided up to Nadia with a small envelope on a silver tray. She quickly read the note, then said to the waiter, "Our regrets, but we have been called away. Please ask the front desk to have my automobile brought around."

"Both of us?" I blurted out, only to receive a scathing look aimed by an arched eyebrow. "Get your coat and meet me in the lobby."

"Aye, aye. And the reason why?"

"Someone just tried to kill Henry Bowen."

We left the Empire Room and parted company at the elevators, where I overheard Miss Ravenwood tell the operator she was going to the *Greek Room*, a fancy name for a penthouse suite, I assumed.

I went to my own quarters and retrieved a hat, overcoat and revolver, which I secured in a pocket holster. In no time at all, I met her in the lobby, and then we were off in Nadia's motorized chariot.

I should have timed the scant minutes it took for us to arrive at the Bowen mansion. There was one police sedan present, but parked across the street, and no ambulance in attendance. For the scene of an attempted murder, it was bizarrely quiet.

When Miss Ravenwood and I reached the front doors, they opened right away to reveal a uniformed policeman looking young and rather out of his depths. We got the up and down look. "Who're you?"

"The people you call during an emergency," Nadia snapped. "Where's Henry Bowen?"

The officer took a quick look off to his right, and Nadia barged in, with me in her wake. "Thank you, Officer." She moved with alacrity as we approached a set of double doors, and she admitted herself into a wood-paneled den. Gilded framed portraits hung on the walls, and comfortable chairs set about carved wood tables bearing an array of *après dinner* selections of drinks and smokes. There was also a frazzled-looking Henry Bowen in his dress shirt, collar unfastened and tie undone, nervously smoking a cigarette.

Alongside his chair knelt his sister, Mary, in a modest floral-pattern nightgown. "You came," she called out when she spotted us.

Henry narrowed his eyes. "What the...Mary, you telephoned for these people?"

She leapt up and rushed to Nadia's side, possessively taking her by the arm. "I did. You need them."

The older officer looked to Henry. "Mr. Bowen, should I have these people leave?"

Henry looked to Nadia and me. "No." He sighed. "They...have some insights into what's been going on here lately."

I looked about the room. "Where is everyone? You'd think Manhattan's Finest would have a whole brigade out here by now."

"They don't need a brigade," a quiet voice came from the entryway. "I'm here."

I turned and saw the origin of this enormous boast.

And I was forced to agree.

Chapter Eleven:

J ohnny Broderick, detective with the New York City Police, would fool you at first glance. He was too well dressed and soft spoken to be a copper, you'd think. Then you would notice the once broken nose on his otherwise placid features, and his hands crisscrossed with scars from busting up people's faces. When it came to cops, he was the real deal, as some gangsters attempting to break out of The Tombs found out last year. Johnny had walked in, and they got carried out and buried.

What was odd was seeing him here on Park Avenue. The press didn't call him *Broadway Johnny* for nothing. Reporters loved him, and he operated in quite the opposite manner to Nadia Ravenwood and me. *He takes the spotlight; we keep to the shadows.* Regardless, there've been a few occasions involving certain celebrities where our paths had crossed. But last I heard, he'd been assigned to a special unit called the *Industrial Squad,* keeping racketeers and Communists from interfering with businesses and commercial matters.

And if someone just tried to murder Henry Bowen, then I suddenly wanted to know what business Bowen was involved with.

But now was not the time for a little polite chit-chat, as Nadia and Detective Broderick nodded to each other. He looked us over, taking in our formal attire with a slight smile. "Miss Ravenwood, nice to see you again. Catch you at a bad time?"

"Detective. What brings you away from Times

Michael Siverling

Square?"

"I called him," Henry said. "The detective has been helping me with certain professional matters."

Nadia gave him the evil-eye. "And are these professional matters attempting to kill you?"

Whatever Henry Bowen was involved with, he had a direct line to reach Johnny Broderick and had enough pull to get him out here on a moment's notice. That was an impressive amount of influence.

"So what happened here tonight?" Broderick asked.

Henry looked to Mary. "This is nothing for you to hear, dear. Please, go back to your room."

I watched Mary take a breath, as if preparing to fire back with an argument.

Nadia intercepted to her. "Your brother made an excellent suggestion. You should go. I'll come and see you before I leave."

What Henry hadn't seen was Nadia's conspiratorial wink to Mary, who apparently got the drift and nodded then walked up to her brother. "Goodnight, Henry. I'm so glad you're all right."

"Everything will be fine, Mary. You'll see. Detective Broderick will take care of everything."

Mary looked over to Nadia. "Miss Ravenwood, too."

"Of course."

After Mary's departure, Nadia asked, "So what happened, Henry?"

He got up and poured himself a brandy from a crystal decanter, then tipped the glass to us, a silent offer to help ourselves. Nadia and Johnny declined. He didn't smoke or drink, and was, by all accounts, a good family man, which made him all the more inhuman, as far as I was concerned. The remaining officer and I took the hint and declined the alcoholic refreshment, as well, far more reluctantly, I might add.

Henry took a swallow, then: "I was upstairs in my study, working at my desk." He stared in his drink as if he didn't believe his own words. "I'd just returned home from my club."

"Which club?" Nadia asked.

Henry scowled at the interruption. "Engineers Club, if you must know. In any event, I heard an automobile horn honking outside. I went to the window, and the next thing I knew, a pane broke. Frankly, I just stood there until another pane shattered, and I heard something *smack* the wall behind me. Then it hit me...bullets...I was being shot at."

"Thank God you weren't hit." Nadia's voice was actually laced with concern.

Henry Bowen's outrage as he recounted the events was palpable. "Not for a lack of trying. I dropped to the floor. Then, as I lay there, I get showered with broken glass as more shots were fired, one after the other."

One shooter, I thought.

"Then I heard a car drive away at high speed. God knows what the neighbors are going to think."

Nadia turned to Detective Broderick. "I know it's a crime scene, but may I see Mr. Bowen's study?"

"It's official police business now. I'm certain you understand. I intend to post a man here before I leave."

Henry Bowen held up his hands. "You see, Miss Ravenwood? This has nothing to do with my brother's situation."

Now Broderick looked puzzled. "What situation?"

"Certain family matters are officially private business." Nadia smiled sweetly. "I'm certain you understand."

Detective Broderick glanced at Henry, who sheepishly looked away. "All right. As long as your family business doesn't have anything to do with my department, then I suppose we'll just stay out of it."

"Very well. In that case, I'll just say goodnight to Mary, and then we'll be on our way."

I caught the subtle flick of her finger that silently told me to delay as long as practical. "Henry, I'll take that drink now, if it's still offered."

Nadia and Johnny, along with the remaining uniformed officer, departed, leaving me alone with Henry. I took a drink and a cigarette from him and then sat down. "Hell of a thing, being shot at."

He just stared out at nothing. "I still can't believe someone wants me dead."

"Any idea who'd be using you for target practice?"

Henry took a breath, then held it as a mottled guilty look flashed across his face. "I'm certain Detective Broderick wouldn't want me to say anything."

I nodded in agreement, and then waited for what felt like a year before Nadia Ravenwood came along to collect me.

Chapter Twelve:

W e took our leave with a rattled Oscar the butler seeing us out. Across the street, Johnny Broderick was staring toward the mansion. Nadia took my arm. "Let's join him."

We waited for a solitary car to make its way past us then hurried across as Johnny Broderick watched our approach. "Penny for your thoughts, detective," Nadia said playfully. "Or rather, for those brass casings in your pocket you've picked up."

Johnny sneered. "Just can't keep yourself away, can you, Miss Ravenwood?"

"I'm just trying to be helpful."

I took a stance next to Broderick, looking across a manicured lawn at the house, placing the windows of the study from my brief visit there. "That is one hell of a shot. How many hits?"

Before Johnny could say a word, Nadia spoke up. "Seven. Three high up on the opposite wall and four to the ceiling. I could see where an officer dug one of the bullets out of the wall. You can also see on the floor by the window where Henry dropped. There's an outline of his body in broken glass."

Broderick's face reddened with anger. "You went into the study...after I told you no?"

"It was just down the hall from Mary Bowen's room."

I took a step into the street and crouched down to stare at the second story window a good hundred yards away. "Shots fired from inside an automobile?"

Broderick remained quiet.

I kept going. "Seven shots, rapid succession. Henry didn't say he heard gunshots, so, maybe one of Maxim's silencers at work? They make those things up in Connecticut."

"Most likely." Nadia turned her full attention on Johnny Broderick. "Now...if only we knew what kind of gun fired those shots."

I'd seen lesser men melt under those lovely eyes. Not Johnny. As I'd said, he's not human. "Nothing doing, Miss Ravenwood. You work your side of the street, I'll work mine."

He tipped his hat and sauntered away down the sidewalk. Nadia and I watched him go, then: "I've got my foot on a spent cartridge Johnny missed," she whispered. "If you would be so kind?"

I knelt down and recovered the object in question. I used my cigarette lighter to get a better look as Nadia and I stood close. In the palm of my hand lay a flattened cartridge, looking to be about a .38 caliber, but short so as to feed into an automatic. "Looks like a pistol cartridge."

Nadia looked across the street to the Bowen mansion. "Could you make a shot like that with a pistol? Seven times?"

"Maybe once in seven tries. That is some damn impressive shooting."

"And yet, no one was hit. Interesting, no?"

"Yeah."

"I'm hungry. Let's catch a late dinner."

And just like that, we were soon back in the warm, rich embrace of the Waldorf Astoria. Nadia and I were the best dressed people in the room, mainly because we went to the drawing room of her Greek Suite where we ordered room service of cold lobster Bagration with a romaine and pear salad. Once dinner was cleared away and Nadia had time to indulge herself with one of her Turkish cigarettes, she eyed me across the small table. "What time is it?"

"Coming up on midnight."

She sighed. "Right before I left the house, I asked Henry to telephone me when Richard came home tonight. Either he's forgotten, which under the circumstances is understandable, or Richard's yet to arrive."

"What do you want to do?"

"I want whoever actually killed May Scott to be neatly caught, and for it not to be Richard. On the other hand, I'm afraid his brother's business may indeed be connected somehow. It's too much happening all at once to one family."

"Agreed. But how are they connected?"

She rolled her eyes. "I don't know. When I went snooping through Henry's study, the papers he had out on his desk were production reports from at least three different armament manufacturers."

"Armaments? Not much call for those these days."

"Spoken like a true American. Spin the globe and place your finger anywhere, you'll land on trouble. Right now, China is in the throes of a Civil War, and before that, there were uprisings in Turkey, Mexico, the Dutch Colonies and so on."

"Your dad always said war was good for business if absolutely nothing else."

"Yes, Father had his insights and didn't mind making a penny or two in the process. Regardless, the Bowen Brothers are both in trouble. Makes me want to spirit poor Mary away from all this. She confided in me that Henry is considering sending her away to a finishing school. That may be a good thing for her right now."

I couldn't help but laugh. "Really? Your father told

me, at great length, how you escaped from every boarding school and convent he placed you in."

"It taught me a measure of self-reliance."

No doubt. Especially the time after she slipped away from a school in Paris and was found running in the streets with a band of Apaches, or the time, in London, where she was adopted into the female Forty Elephants gang. Replace *self-reliance* with the words *criminal abilities* and you get an idea of the kind of education Nadia Ravenwood received. If she hadn't chosen to take over her father's business of getting people out of trouble for a profit, she'd no doubt be running her own criminal empire by now.

"Regardless," she said. "We should probably see to our rest. God knows what tomorrow will bring."

I bid her goodnight and went to my own room, where I indulged myself with a hot bath and cold scotch whisky. The next morning, I arose and dressed, looking forward to whatever kind of sumptuous breakfast the Waldorf Astoria had to offer.

My mistake was stopping at the lobby newsstand, only to see all the morning papers proclaiming the horrors of a socialite murdered in Chinatown.

Chapter Thirteen:

I found Miss Ravenwood wearing a rich royal-blue velvet day dress and matching beret, complete with her signature black feather, in the glass-enclosed rooftop-garden café. I was forced to ignore the splendid view of the surrounding city to focus on the story beneath the headlines of the Herald Tribune, which I'd already glanced at in the lobby.

"Took you long enough this morning."

"Apologies. I take it you've perused the news. Want to give me the gist of it?"

She took a sip of her Turkish coffee. "Young Socialite found brutally murdered in Chinatown. Police announce arrests are imminent, Mayor Walker to issue statement, the usual sort of thing."

"You think Richard is the police's target?"

"Unless that Detective McDonough found a more suitable suspect." Nadia finished her coffee with a sigh. "Let's go talk to Mary, see if she's heard anything."

"I haven't had breakfast."

She tossed me a roll from the basket on the table.

I looked at it disdainfully. "What...no honey?"

"Not today, sweetheart."

We parted at the elevators and rejoined in the lobby with overcoats, and in my case, a hat and revolver, for now I had to add hidden marksman of uncanny ability to my list of worries. We drove directly to the row of Park Avenue mansions and had no trouble seeing which one was ours: all we had to do was pull up to the one with police cars.

Actually, there were only two police sedans present as we parked well shy of the house, along with a truck with ladders mounted on the side and a painted door advertising Joseph and Son Carpentry, no doubt getting to work on repairing the shot-up study without delay.

The air was cold this morning, with a chill wind that blew along the streets of the city. This didn't dissuade the numerous citizens, both upper-crust locals and those not so much, from strolling along the opposite side of the street in a kind of slow-moving rubbernecker's parade. I had no idea that so many dogs required walking at the exact same time. But there was one type of person loitering around the black iron portcullis of the Bowen manor that drew our attention: Reporters, the personal bane of Miss Nadia Ravenwood. There were two of them, one armed with a camera.

I heard Nadia whisper a curse in French, then: "I was hoping to find out the latest news, not become a part of it. I'm not getting in the middle of that mess."

"Well, you do have a habit of interposing yourself between newsmen and juicy stories. It's a wonder you don't have your own troop of reporters following you around just to see whose business you're up to."

"I suppose we could just telephone Mary, but I don't want to be at the mercy of either Detective Broderick or McDonough's prying ears. Suggestions?"

"Hard to think on an empty stomach."

"Then imagine the lovely luncheon I'll provide at the chophouse of your choice once you figure out a way to get us into the residence."

"When the Mountain won't come to Mohammad..."

"I get it." Nadia kissed the tips of her gloved fingers then gently slapped me with the same. "Well, aren't you the horse to bet on."

"I've a feeling you'd take better care of your horses."

It took a short drive to find a telephone booth to call a message service, and then a bit of a wait to send the telegram, but soon Nadia and I met our favorite member of the Bowen household: Mary Bowen with an escort consisting of one of the maids who looked like she'd seen several ghosts. You'd think she would have been more at ease at our rendezvous: the Little Church Around the Corner being a perfect combination Sanctuary and Hide Out. The quaint, gothic chapel itself was like an oasis in the midst of the frantic pace of the city, as if it had been magically transplanted here from *Olde England*, complete with garden and gazebo.

Mary bounded up to us, her voice echoing through the church. "Oh, I'm so glad to see you. I wanted to call, but Henry wouldn't let me near the telephone. I heard this morning that they're going to arrest Richard...for murder."

Nadia took Mary by the hands and sat her down in a pew. "Quietly, dear. You never know who could be listening. How did you manage to get away to see us?"

Mary undid the ribbon that held her wide straw hat to her chin. "I got your telegram. I've never received one addressed to me before. I didn't tell Henry I was coming to see you, just said I wanted to go to church to pray for Richard."

"And so you shall, but always remember that telling the truth is important."

I noticed Nadia didn't add her own personal motto: *when the truth is convenient.* I took the opportunity to quietly hand the maid an honorarium that made her eyes open wide, then relax as she nodded acceptance of the arrangement and then proceeded to look away at nothing.

Nadia said to Mary, "So, what, exactly, is going on with Richard?"

"That Detective, the old one, not the one from last

night, showed up at the house, told Henry he was there to arrest Richard and take him away. Only Richard was already gone. They checked his room, and I heard it looked like he came in late from the back of the house then packed a bag and left."

"And you have no idea where he may be?"

Mary ducked her head and whispered, "They did find something in the garden outside Richard's room. Footprints by his window. But what was strange was the thing that was scratched into the window glass."

"What was it?"

"An arrow. Pointing upwards. And no one knew what it meant."

Chapter Fourteen:

We left Mary and her escort in the quiet of the church and walked out to the noisy, bustling world of the city. "So, early luncheon?"

"Not quite. I want to pay a call at the Scott residence and see if the victim's family can shed some light on the situation."

"You don't think Detective McDonough has already covered this ground?"

"Oh, he would have. But he is not we, and we are better at this sort of thing."

"Especially when well fed," I added. My entreaty fell on deaf but shell-like ears.

Nadia Ravenwood had already secured May Scott's address by checking the Social Register while *I was lazing away the morning* as she phrased it. The address led to an upper-end row of homes not far off Park Avenue, predictably within strolling distance of the Bowen mansion. The black wreath on the door was a sad signpost.

We were admitted by a somber butler to find a small gathering in the parlor, where grief had settled like a blanket of freezing snow. In the corner an older woman, attired in black, who was the focus of the people clustered together amidst the dull drone of quiet voices. Nadia took a quick survey of the mounted photographs along the papered walls, then hunted amidst the people for one in particular, where she swiftly yet smoothly inserted herself into the cluster to whisper into the ear of a young woman. The woman followed Nadia back to me in the hallway, and together we stepped back around the base of the stairway as Nadia made introductions:

"Miss Eve Scott? This is Mr. Stephen Locke, and I am Nadia Ravenwood. We are here to see that justice is done."

The woman was young, early twenties at best, wearing a dark blue dress with light hair that fell in loose waves to her delicate jaw line and light eyes that now displayed confusion. "I don't understand. Are you with the police?"

I'd noticed Nadia hadn't identified exactly who we were seeking justice for. "No, Miss Scott. My associate and I are simply more effective. We'd like to speak with you as we do not wish to disturb you mother at a time like this."

Eve looked to Nadia, then me and back again. "What do you want to know?"

"What can you tell me about Richard Bowen, especially his behavior in the last few days?"

"I told May to stay away from him," she whispered in a strained voice. "She wouldn't listen. She never got over him, even after he came back from the war all bitter and broken. And he didn't even want her. He kept pushing her away. Until recently."

"What happened?"

Eve took a look over her shoulder, as if making sure we were still unheard, then whispered conspiratorially, "Everything was going fine. May had finally come to her senses last year, and Richard stayed away. May even got engaged. Then, a couple of weeks ago, Richard calls and wants to see her. I told her not to, but she didn't listen. I thought Wally was going to go insane."

"Who's Wally," I asked.

"Walter Reeves. He loves May dearly. Or did. Sorry, I'm still not taking it all in."

Nadia put a hand on Eve's arm. "We understand. But

anything you can tell us can help. Why did Richard all of the sudden want to see May again?"

Eve shrugged, then signed. "I'm not sure. May would come back from meeting him all excited, telling me about how he'd changed, and that he'd finally found a purpose. She thought it was an answer to a prayer."

"How did Walter take this?"

Eve looked up with a shrug. "He didn't. May told me he said she'd clearly taken leave of her senses and ought to see a doctor. She gave him the push off."

"Walter didn't take it well?"

"There were scenes. Walter has a bad temper."

"But everything between May and Richard was going well?" Nadia asked.

Eve shook her head. "Until that last night she saw him. He came by for her and I saw them off. I still wasn't convinced, and when I saw him that night, I was worried all over again."

"Why?"

"Richard was, uneasy. He barely looked at May and seemed in a hurry to be away with her. I told her I'd stay up until she came home..." A look of pain, sharp and swift, cut Eve's words short. She took a breath. "May telephoned later, from the restaurant, and said that something was wrong with Richard and that she'd be late coming home and would call me later." Eve looked away. "I never saw her again."

Nadia took her hand. "Thank you. I can only imagine how difficult all this is."

Eve drew herself up. "Excuse me. Mother needs me."

Eve saw us to the door and out to the porch.

Nadia gave Eve her card.

Eve said, "I don't know what you can do, really, but I would appreciate hearing from you."

Nadia was about to reply when Eve's eyes grew large as she spotted something behind us. Turning toward the street, I saw a man in a dark coat and tall hat exit a Chrysler Imperial, marching a quick-step right at us, huffing like a locomotive, anger radiating from his eyes.

"Oh, God. What's Wally doing here now?"

That's when I saw he held a walking stick.

Chapter Fifteen:

My mind immediately went to my fear of long sharp blades, but my revolver was in the pocket of my trousers beneath a buttoned overcoat. Thanks to the Army I had a large bag of dirty fighting tricks drilled into me during the War. I charged down the steps and ran right at him, grabbed hold of the arm that held the stick and spun him around in a hip throw to make him crash down onto the concrete walkway. He landed with a satisfying *thump,* and I held back from finishing him off with the combination of fist, elbow and boot blows I'd been taught to use. I grabbed onto the walking stick and gave it a twist and pull to withdraw the internal sword.

Nothing came out.

I squinted at the weapon, looking for hidden catches and such, but the stick was just that: a stick. Still, it had a hardwood shaft and metal grip that could have done some real damage. And that was the story I was going to go with.

Walter Reeves was rolling himself back and forth, like an overturned turtle as Eve Scott came up with arms crossed, staring down at him. "Wally, what on earth are you doing here?"

It took a moment for Walter to find his hat and get his feet under him, and once he stood, he was looking none too steady. Getting a better look at him, I saw he was a pretty good-sized specimen, tall and broad. His hair was slicked back and black from pomade, and his moustache was meticulously trimmed. Walter looked around until his eyes found Miss Ravenwood. He pointed an unsteady hand at

Eve and demanded of Nadia, "What has this woman been saying about me?"

"Go home, Wally," Eve said, though not in an unkind tone. "There's nothing for you here."

He drew himself up. "I loved her. Do you hear me? I loved her. And you let her go off with that Richard bastard."

Nadia took two quick steps up to Walter, moving in close, close enough to conceal her push dagger that she pricked his tummy with as she grabbed his shoulder. "This is a house in mourning, you stupid lout. Now shut your mouth and walk away, or I'll let my friend loose on you again."

He paled and stumbled backward, almost falling again, looked from Nadia to Eve to me and saw no reprieve anywhere. I tossed his stick out into the street as a motivator to move him along, and we all watched as he scurried to retrieve it, and then he climbed into his car and, in a grating clash of gears, tore away from the curb.

Nadia quickly hid her knife before turning to Eve. "Just how jealous was Walter of Richard?"

Eve sadly shook her head, hugging herself against the cold October morning. "He really loved May. A lot. Maybe too much. Thank you for chasing him off. I really didn't want Mother to see a scene like that."

"Of course, dear. Please telephone if we can be of further service."

We took our leave, and when we were underway in the Rickenbacker, I said, "So, you think maybe Walter could have killed May in a jealous rage?"

"We've seen that, and worse, before. Now, my hero, where would you like to have your luncheon?"

I was soon being spoiled in the Red Room of the Restaurant Crillon with steak medallions in hollandaise and a side of *Maryland Morsel*: deviled crab meat in an anchovy pastry. I was allowed time for my indulgence, and when I ultimately declined the fruit and cheese plate, Nadia resumed our professional relationship. "This case, or rather, these cases, are quite the mess."

"We could withdraw from the field. After all, since we returned Richard from the clutches of the opium den, Henry hasn't actually engaged our services."

Nadia hissed a curse, in German, this time. "You're right. I just keep thinking about Mary, and how sorry I feel for her to be trapped in all this. Very well, let's return to the Bowen estate and straighten out our official status, at least. It'd be nice to be able to find Richard and bring him in for his arraignment so he doesn't run the risk of an overenthusiastic police officer hurting him, or worse, during an arrest."

We motored back to the Bowen residence, happy to see no police cars present this time. When we rang, Oscar was less than pleased to see us. "Are you quite certain you have business here, sir and madam?"

"That is what we are here to discover. Is Mr. Henry Bowen at home?"

"Wait here. I shall see."

We weren't left on the doorstep long before the door opened again and Mary Bowen's face appeared. She put her finger to her lips and whispered, "Henry spoke to Richard on the telephone. Richard wanted money, and Henry said he had to go to the bank to get it."

"Do you know how Henry intends to get the money to Richard?"

Mary huffed in exasperation. "No. But I think Richard is supposed to call again later when Henry gets home to tell him."

Mary cast a look over her shoulder then gave a quick

wave as she shut the door. Moments later, Oscar appeared. "I regret to inform you that I have no instructions for you. Please be on your way."

"Do tell Mr. Henry Bowen we called," Nadia said sweetly.

Oscar shut the portal.

"Now what?" I asked.

"I want to get a look at that arrow etched in the window that spooked Richard enough to make him take off."

I followed Nadia around to the side of the house to the brick wall of the mansion garden. There was a black iron gate that was open, due to the fact the lock clearly suffered recent damage.

We crept into the garden proper and past the marble fountain to the window of Richard's room. The flowerbed under the sill had been torn up, the result of police making plaster castings of the foot impressions the mysterious visitor left, no doubt.

And there, on a single windowpane, was an upward pointing arrow cut deeply into the glass.

Chapter Sixteen:

Nadia stepped up to the window, removing her glove and tracing the lines on the pane with her finger. "Deep, very fine cuts. Probably used a diamond tipped drill as a quill. And look here...it's actually pointing to the two o'clock position. If you look on the other side, you can see where whoever cut this started to make it point to the ten o'clock position, then changed when he realized it would be read from the other side."

"So?"

"This is a code. Probably a specific warning to Richard Bowen."

As we quietly retreated, Nadia grinned, positively happy.

"What's tickling you?"

"We have another piece of the puzzle."

There were countless detective stories where the main character relished bizarre mysteries, the more twisted, the better. I would count a real-life person with this viewpoint as hopelessly deranged. Puzzles were vexing, nagging problems best avoided altogether. But here was Nadia, happy as a clam.

"Would you please explain yourself?"

"Look what we have here: Wounded soldiers, exceptionally good pistol shots, and rather common burglars."

"Yes? So?"

"Now all we have to do is find a connection among them."

As I had said, *vexing*.

At Nadia's car, she stopped. "But the immediate problem now is finding Richard Bowen."

"Brother Henry is supposed to be out collecting money. For a getaway, I imagine. Which is a stupid move on Richard's part."

"Unless he is guilty. And I can't picture that...yet." She opened the car door.

We drove up Fifth Avenue, and I was grateful the congested midday traffic constrained Nadia's normally reckless driving as she muttered curses, this time in Russian. The talk of soldiers brought to mind a small miracle I'd once heard about. Almost a decade ago, members of the Army's segregated black regiment, the fearsome *Harlem Hellfighters*, were given a grand parade when they came home after the War. For one day, all of New York came out to cheer the men who marched along Fifth Avenue, celebrating their bravery and sacrifice.

But sadly, the gratitude for these men faded all too quickly.

Nadia pulled out of the slow crawl of traffic across from the New York Public Library. "I'm going to check a few things. You get to a telephone and see if we've received any messages."

As Nadia braved the crowds on the sidewalks, I jumped into the throng and made my way to the towering Radiator Building and found myself a comfortable telephone booth in the lobby. Cocooned from the noise of the city, I had the operator connect me with the Ravenwood Brownstone, only to have Mr. Ivanov, her butler, curtly tell me no one has called for The Miss today.

I then tried to reach Henry Bowen, only to be told by a smug-sounding Oscar that Mr. Henry Bowen was not at home. To me, in any case. I decided to not ask to speak with Mary Bowen as I didn't want to get her into any trouble with her brothers and felt confident that the clever little girl would manage to get a message to us if it was important.

I then took a chance and called for Henry Bowen at the *Engineers Club* that he had mentioned the other night. But the person on the other end of the line assured me they had no such member by that name on their rolls.

Again, as I said, *vexing*.

I made my way back to the Rickenbacker. In the stillness of the car, it was rather like being in an oasis of calm surrounded by a river of people and vehicles. Eventually, I spotted Nadia as she rushed up and jumped in behind the wheel. "Any messages?"

"No messages, but I've got proof that Henry Bowen is a liar."

"Oh?"

"Remember when he said he was at his club before he came home and got shot at? A club he identified as the *Engineers Club*? Well, they say he's not a member."

Nadia Ravenwood had a beautiful smile, and it lit up like I'd just given her a Christmas present. "Ah..." She sighed. "Lies can be most revealing."

"What'd you get?"

Nadia pulled out a small piece of paper with a simple arrow drawn on it. "This may also be telling. It's a Nordic Rune, a symbol. And in this case, it's the symbol of the Norse God Tyr."

"Him again?"

"Yes." Nadia grinned happily. "Intriguing, no? Here Richard Bowen is reading up on a particular Norse god, and then someone happens to come along and scratches that god's symbol on Richard's window, starting a chain of events, beginning with Richard's elusive behavior and disappearance."

"Yet it brings us no closer to finding him."

"Well, now I suppose we'll have to try the criminal side of things."

"What do you mean?"

"We know a burglar is involved, so let's go talk to someone in that social circle and see what we can find out."

"Who'd you have in mind?"

"Owney Madden.

"Madden? The last time you met with him, you busted a bottle of champagne over his bodyguard's head. It was also the first time you met him."

"Oh, that was ages ago."

"That was last month."

Nadia Ravenwood simply smiled and put her car into gear, doubtlessly driving us to our own funerals.

Chapter Seventeen:

There were thousands of speakeasies in New York, all thanks to Prohibition, and they're all run by gangsters. For the most part, they're the place for a fun, frolicsome evening with the best jazz music and latest dance steps. Unless you make the mistake of crossing the management. Nadia and I did just that last month, getting an unasked for meeting with Owney *The Killer* Madden in the process. In true Ravenwood fashion, she not only walked away from that potential disaster, but Madden had invited her back.

The *Club Intime* was a little basement speakeasy in the Times Square district underneath the Hotel Harding, which Madden also owned and where he put up his friends, associates, playmates, and heavily armed cohorts, some of whom we found dutifully loitering around the back alley while a covered truck was being unloaded. As it was late afternoon, I could only assume all the Treasury Agents and Prohibition cops in the area had decided to knock off early.

Nadia and I strolled right up to the steps leading to the basement, where a sour-faced individual appeared less than impressed with Nadia's card and our request to speak with the management, but he grunted assent and disappeared within. I was hoping this would be as far as we would be allowed to go, but then we got a surprise when the club's door opened up.

The dark and surly man was replaced by a woman with platinum curls that had yet to set and fell in loose springs surrounding a face of bold beauty with blue eyes that shone like lamps. She was wrapped in a silken dressing gown of peacock blue with a white, feathery trim. She glanced at me, gave Nadia Ravenwood the once over, and purred, "So what do you want with my sweet, vicious little Owney?"

For a moment, I thought we were seeing 'Texas' Guinan, Queen of Night and hostess of *Club Intime*; this woman, who could be a close twin, was someone else. Then it hit me. "I think I caught your act at the 63rd Street Theater."

She smiled like Alice's Cheshire Cat. "Care to say the name of the show out loud? Or does your Mama here disapprove of such things?"

Before I could say the simple three letter name of the play, Nadia chimed in. "I heard they shut that show down. Morals charge, wasn't it?"

"Best publicity a girl could have. Now, like I said, what do you want with my Owney?"

"Business matter," Nadia barked.

"Honey, I've been his business."

"Of that, I'm certain."

The two stood and stared at each other in a wordless duel of will, blue eyes against dark, until the woman made an expansive shrug. "Okay, honey, I was just curious. He said you two can go straight to the back."

She stepped aside and let us in, only for us to be approached by the first sour-faced bruiser who greeted us. He pawed me over, looking for weapons, but not being entirely stupid, I'd left my revolver in Nadia's car. She wasn't treated in the same way and was allowed to proceed, probably a very lucky thing for the poor mope.

Once through the club, smelling of stale booze and burnt tobacco, we were allowed to go into the back room that was loaded with enough crates of alcohol and barrels of beer to refloat the Maine, where Owney Madden himself stood to greet us.

"Miss Ravenwood. I hope Mae didn't give you a hard time."

"Not at all, Mr. Madden. It's good of you to see us. You remember Mr. Locke?"

Madden gave me a brief nod, waving at some chairs at a card table. Once we were all seated, he asked, "Can I get you anything?"

If you didn't know better, all you'd see was a quiet, well dressed man being polite. But this quiet man has a lifetime's worth of scars drawn across his skin and was still carrying all the lead bullets that the doctors couldn't cut out of his body. Forget these things, and you might make the mistake of forgetting this man was an ice cold killer.

Nadia and I declined refreshments, and Madden lit a cigarette. "So what can I do for you?"

Nadia held up one of her cards with a simple arrow drawn on it. "This mean anything to you?"

Owney Madden took the card, then tossed it to the table. "Maybe. Why?"

"We're thinking it's a sign, a symbol for a group."

"That so?" Madden's eyes were like glass marbles, deadpan, like he was playing a hand of poker. "What's your stake in this?"

"One woman's already lost her life, and the family of a young girl may be in danger, not to mention the girl herself. She's my main concern."

Madden sat back, blowing a puff of smoke toward the low ceiling. "I did some checking on you, you know, after you came into my club the first time. Word is, you work for the swells, keeping all the dirty secrets buried."

"That's part of what I do." Nadia held her chin up proudly.

"Yeah? What's the other part?"

"Making certain people get what they deserve."

He nodded. "I imagine that keeps you busy." He picked up her card from the table. "So, getting a line on these guys, what's this worth to you?"

"What do you want?" she anteed up.

"You ever consider working for someone like me?"

"For which job...to bury your dirt or to see you get what you deserve?"

Madden just stared, then a soft wheeze came out of him, like one of his old bullet holes sprang a leak. "You think you're funny?"

"You've seen me when I'm serious. Care to see it again?"

"Okay. I can't promise anything, but I might be able to get you something. Check with me later, okay?"

Having made our deal with the Devil, Nadia Ravenwood and I took our leave from Hell.

Chapter Eighteen:

We used the telephone booth in the lobby of the Hotel Harding to see if anyone left messages for Nadia at her Brownstone, which resulted in a *no*, and if Henry Bowen was at home, only to get stonewalled by Oscar who claimed Henry had yet to return. Nadia hung up. "Oscar could be lying. If Henry went for money, the banks have been closed for hours."

"Perhaps he's gone to the place he goes when he tells people he's at the Engineers Club?" I got a dark-eyed scowl for that remark.

"Regardless. We have no other leads on Richard Bowen's whereabouts. We may as well go back to his house."

The traffic proceeded at the stately pace of a log-jammed river, much to my delight, and Nadia's frustration, where her curses ventured into either French or some Persian tongue. Eventually we arrived at the well-traveled block of Park Avenue and saw a surprising sight: the green Chrysler Imperial that Walter Reeves drove. As we motored past, I saw through the windshield that there was no one behind the wheel.

"Let me pull up around the block." Nadia turned the corner.

There, pedestrians were out and about under the streetlights, including one figure loitering at the garden gate of the Bowen mansion. He wore a fur-trimmed greatcoat, top hat, and leaned on a cane: Mr. Walter Reeves himself.

Nadia Ravenwood swerved to the curb and exited her

automobile in a graceful rush, leaving me to scramble out and run around the car as fast as I could.

Walter Reeve's eyes swiveled from Nadia to me and back again, then his feet did a shuffle as if he couldn't decide which way to run.

I was in no mood for a footrace. "Don't you dare make us chase you."

"Stay back." He brandished the point of his walking stick. "I'm armed."

Nadia stopped and raised her hands. "We only want to talk, Walter."

"You threatened me with a knife...and that one..." he poked his chin in my direction, "laid hands on me."

I shrugged and smiled as I put my hands into my overcoat pockets to get a grip on my .38 revolver. I hadn't made the mistake of keeping my gun out of immediate reach twice in one day. Walter said he was armed, but so far he just swished his cane around like a fencing foil.

Nadia dropped her hands to her side. "Walter, what are you doing here?"

"I am going to see that blackguard Richard Bowen face to face and have it out with him."

I was taken aback. Who used a word like *blackguard* anymore? Slowly, puffed up Walter grew less threatening and more comically tragic, as if he were acting out the lines from a melodrama. Only the tragedies of death were real, I reminded myself. Thus far, we'd managed to escape anyone else's notice.

"How long have you been standing out here?"

Walter lowered the point of his walking stick. "Ever since I left May's house."

"That was hours ago." Nadia glanced at me as she said that, then looked back to Walter. "Have you seen Henry Bowen come home?"

"No. I looked into the carriage house. No cars there, and the only lights that came on were all downstairs."

"All right, Walter, listen to me. My friend and I are here to see that the police don't harm Richard once they get their hands on him. Justice will be done. I promise you that."

"But...what am I supposed to do in the meantime?"

"Go home. Leave everything to us."

He scowled. "Why should I trust you?"

At that, I jumped in. "Because this is what we do. And we do it very well. Otherwise, we would never have been able to stop such a man as yourself when you came at us earlier today, eh?"

Confusion crossed Walter's face as he tried to settle on either being angry or flattered. Flattery won out. "Yes. Of course." He fumbled out a business card with hands that shook a bit. "Here. I would be most grateful. Grateful and generous, mind you, if you keep me informed of your findings."

Nadia exchanged cards with him, and with that, he tipped his hat and walked off. He stopped, though, and halfway turned back. "I loved her, you know. I truly did." And then he resumed on his way.

Nadia Ravenwood looked at me. "I'm glad you didn't shoot him."

"God. That man is obsessed."

"I hear love will do that to you."

Before I could inquire further about her knowledge of love, she bent down and picked up a tiny item off the sidewalk. In the light of the streetlamps, I saw she was holding a little unfired .25 caliber cartridge in the palm of her gloved hand. "Hello," I whispered, "What's this?"

"This may have come from our friend Walter Reeves. He did say he was armed."

I took the cartridge from her hand. It was a common mistake when handling automatic pistols to rack a round into the chamber when it's already loaded, kicking an unfired cartridge out of the gun. The brass and metal jacket of the bullet was new, and it looked like dear old Wally wasn't bluffing when he said he was armed. The pistols these cartridges fit are usually inaccurate and fairly weak, but I still wouldn't want to get shot with one. "You think old Wally was waiting around to assassinate Richard?"

"Not beyond the realm of possibility," Nadia replied. "But at least he's not a member of the group who broke into the garden." To prove her point, Nadia pushed the gate, showing it remained unlocked. "He'd have concealed himself better if he'd known the gate was open."

But we weren't left with anymore time to ponder, as I saw a late model roadster pull up to the Bowen house. Nadia and I rushed up to the corner just in time to see a masculine figure in a heavy overcoat and cap move with alacrity to the front door, where he was admitted right away. "Well, that couldn't be Richard moving like that."

"Shall we find out?" Nadia grinned.

Chapter Nineteen:

I kept a lookout as Nadia rummaged through the coupe's carriage. When she popped out, she said, "It's registered to Henry, all right. Doesn't mean he was driving it."

"So, do we knock on the front door like respectable people?"

"Or go around the back like the sneaky people we are."

I fetched the skeleton keys from the bag in the car and brought back the .32 Browning pistol for Nadia. "Take this. People keep showing up with guns around here."

I watched her as she expertly checked the load and the safety. Nadia Ravenwood did not care for guns, finding them noisy and unpleasant, but she knew full well how to use one. We faded back along the garden wall until we reached the gate, then looked about to see if any people took an interest in us. I should have brought some oil from the burglary kit, as the gate squeaked a bit, but we eased our way inside without raising an alarm.

I tried to recall as much of the layout of the mansion as I had seen, making a guess where Richard's ground-floor room was located. There was an extension from the rear of the house that, at first, I took for a glass-enclosed solarium. I was shocked to suddenly see lights blaze forth from an overhead crystal chandelier and realized this was a formal dining room with a view of the garden.

Nadia took my arm and whispered in my ear, "Perfect. They'll be blind to us out here."

It was quite the opposite for us, for it now resembled a stage where a play was about to commence, only like modern moving pictures we could see the actors but not hear them. And due to the reflection of the light, they could not see us at all. It made me feel like that 'Invisible Man' character Wells wrote a story about.

Nadia and I stood boldly before the tall glass panels as Henry Bowen came into the room followed by Oscar. Henry looked flushed, with his tie askew while Oscar just looked unhappy and contrite. Henry checked his pocket watch and made an angry gesture. Something wasn't going to his liking.

Then, the two of them startled, and Henry made a slashing motion toward the front of the house. Oscar hurried away with unceremonious alacrity.

"Quick," Nadia said. "Get the stethoscope."

I moved back through the darkened garden, slipped though the gate to the car to retrieve that modern boon to both medicine and safecracking then hurried back, glad I didn't trip over any of the pottery lying about. When I got back to Nadia, I stopped cold.

There were two more men in the room, one I recognized, the other I didn't. The first was the florid-faced, mustached gentleman with the white eye patch Nadia had gut-punched back at the opium den. The other was short and stocky, had a round face under a cap, wore a scuffed leather coat, and stood back by the entrance.

Nadia and I crept closer to the edge of the window, and I held the end of the stethoscope to the glass as Nadia and I literally put our heads together, sharing the ear pieces as I attempted not to be distracted by her Egyptian 'Lotus Flower' perfume. The muted voices came to us:

Henry: "What are my assurances? I have the most to lose."

Eyepatch Man: "I would say that is true for your brother, not so much for you. You're only risking money."

Henry: "With no guarantees?"

Eyepatch Man: "That is the deal. Take it and take some risk, or back out and be ruined. Your choice."

There was silence for a moment, then Henry nodded, hanging his head in acquiescence. Without further comment, everyone left the dining room. Nadia and I removed the stethoscope and made our way back to the garden gate, staying just inside the walls.

"That was less than informative."

"At least we know Henry Bowen is in cahoots with Richard's new playmates."

"To what end? Come on, let's follow them."

We returned to Nadia's Rickenbacker and fired it up, then moved to the corner of Park Ave and spotted one of Ford's delivery trucks with a canvass covered bed. Nadia Ravenwood let it pass, and soon we were following behind. We proceeded south, toward the Lower East Side and eventually took Fourth Avenue past Union Square. Even at night it's quite the sight to see the landscape change from the affluent to the tenement. We reached the Bowery, where the traffic and pedestrians picked up with people out and about under the elevated train tracks until the truck pulled off on Canal Street and came to a stop at the front of a garage. Nadia and I stayed well back as we watched the driver and passenger be greeted by others as the bay of the garage admitted the truck, pulling the gate down closed behind.

"What's the address?"

"Only one way to know for certain." Nadia engaged the engine and slowly drove down the street.

I strained my eyes in search of a number on the garage.

Unfortunately, we'd started moving too soon, as four men exited the garage and cut across the street as we passed by. I craned my neck around to see where they went, and I'd have never guessed the answer.

As Nadia pulled the car over, I watched the procession enter a building where a wan electric light lit a cross and the words: *All Night Mission.*

Chapter Twenty:

By the look on Nadia's face, I knew we were going in. "Never too late to get religion, I suppose."

"I'm sure you noticed how close we are to Chinatown."

"Yes. I'm certain that'd be convenient for some people."

"Now, how do we get inside the Mission?"

"We're both a little overdressed for the place. Besides, I recognized one of the men at Henry Bowen's house tonight. The man with the eye patch we met back at the opium den. I'm certain he'd recognize us, as well. You left him with quite a stomachache, as I recall, with that knuckleduster of yours. It's not a good idea to go in there and faceoff with him again."

Nadia fumed quietly. She hated being restrained when on the hunt, like a falcon straining against her jesses. "Very well. Let's go brace Henry Bowen and see what he has to say for himself."

"He lied about the Engineers Club for some reason."

Nadia took us back toward the land of plenty of money. "I'm also thinking about Henry surviving all those gunshots. I can't decide if that may have been some form of warning to him..." She glanced at the rearview mirror. "Or if he was complicit in a charade to throw suspicion off of himself."

"Or if someone was indeed trying to do away with him."

"Our man with the eye patch has made some sort of

deal with Henry, so I don't think he would want him dead. Not yet, anyway." A rearview check again.

I realized she was driving at a reasonable pace. "Let's not forget Henry has something going on with Detective Broderick, whose specialty is with labor insurgents and other anti-business types."

"Which has *what* to do with a group of wounded War Veterans?"

I grumped. "Makes me wonder why we're still on this case."

"Trust me. Someone's going to pay us for our trouble, one way or..." Another quick glance at the mirror made her curse in Russian. "We've got a tail, been following us since we left the Bowery."

"What?"

"Don't turn your head," she spouted. "I've seen the same headlights behind us since I turned left on Canal Street."

I winced, remembering one of Nicholas Ravenwood's cautions in regards to spying: *"Whatever you're doing to someone, someone could be doing the same to you."*

"Let's see, shall we?" Nadia pushed her motor to go faster then suddenly turned right, shoving me against her as she kept an eye on her mirror. "Oh, yes. We have unwanted suitors indeed."

I was about to ask what her plan was when she executed another quick turn and accelerated, only to stomp on her brakes, bringing her car to a screeching halt before the iron fencing of Gramercy Park. She and I flew out the doors as the straining motor of an older Model-T chugged toward us. That's when I saw the long barrel of a rifle protrude out the rear side window.

In truth, I don't know who fired first: I was aware of pulling the trigger on my .38 revolver when the thundering sound of a jackhammer erupted, along with stuttering flames, from the passing Ford. My peashooter was no match against that cannon, so I threw myself down to the cold, hard concrete as the measured whip-crack sound beat the air until the Ford's motor labored on down the street.

I heard tires squealing and sat up in time to see the Model-T turn down a side street and drive out of sight. My heart was beating hard. I looked up to see Nadia Ravenwood standing over me, gun in hand at her side. "Are you hurt?"

"My nerves a little." I got to my feet and saw the gold and black Rickenbacker spewing steam and bleeding hot oil. Not a panel hadn't been pocked, not a window remained intact, the result of a Browning Automatic Rifle. Nothing else sounded like that cannon. It fired hunting rifle rounds and held twenty at a time. I placed a hand on a rear fender, since my legs threatened to quit supporting me, and caught my breath. "Are...you...okay?"

"Do I look okay?"

"You look pretty when you're angry."

Nadia stared at the Rickenbacker. "Another warning shot?"

"Who knows? Ah...do you hear that...or are my ears still ringing?"

"I hear sirens."

We didn't have to wait long. Uniformed officers from the 13th Precinct swarmed us. They were suitably impressed by the amount of gunfire damage visited upon Nadia's car. She made liberal use of her card signed by the Police Commissioner to command the Officers of the Law into bending the rules so as to not have our names appear in any official paperwork and simply record the event as the shooting of an innocent automobile. After making arrangements for the Rickenbacker to be towed to a mechanic, we engaged a taxi to take us to our home away from home, the Waldorf Astoria.

All during the ride to the hotel, Nadia was quietly fuming. I knew the look. Her father's temperament was like an ice berg, cold and deep. Nadia is much more like a smoldering volcano. In other words, in times after great stress or excitement, Nadia had been known to act out a bit. And by *a bit*, I mean a full throated, furniture smashing fury.

Once we were back inside the opulent embrace of the Waldorf, I let Nadia get a head start to her room as I loitered a bit in the lobby. After a while, I went to the elevators and directed the operator to deliver me to the floor of Nadia's Greek Suite. I stayed outside her door as I heard, faintly yet distinctly, the sound of Nadia cursing up a storm, in good old fashioned English this time.

When her rage had passed, I simply went back to my own room, wondering what horrors tomorrow would bring.

Chapter Twenty One:

I confess it took more than one application of scotch whisky to settle me down for the night. When I checked over my revolver, I saw I had only fired two shots before I tried to dig a hole to China through the sidewalk. The thought of Nadia Ravenwood, standing straight up and methodically emptying her father's pistol at the attackers in the Ford, was a vision that left me cold: If they had turned the vicious fire of their automatic rifle on her instead of her car, she'd have been cut in half.

I arose before the clanging of my alarm clock and readied myself for the day, making certain to call for an order of breakfast; I wasn't getting caught short two days in a row if Nadia decided to go off early on a tear. Although I was wondering if her lack of a private automobile would slow her down at all.

My preparations were not in vain. The telephone rang for attention, and the hotel operator connected me with Nadia in her *Greek Room*. "We're going to have company this morning."

"Oh? Who are we to expect?"

"The police. As in Detective Johnny Broderick. He'll be coming here."

"I'm ready."

"Good. Come on up."

When I arrived, I was pleased to see the drawing room in good repair with nothing broken in view, considering the sounds Nadia made when she got behind the door last night. Another good sign was there was but a single remnant of her Turkish cigarettes in the brass tray, showing she was still in control of her few vices. She emerged from the bedroom surprisingly attired in full riding kit: Broadcloth shirt with tie under a suede leather vest over whipcord breeches and tall leather boots.

"You're looking well this morning."

Nadia rolled her eyes. "Horrid night's sleep."

"I need a word."

She stopped and frowned. "Very well."

"You are, without a doubt, the cleverest investigator around. When it comes to wriggling secrets out of people or picking locks or pockets, you are without a peer. But before your father taught me the lessons of being a spy, I was a soldier. And the first thing a soldier learns is when someone is shooting at you, you get the hell out of the way. That's what makes the difference between being a good soldier and a dead hero."

She stared at me, deadpan. "So, you're saying...if I got killed...you'd miss me?"

"Damn it all, yes. The next time someone fires a gun in your direction, duck."

There was a moment, just then, when it seemed that time stood still and the world got small, until there came a knock at the door and the spell was broken.

"Ah. Breakfast." She strode to the door. "Have you had yours?"

"Yes. Smoked salmon with eggs, thank you." I watched as the waiter arranged a silver decanter and demitasse along with a basket of brown bread and honey over snow white linen. Once all was set, Nadia tipped the man and then dug into her meal like a plowman.

Heartwarming to see her so full of life, like nothing fazed her, not even death. "So...what is the plan for today?"

"First, we'll see if we're going to be arrested for

anything. The good detective Broderick did not sound happy over the telephone. Coffee?"

"That Turkish stuff you can cut with a knife? Thank you, no. Presuming we retain our freedom, then what?"

"Get after Henry Bowen. He's the link between those thugs we followed and who in turn followed us and shot up my car, and his brother, Richard. He's still unaccounted for."

"If he's on the lam, he'll be hard to find."

"Perhaps. And perhaps he's been kidnapped by his no-good friends. Maybe he's dead. Let's see what information we can wriggle out of the good detective while he's grilling us about last night."

We had not long to wait, and Detective Broderick did not come alone, for when we opened the door, I was pleased to see Detective Barney Ruditsky standing in the hall, as well. The two detectives made a bit of an odd pair: Broderick with his good looking, if impassive face, versus the amiable homeliness of Ruditsky. Broderick dressed much better, as well, and it was easy to wonder if those rumors of his being open to bribes might be true.

When offers of coffee were declined, we sat ourselves down in the lavishly appointed room, with Ruditsky looking around in open admiration. "Not a bad little home away from home you got here, Miss Ravenwood."

Broderick got right to the point. "You two got yourselves involved in a shoot up last night."

Nadia and I exchanged glances. "Could you be more specific?"

The detectives traded looks, as well. "We got the body of a man shot to death last night, two blocks from where your car was riddled with bullets. You going to say that was some kind of coincidence?"

Nadia stared at Broderick "If you have accusations to

level, then do so. If you do not, then do us the courtesy of telling us what you know of the matter. Mr. Locke and I will be more than glad to help you solve your case."

Ruditsky held up his hands. "Look, Johnny here just asked me if you two were on the level, and I vouched for you, especially after that homicide case last month. I told him you were very helpful. But it sounds like you're tangling with some dangerous people, and I think you're going to want our help."

Ruditsky still held some gratitude, and well he should, since Nadia and I saved him from a recent wrongful arrest situation. However, gratitude faded fast.

I had to ask, "What dangerous people are you talking about?"

"Gangsters," Broderick said flatly.

Chapter Twenty Two:

Nadia smiled. "Gangsters...is that all?"

Granted, she was a consummate actress with whom I would not want to bet against in any high-stakes card game, *besides the fact she cheats.* I'd venture to say I knew her better than anyone, and still, I could never tell what was going on in her mind. If Broderick was trying to discourage her from our current pursuit, he was going about it entirely the wrong way. "What gangsters, exactly?" I asked.

"Labor racketeers, and worse, we have evidence they've joined up with anarchists."

Detective Johnny Broderick's involvement suddenly made sense, as the police Industrial Squad was made for such threats. I looked to Ruditsky. "You in on this too?"

"Nah, I just wanted to tag along this morning to see what you and Her Highness were up to."

That was a shame, as I trusted Ruditsky; Broderick, not so much. Barney Ruditsky was so dedicated that he and his wife once stopped an armed robbery when they were out celebrating their wedding anniversary.

Nadia didn't look impressed. "Tell us about this man who was killed last night."

Johnny Broderick got tight jawed, but Ruditsky gave him a nod.

Broderick huffed. "A guy gets dumped out of a moving car last night over in front of St. Marks church, and the cops get called. But because the church is in the 9th Precinct, they don't tie it up to a shooting just a couple blocks over in the 13th until early this morning. Turns out this man has ties to the anarchists I've been after."

"This man have any missing limbs of note?"

Johnny just stared at her as Ruditsky grinned and whispered to him, "Told ya. She's a witch."

Detective Broderick opened his mouth, doubtless to ask where Nadia got her information but she beat him to it. "Go, on, please."

He stopped, as if getting a grip on his emotions, then: "So when the boys at the 9th see this man's been shot, he gets shipped to the Medical Examiner right away. Turns out he's got three slugs in him: two .32s and one from a .45."

I cut in. "Wait. A .45, you say?" That was strange, as I was shooting a .38. If this was one of the men we tangled with last night, then those .32s certainly came from Nadia's Browning pistol, as she was too bullheaded to duck. "Where did a .45 bullet come from?"

"Coup de Grace," Nadia said.

"Beg pardon?" Broderick asked her.

"My bet is that .45 came from close range. Am I right?"

"Point blank to the temple."

"What of his other wounds?"

"One of the .32s penetrated a lung, but it wasn't fatal."

Nadia nodded. "So, his partner decided to keep him quiet in case the police caught up with him in a hospital, ends his misery, and then leaves him at a church, his silence assured."

Broderick leaned forward. "Since you know so much, any idea about who plugged him?"

"Detective..." Nadia glared at him, "I'm happy to

discuss your suspicions, and even your accusations. All I will say at this point is that my car was shot up, and we don't know any more than that. How far do you want to take this?"

"I don't know. Yet. So let's start with this. Why are you still sticking your noses into police business? I told you to stay out of it."

"We're working on behalf of our client, Mr. Bowen."

"Nothing doing. He doesn't want anything to do with you."

Nadia arched a slick eyebrow. "I didn't say our client was Henry Bowen, did I? He's on again, off again. We're working on behalf of Richard Bowen."

"Richard? He's wanted for murder. Every cop on a beat's got his eye out for that guy."

"Nonetheless, he's still our client. And until we hear it from him, that we are dismissed, then we are still employed on his behalf."

I knew she was bending the truth a bit, but that was her way.

"So what were you doing last night before your car got all shot up?"

"Looking for Richard, of course. What else would we be doing? As to why we were targeted, and by whom, your guess is as good as mine."

"Did you happen to shoot back at the men who were shooting at you?"

"What do your witnesses say?"

"Witnesses? There are no witnesses."

"Well..." Nadia smirked, "pinning anything on us would be a problem for you then, wouldn't it."

Broderick leaned back in his chair, seemingly at a loss. "That little card of yours from the Commissioner only gets you so far, lady. And in this town, Commissioners come and go pretty fast."

Nadia sipped her coffee, the embodiment of innocence.

"Okay." Broderick exhaled, sounding tired. "Give me something, at least. How did you know the dead guy was missing a hand? Did you happen to see him last night?"

Nadia smiled. "I didn't say a hand. I just knew something of his person was missing. Tell you what, I'll trade you, fact for a fact. Who are the gangsters who are supposedly working with the anarchists?"

The two stared at each other. I'm not certain if anyone blinked until Broderick said, "Orgen."

Nadia's dark eyes scowled. "Orgen? That tells me nothing."

"It's a name. And if you find out about the man with that name, I hope you'll have the good sense to stay away from him. He doesn't like people sticking their noses in his business, and he isn't shy about getting rid of them. Now, your turn."

"Very well. You're looking for a group of men who have something in common. They're all ex soldiers and they've all been wounded in the War in some way. They've bonded together in a common cause, but what that is, I don't know. They've chosen a symbol for themselves, one that represents the Norse god Tyr. It's an arrow pointing upwards at two o'clock."

For a few moments, Broderick and Ruditsky just stared at Nadia as if she produced live pigeons out of thin air, until Broderick asked, "And you know this how?"

"People talk to me."

Broderick shook his head, as if trying to take it all in. "One thing is for certain." He and Ruditsky stood in preparation of taking their leave. "I sure wish you'd keep out of this mess."

"Speaking of the Bowen's earlier..." Nadia interjected, "how is Henry tied up in your investigation?"

It was Johnny Broderick's turn to smile. "What else have you got to trade for that little piece of information?"

"My undying gratitude."

Broderick got serious. "Make sure that's not the only thing that stays undying." And with that, he and Ruditsky left.

After they'd gone, I asked her, "What's an *Orgen*?"

"Someone I'm certain our friend Owney Madden can tell us."

"He's not our friend."

"Regardless, we'll have to drop in on him again. But Henry Bowen should be our first stop."

"Shall I call downstairs for a taxi?"

"Nonsense. I arranged to lease a car this morning."

As she turned to leave, I reached out and touched her arm. "Nadia? Are you all right?"

"Yes. Why?"

"You just heard that you shot a man. And he died, whether there was a witness or not."

She looked away, out at nothing. "I didn't actually see it happen, you know, all the muzzle flashes and noise...it doesn't seem real to me."

"Nadia, we weren't the target. The car was...don't you see? Somebody doesn't want us dead. They want us off the case."

"Well, that's not happening. Besides, I didn't kill anybody. His own comrades actually did him in."

"But are you okay?"

She gave me a familiar, sardonic look, letting me know she was going to be fine. Or at least pretend to be.

After retrieving coats and hats, we made our way to the front street entrance, where I was introduced to my latest nightmare: A red, two door Packard roadster.

"It only has ninety horses under the hood," Nadia said wistfully as we climbed in, sharing the only seat. "It's cozy, too."

"So is a coffin."

Chapter Twenty Three:

There were patches of blue sky to be seen over the manmade mountains of the City. I enjoyed the view as best I could as Nadia Ravenwood tested the ability of her new motor toy to scramble my stomach. "The wheel handles nicely." She zipped around an overly burdened delivery truck to the accompaniment of the driver's angry curses punctuated by his horn.

But the distance to the Bowen mansion was life-savingly short, although Nadia chose to drive the long way around and come up on the garden side down from Park Avenue. "Are we sneaking in through the back again?"

"No, I just want to get right up to the front door before anyone can see us coming. Also, I wanted to make certain Walter Reeves wasn't loitering around again today."

Seeing no sign of Walter or his sporty Chrysler Imperial, Nadia and I walked around the block and up to the door, then rang the bell for admittance. The first surprise came when it was not sour-faced Oscar who answered, but a tall dark-haired gent in a neat pinstripe suit and tie, making me think he must have been one of Henry's banker associates. "May I help you?"

"Nadia Ravenwood and Stephen Locke to see Mr. Henry Bowen. That is, unless Mr. Richard Bowen is available."

The man twitched a smile under his neatly clipped moustache. "Won't you come in? Please allow me to help you with your coats and hats."

I enjoyed this vast improvement over Oscar's rather

belligerent butler behavior. Then I stopped; my revolver was inside my overcoat pocket, and I had no graceful way to retrieve it. The man simply raised an eyebrow. "Problem, sir?"

I fished my revolver from my coat. "It's my lucky charm."

The man didn't blink. "I'm afraid you have to hand it over. I'm looking after Mr. Bowen's safety these days."

Nadia made a subtle gesture that told me to go along, and I opened the cylinder and removed the bullets, then handed the gun to him and pocketed the ammunition.

"I shouldn't worry. You'll certainly have no need of a weapon in this house."

"Odd," I said. "Considering just the other night someone shot the place up."

"We have security now." The gentleman turned to Nadia. "Nothing to declare?"

She just returned his gaze placidly, and I was sorry he didn't press the point. Not only would Nadia never willingly hand over her dangerous 'little sisters', but one may as well stick their own head inside a bag of angry cats as to try to make her.

"Wait here in the reception room, and I'll see if Mr. Bowen will come down."

Nadia and I were left inside a comfortable, well furnished area with a view of Park Avenue, but were now insulated from the rest of the house. A fact I confirmed when I checked the door and found it locked. "Security, indeed."

"Not to mention rude. Still, I can't blame Henry for taking precautions after what he's been through. What do you make of the new man?"

"He's unctuous enough to be a snob's servant, but he looks a bit too physically fit and knows firearms too well for my liking."

"Former soldier, perhaps?"

"Sure. Or police. Or gangster."

"Nice how you narrowed the field."

We stopped as we heard the lock being turned and saw Mary Bowen as she quickly slipped in and closed the door behind her. "It is you," she whispered.

"Hello," Nadia said. "So what have we missed?"

"Everything. Richard still hasn't come home, and since last night there's this man named Mr. Baker who Henry says is in charge of the house. Everyone has to do what he says, and he's locked up the telephone. I'm not allowed to go to my lessons. Henry says it's just for a while, but I don't like it."

"Mary, you'd best get moving. You don't want to be caught here. You still have your pass key and remember my telephone number?"

Mary nodded

"Go. I'll find a way to get in touch with you."

Acting as a good soldier herself, Mary went without further word, leaving Nadia staring darkly at the door. "I hate the idea of leaving that girl here. I really do."

But Mary didn't depart any too soon as the door was again unlocked and the butler stepped in. "If you both will follow me, Mr. Bowen will see you now."

Nadia moved quickly as she walked past the man. I followed close behind. He led us to the same den where we saw Henry recovering from his shooting affair. There was definitely far less brandy in evidence.

Henry sat at an inlaid writing desk, and as we entered and said without preamble, "I'm prepared to pay you for your services to date and be done with you. Please name your price."

"I'm sorry, Mr. Bowen, but I'm here on your brother's

behalf, and until I find him, I wouldn't think of taking your money."

Henry's face colored as his eyes blinked, It seemed as if he couldn't understand the words that were spoken to him. "But, I'm the one who hired you originally. You work for me until I say otherwise."

"That was true then..." Nadia shrugged, "but since the police interrogated Richard and placed him under suspicion of murder, I've worked on his behalf exclusively."

"You can't. I won't allow it."

Nadia spread her hands. "It's not up to you anymore."

The problem was Richard Bowen made it very clear that he wanted nothing to do with Nadia and me right after his interrogation by Detective McDonough. But since there were no other witnesses to that event, Nadia simply got away with her boldly stated lie.

The tension grew like a rising tide.

"So, if I am to be dismissed, it'll have to come from Richard Bowen himself. In person."

Chapter Twenty Four:

Henry's face turned so red I thought it would explode. "So, if you no longer work for me, why are you here?"

"I was hoping for word of Richard," Nadia said. "Has he contacted you at all since he disappeared?"

"What? No. No, he hasn't."

"And no one else has contacted you about him?"

There was a heartbeat's hesitation as Henry stumbled his reply. "N-no."

"And will you call for me when he does? After all, I'm only trying to help your brother."

The new butler, who had yet to introduce himself, stood by the door. "Just what will you do with Richard when you find him?"

Nadia turned and fixed him with her best dark-eyed glare. "And who, may I ask, are you to ask such a question?"

"My associate," Henry jumped in. "Mr. Baker. He's here to help me with some matters. He has my complete confidence."

"In that case, Mr. Baker, I intend to see that Richard Bowen is safely delivered into the hands of the police and is assured of the best possible legal counsel. It's what I do for clients who manage to get on the wrong side of the law. Speaking of such, would you care for my card?"

Mr. Baker smiled.

I imagined hyenas smiled in the same manner.

"Thank you, no. I have my own remedies for trouble,

Miss Ravenwood."

Nadia shrugged off his comment as a matter of no concern, and turned back to Henry. "I have one other issue to broach."

"Miss Ravenwood, I really do not have the time—"

"It's about your sister, Mary."

Henry looked as shocked as if Nadia had slapped him. "Mary? She has nothing to do with anything."

"I worry for her safety. After all, you were violently attacked here in your own home. What if those assassins had shot up the rest of the house?"

"What? Miss Ravenwood, I have the protection of—" Henry stopped, eyes widening. Clearly, he'd almost uttered something he didn't want us to know. "The police...I've got Detective Broderick's word that my safety and the safety of everyone in this house is assured."

Nadia scoffed. "The same police who cannot find your brother?"

Henry had had more than enough. "Miss Ravenwood, I shall ask you to leave now. I am done speaking with you."

"Let me take Mary with me."

No one, including me, knew what to say to that. But as if on cue, Mary rushed into the room. "Really? I could go with you?"

"Mary," Henry shouted. "What have I told you about sneaking around and eavesdropping?"

"I want to go with her and help find Richard."

Mr. Baker looked at Nadia with measuring eyes. "Just what are you proposing?"

Nadia ignored him and kept the pressure on Henry. "I can keep the girl safe. Truly safe. For as long as necessary. That way, you will have one less worry."

Henry looked to Mary, and something I hadn't yet seen in his eyes appeared: something that may have been love. "All right...but only for a little while. Until things get settled. If that's what you want, little Bo."

Mary rushed up and threw her arms around Henry. "I asked you not to call me that anymore."

"I suggest we go right away." Nadia took Mary's hand. "We can send for her things later, but the sooner we're gone, the better."

"Certainly." Mr. Baker bowed and escorted us to the vestibule. As we gathered our coats, I couldn't read the expression on Henry's face, but Mr. Baker's was clear when he returned my revolver to me. He and I looked at each other face-to-face, each nodding to the other as Roman Gladiators about to fight to the death.

As we walked away from the house, Mary was somber. "Are you sure me leaving Henry now is the best thing?"

"Henry loves you, dear. And I'm sure he saw that letting you go is the best way to keep you safe."

"Henry and Richard are in trouble, aren't they."

"Maybe. But we can try to get him out of it, yes?"

It was an encouragement I hoped Nadia wouldn't regret.

Our getaway was complicated by the fact that Nadia's new motorized toy didn't have room for the three of us. The laws of hospitality and Chivalry dictated that I was stuck in the rumble seat, crouched, holding on to my hat with one hand and the carriage with the other as Nadia did her best to recreate the Indianapolis 500.

Chapter Twenty Five:

I was hopeful I'd survive the trip, until I realized Nadia was driving not to our hotel rooms, but her Upper West Side Brownstone. I was tempted to escape during the times we were stopped for traffic, but ultimately resigned myself to a test of endurance.

When we finally arrived, I was trying to find some sense of feeling in my hands and face as Nadia Ravenwood assembled her house staff and introduced them to Miss Mary Bowen. The girl was looking a bit shy, as well she should, as Nadia's house staff resembled a gang of cutthroat brigands barely disguised as servants. Which, in fact, they were.

It was Nicholas Ravenwood who, throughout the years, gathered them together from across the globe. From Mr. Ivanov, the butler, who fought against the Bolsheviks in the Russian Civil War to Mr. Li, the chef, who in his youth took part in the Boxer Rebellion, to little Miss Murphy, the maid, who couldn't go home to Ireland due to her activities during the Easter Rising, Nicholas took them all in. And their loyalty was now given to Nicholas's daughter, Nadia.

After introductions, Nadia sent Mary off with Mr. Ivanov for a tour of the house to conclude in Mr. Li's kitchen, and when that was underway, I saw Nadia whisper to Miss Murphy, who nodded and smiled with a rather wicked gleam in her eye, and then rushed off to do the mistress's bidding.

I was shivering. "If you won't be needing me for a bit,

I think I'll try to thaw out somewhere."

"Come up to the Reading Room. I'll turn up the radiator."

The 'Reading Room' was a bit deceptive. Granted, it had a bookshelf with not only the Classics but some new, popular works, as well, and a collection of *Judge, Photoplay* and other newsstand fare usually left lying about, but primarily it was the place where Nadia kept all the modern entertainments: the radio, a phonograph with an eclectic selection of recordings, and the telephone.

It was to this last device that Nadia went, asking the operator to connect her to a number I'd come to know and dread.

When the connections were made, my fears were confirmed. "Auntie Kit? Nadia Ravenwood here. Could you spare some time today? I'm in want of a guide. You're free? Splendid! My place. See you soon."

"Just what, in God's name, are you planning to do with her?"

Nadia fetched one of her Turkish cigarettes, indulging herself early, I noted. "Kit can take Mary shopping for clothes and necessities."

"Perfect. Then I'm sure afterwards she can take Mary to her first speakeasy. It will all be quite educational, I'm sure."

She sat on the sofa and sent a cloud of smoke to the ceiling. "You exaggerate wildly. Besides, I'll send Miss Murphy along as well."

I lit one of my own Chesterfields. "You never had dolls of your own growing up, did you?"

This time, she sent a cloud of smoke my way. "You think that's why I dragged Mary over here?"

"It's a thought."

"But I did have dolls. Every Christmas, wherever

Father had placed me, when he wasn't coming to see me himself, he'd send a great big beautiful doll as a present. The other girls would be quite jealous when they got back from seeing their families."

"Oh. Did you have a collection?"

"I always burned them right after the holidays."

I mulled this over. "Perhaps we ought not have children around this place."

Nadia laughed. "Truly, if Henry is in a situation where he's being forced to do things he doesn't want to do, then his sister is in harm's way. Did I mention that his Mr. Baker was carrying a pistol under his jacket? I verified that little fact when I passed him in the doorway."

"I'm not surprised. You didn't happen to lift his wallet as you went by, did you?"

"He was a bit too alert."

"Pity. He may be carrying around some incriminating information. Ah, well. What is our next move?"

"After Auntie Kit comes for Mary, you and I are off to the Bowery. By the way, you're overdressed for that occasion."

I waited until we'd finished our smokes then went to my room. I kept a variety of attire in a variety of conditions, from evening wear to old worn apparel. I changed into poorer, though more comfortable, clothes with sturdy, scuffed hiking boots and topped off the look with an old cloth cap and well worn trench coat that had a patched bullet hole on the front pocket, a souvenir I brought back from Europe.

I delved into my travel-scarred trunk and came up with a relic from the War: a .45 Colt pistol. This was an ugly, brutal weapon, much like the Browning Automatic Rifle the unknown enemy chose to use against Nadia and me. It was also a reminder of what Nicholas Ravenwood taught me. He always said that the spy business was one of silence and secrecy, and that violence was absolutely the last resort. While he himself was an excellent shot, he very seldom carried a firearm, and once said that a spy should be able to kill a man, if necessary, with a knife or bare hands. But this job was feeling less like spy work and far more like a war, so I decided to bring the Colt and a couple of extra magazines along to even up the odds.

Because whatever way we were headed next, Nadia and I were bound to find trouble.

Chapter Twenty Six:

I rejoined Nadia and Mary in the parlor, where Auntie Kit had just made her appearance. If there was anyone on earth whose presence could overmatch the exotic treasures of the Ravenwood collection, it was Auntie Kit. Her true name was Catherine Krupp, and she was happily and prosperously widowed. She was a woman of mature years and immature manner with wide-apart gray eyes and a wider smile. Her processed platinum-bobbed hair and makeup seemed suitable for a Broadway performance. She didn't simply walk, she promenaded, waving her ebony cigarette holder like a conductor's baton. Today, she was clad in a jungle's worth of leopard prints. "Stephen. Darling. Give us a kiss."

I braved her cloud of French perfume and received my punishment stoically. "Nice to see you, Kit," I lied.

"And who is this little confection?" Auntie Kit inquired of Mary.

She dutifully stepped up and performed a short curtsey. "Mary Bowen, ma'am."

Kit's Cheshire Cat smile froze for a moment. "Ma'am?" she said in her rich contralto. "Oh, we are destined to be so much better friends than that. And what on earth are you wearing? Are you a runaway from the Navy?"

Mary was wearing her sailor's tunic over a long, pleated skirt. "What's wrong with what I'm wearing?"

"For a child, it's charming. For a young woman, it simply won't do. Now, get your coat, dear girl. We have a date with Saks."

As a somewhat bewildered Mary exited, Nadia turned to Kit. "I'm sending Miss Murphy along with you in case of trouble."

"Trouble? You don't think I can handle a little of that on my own?"

"I think you can be the cause of a great deal of it, Kitty. But in this case, Mary's brothers are tangled up with dangerous people, so I want to send some of my own along for protection."

"In that case, how about that yummy Mr. Ivanov? Or your mysterious Mr. Li?"

Nadia raised an eyebrow. "And who would protect them from you?"

Kit looked away, murmuring under her breath, "Slander and libel, that's all I get."

We waited until a somewhat hesitant Mary and Miss Murphy were swept away by Kitty. "All right, Stephen. Our turn."

I placed my Colt and extra ammunition into our black bag, noting that the Browning pistol was not in evidence, signaling Nadia was already carrying it. Instead, I saw an ugly, bound together package wrapped in butcher paper with a fuse protruding out. "What the hell is that?"

Nadia spared a quick glance. "Ah. A little something Miss Murphy whipped up for us."

That caused my blood temperature to drop several degrees. Miss Murphy, during her time in Ireland's Troubles, had been a newly minted nurse who tended to the wounds of her rebellious countrymen. She also turned her talents into making explosive devices of various types. And here I was about to drive around town with one of her little specialties inside the car. "Just what are your intentions for our outing?"

"You'll see."

Nicholas Ravenwood was the consummate spy, and he always said it was like every other profession in that it had rules and guidelines. One of those rules was that information should not be shared until absolutely necessary. Personally, I don't think Nadia gave a hoot about rules of any kind. She just liked surprises, as long as she was the one doing the surprising.

We sped through the early afternoon traffic as best we could, heading downtown, keeping well away from the Great White Way and closer to the West Side docks until we caught Canal Street and drove past Chinatown to the area near the *All Night Mission*. This was a fairly busy and well traveled area of the Bowery district, close to the elevated train tracks.

As Nadia parked the car around the corner from the Mission, I asked, "Now what?"

"Now you take that little device Miss Murphy made up and put it in your pocket."

"What if it goes off?"

"Then I shall have stern words for her."

We stepped to the sidewalk, letting the people walk around us as we stared down the street. Once away from the eye-catching automobile that was Nadia's new toy, we blended in better, with Nadia in a long midnight-blue overcoat that covered her riding apparel. "The problem is, we don't have a way to safely check out the Mission. We've seen the man with the eye patch go in there, and he's seen us at the opium den."

I craned my neck around for high ground. Most of the roof tops here were only three or four stories tall, so climbing up on one across the street would provide a good vantage point. On the other hand, the mechanics' garage on that side was already known to be used by our unidentified enemies. "I supposed we could loiter at the barber shop or billiards hall over there and watch who comes and goes?"

"I've got a better idea. You stay put by the lamppost and keep watch. Give me the package."

I did a subtle handoff of Miss Murphy's infernal device, and Nadia made it disappear inside her coat. The woman was a magician when it came to making small items vanish from view, or your pockets, for that matter. I struck up a cigarette and kept the All Night Mission in sight. But before ten minutes had passed, Nadia was again by my side. "What's up?"

She had a mysterious smile on her lips as she whispered, "Keep watching."

Other than the parade of people and vehicles sputtering up and down the street, nothing of note occurred. Until a somewhat ragged young man came sauntering out, moving halfway up the block until he broke into a run as he cut through the cars and trucks on the street, crossing over to our side where he resumed his causal stroll. As he passed by us, Miss Ravenwood tossed a gleaming coin in the air and he snatched it up, never breaking stride.

"Who's your new friend?"

"Just an industrious young gentleman who wanted to make a not so honest couple of dollars. Now, just watch."

I did as instructed, and then the show began.

Cries of "Fire" were shouted as men came spilling out of the Mission, coughing and wiping their eyes, followed by tendrils of black smoke. Traffic came to a screeching halt as people rushed to gather by the doors, filling the road as they called out and pointed upward, where smoke came billowing from the upper windows.

"So, not a bomb?" I whispered into Nadia's ear.

"More like a plumber's rocket, all smoke and very little fire. I figured if we couldn't get in to see who's there,

I'd invite them to step outside."

We had to stand on the back of a delivery truck to see over the crowd, but I got a glimpse of one familiar face, though it took a moment to recognize her by her scowling expression. There, with her shiny platinum hair covered by a bonnet and wearing a simple gingham dress, stood the woman I'd seen cradling the unconscious Richard Bowen in the shabby opium den. Only now she was surrounded by a cadre of hard-faced men, circling protectively around her.

Many of them could clearly be called *walking wounded*.

Chapter Twenty Seven:

We stepped down from the bed of the truck as the clanging of the fire engines could be heard. Nadia hissed a string of curses in French. "Damn it all. I really want to talk with that woman."

"She's too well guarded at the moment. And they're going to discover your little smoke bomb sooner than later, which will keep them feeling suspicious, no doubt."

As we were discussing our options, I spotted one of the men make a quick salute and leave the circle, heading away down Canal Street toward the Bowery. "Looks like one broke away from the herd."

"Here's your chance to play Cowboy. Let's go round him up, shall we?"

Despite his reliance on crutches, the man moved with speed and more than a measure of grace, deftly dodging his way through the crowd as we followed behind and across the street from him. He kept up his rapid pace, and I took a few glances behind us to make certain we were not being followed in turn.

The man led us to the warren of Chatham Square, under the shadows cast by numerous twisting elevated train tracks and covered stations lifted over busy intersections. Here, the man, without slacking his pace, went right up to the entrance of a tall building with lettering in Chinese characters affixed to the front and vanished inside.

Miss Ravenwood and I made to follow, until a trio of men materialized ahead of us, barring our path to the door. They were Chinese, dressed in the Western manner, and as we approached, one stepped ahead of the others and took off his bowler hat. "May I help you?" His accent was distinctly British.

It wasn't his polite inquiry that gave me pause as much as the subtle clicking sounds that came from behind the crown of the bowler that kept his hand out of sight. A sound that signified the hammer of a pistol being cocked.

But Nadia blithely stepped up to him. "Yes, you may. I am following the gentleman who just entered that building. Please stand aside."

The man smiled. "I am quite sorry, madam, but the man you were following has vanished. Therefore, you have no further business here."

Nadia distinctly spoke a phrase in Chinese, and even I recognized the words *boo how doy*, signifying a soldier in a Tong's army. But the man's placid features never wavered. "In answer to your, pardon me for saying, poorly worded inquiry, we are not anyone's *Hatchet Men*. Rather, you may consider my associates and I as magicians. In other words, if you persist in your pursuit, you and your friend will, like the man you followed, simply disappear, never to be seen again."

While he was speaking, a window opened up on the third floor and a rifle barrel protruded out. I leaned over to Nadia and whispered in her ear, "I know you said for us to play Cowboy, but this is looking like the wrong side of the O.K. Corral, or possibly Custer's Last Stand."

Nadia's dark eyes glanced here and there, finding no other option. She then uttered another sentence in Chinese as she gracefully bowed, then turned about and retreated back up the street.

I marched alongside. "What did you say just now?"

"Even the finest sword, when plunged into salt water, will eventually rust."

"What was that supposed to mean?"

"I have no clue. It's one of the phrases Father taught me. I just wanted to confuse our new friends long enough to make them sweat."

"Now what?"

"Clearly, our army of wounded men has some kind of deal worked up with one of the Chinatown Tongs. Detective Broderick said he thought that there was some kind of collaboration between anarchists and gangsters, whoever that *Orgen* person turns out to be."

"Tongs, anarchists and gangsters...so now we have three fronts to worry about?"

"Possibly. As for now, we're close to the 5th Precinct. Let's see if Detective McDonough can be of any use."

Unfortunately, we were informed, at the Precinct house, that the good detective was at dinner, but Nadia managed to elicit where: close by at the Nom Wah Tea Parlor on twisty, rundown Doyers Street. We found Detective McDonough in the back of a crowded shop at a small table by himself, where he was in the process of deftly devouring some dumplings with a pair of chopsticks. He had the grace to rise at Nadia Ravenwood's approach, but his scowl was less than inviting. "Unless you're here to tell me you've got Richard Bowen ready to surrender, we have nothing to discuss."

I took up a pair of spare chairs and placed them at McDonough's table for Nadia and me.

She sat across from McDonough. "Believe it or not, Richard Bowen may be the least of our worries."

"The least of... Miss Ravenwood, unlike myself, you haven't got the Mayor's office breathing down your neck over this case."

"But that's just it," Nadia replied. "Richard Bowen is just one case. If I am not mistaken, he may be the one loose string that leads to something much, much larger."

Detective McDonough sat with his usually tight jaw slightly ajar.

"But all this talk of disaster makes me hungry. How are the dumplings?"

Chapter Twenty Eight:

I'll give this to Detective McDonough, he has patience. He calmly waited for our order of Oolong tea, egg soup and dumplings to arrive. I was a tad jealous of the way Nadia wielded her chopsticks, while I had to ask for a fork. Still, McDonough's icy demeanor prevailed until Nadia opened the questions list. "So who runs that eight-story building over at Chatham Square backing up to Chinatown?"

McDonough's eyes narrowed. "Number seven? What's your interest there?"

"It may connect to Richard Bowen."

"How?"

"I don't know, yet."

"Stay away from that place. It's nowhere for a, shall we say, outsider to go."

"Not for the *gweilo*?"

I had to ask, "Gweilo?"

"It's Cantonese for a *white devil* or a *foreigner*. Interpretations vary slightly," Nadia said. "So who are the boss Tongs these days?"

"What has this to do with Richard Bowen?"

"Simple, detective...you help me, and I will help you. In other words, as soon as I have Richard Bowen safely in hand, you will be the very first person I call."

McDonough's eyes narrowed as he weighed a decision to make a deal with this particular dark eyed *gweilo* casually sipping her tea. "All right. But if you go back on me, I'll make sure you regret it, no matter what the

Police Commissioner might say."

"Deal," Nadia said. "Now, who's running things around here?"

Detective McDonough looked around to make certain we were not to be overheard through the murmured conversations of the other diners then he leaned across the table. "All right, here you've got the On Leong Tong and the Hip Sing. They've had it out before, but it's been quiet for a while now."

"I remember hearing about the Tong Wars," I said. "Bloody affairs, yes?"

"The Chinese Theater Massacre happened right on this very street," McDonough said. "But now, On Leong and Hip Sing are working hard to keep things respectable. Old Tom Lee, the man they used to call the Mayor of Chinatown, was On Leong. Now I hear his son Frank Lee is the Ambassador from China to Washington. Pretty good from humble beginnings."

"Doesn't really answer my question, though. Who's running the crime business these days?"

"Depends on what you're looking for. If it's anything to do with opium, I'd say Hip Sing is your best bet."

"So, tell me, detective. What would you say if someone threatened to make a person disappear in Chinatown?"

"Someone threatened you?"

"Heaven's no. I'm speaking in general."

McDonough laughed softly. "Chinatown's riddled with underground tunnels. Has been since before they tore up Mulberry Bend out of the ghettos of Five Points and built Columbus Park. There's a hidden entrance or two along Doyers Street."

"Columbus Park is where May Scott's body was found." Nadia sipped tea. "The question is, was she murdered there? Or was she murdered somewhere else and then dumped there?" She stared at McDonough. "My guess is dumped, wasn't she."

"I did not say that," McDonough spat.

Nadia leaned forward. "You have a muscle in your jaw that twitches when you're holding back."

"Don't play poker with her," I advised him. I didn't add the fact that she cheats.

"Was her body left in such a way as to conceal it, or was it left out in the open to be discovered?"

McDonough leaned back with his poker face firmly in place. "That's a matter for the police to know."

Nadia pressed her point. "Either the killer attempted to cover a crime, or he wanted to put pressure on Richard Bowen, which would be a point in favor of his innocence."

Detective McDonough rose from his chair, took up his overcoat and hat, tipped his chin politely to Miss Ravenwood, and left without a further word.

Nadia grinned. "Ha! We're on to something there. Come on, let's take a stroll in the park."

We paid our bill, and Detective McDonough's, as well. The proprietor wouldn't take money for the detective's meal directly, a long-standing local custom of common corruption between police and Chinese merchants, no doubt, so instead, Nadia offered money for prayers at the temple.

The route we took to Columbus Park went through Chatham Square and under the cold shadows of the elevated tracks. We both kept our eyes on the tall building where those charmingly mannered and murderously intentioned men so politely accosted us. I felt the same skin-crawling sensation as I did back in the War when we were under the threat of snipers.

But we passed through unharmed to the borders of

Columbus Park and strolled along its wide, winding paths amidst the bare-limbed trees and patches of dull late-fall grass. It afforded an unobstructed view all around, like an oasis in the middle of the structures of Chinatown and the surrounding tenements of the other neighborhoods. And with all of that, one thing was clear to see:

This would be the last place anyone would choose to hide a body.

Chapter Twenty Nine:

The sun was setting behind the manmade peaks of Manhattan, and suddenly being out in the open in the park felt like a dangerous thing to do. "We have more than our share of enemies nearby," I said. "Perhaps a strategic retreat is in order."

Nadia made an exasperated sigh. "Too right, as my English friends used to say. Let's get back to the car."

"If your car is still where you left it. The odds in this neighborhood go down precipitously after dark."

We put some spring into our step as we retraced our path down the sidewalks, with frequent glances to see if we were being followed. But when we turned the last corner, I spotted Nadia's Packard with a small crowd of ragged youths leaning against it. My hand had been inside my pocket on the butt of my revolver since we left Columbus Park. Now, I gave it a heft to make certain it would slide right out of its holster.

Nadia strolled up to the ruffians. One straightened and approached her in turn. He was the slender, dark-haired youth who'd pulled off the smoke bombing of the *All Night Mission*. "Everything all clear, Anthony?"

"Not a peep, Miss. The bums shuffle in, the bums shuffle out. But every once in a while, some of those gimpy ones show up, always checking over their shoulder."

"Anything else?"

"Nah. Nobody pays attention to that dump."

Nadia shook hands with the young man, and he looked down to see folded dollars in his hand. He tipped his cap. "Nice doing business with you, Miss."

"You have my card. You know what I want to hear."

With that, he fairly strutted back to his tribe as they peeled off the coupe and formed a cadre around him, and then they strode together down the sidewalk.

"Hiring mercenaries?" I inquired.

"Eyes and ears, Stephen. The bread and butter of our business. I'm content that we have at least a small presence here in the Bowery to keep an eye on things in our absence. Let's go."

We cozied up together inside the Packard's cab and I was glad to get out from under the oppressive cover of the overhead tracks and away from the grimy structures of the Bowery. As we traveled north amidst automobiles and trolley cars, I realized where we were headed. "Back to the Bowen Mansion, yes?"

"Henry is clearly keeping things from us, and possibly Detective Broderick, as well."

"Agreed. But if Johnny Broderick isn't going to beat the information out of him, I don't see what we can do. Especially with Mr. Baker hanging about. And by taking Mary out of the house, we've lost our only spy."

Nadia grinned, tight lipped. "Perhaps not."

This time, we parked well away from the Mansion and walked up to the servant and delivery entrance. Nadia asked of the kitchen staff who answered our knock, "Is Oscar available, please. I would like a private word."

We weren't left waiting long when a wide-eyed Oscar appeared. "What are you doing here?"

"Are you happy with what has been going on under your roof?" Nadia asked.

"Am I...what, exactly, are you asking me?"

"Richard Bowen is missing and suspected of murder, Henry Bowen was nearly killed by gunshots, and now you have a man in your house that I am not entirely certain isn't some kind of criminal. Quite frankly, I am surprised that Mr. Baker hasn't insisted on your dismissal thus far."

"Mr. Baker has made it clear I am to have no duties for the present."

"Yes, that certainly fits with my fears on your behalf. So all I am going to say to you, Oscar, is that if you finally choose to see what is right in front of your eyes, then call on me, and I can help. For the sake of the family you serve, please let me know what I can do."

Nadia deftly placed her card inside Oscar's uniform upper pocket, then spun about and left. As I rushed to catch up, I took a look back and saw Oscar was still filling the doorway. "You left him speechless."

"As long as I left him wanting to do the right thing. All right, enough for one day."

"Back to the Waldorf?"

"Not for me. I have company at home. Still, it may be good to keep you close to the Bowen residence for now. I'll send for my trunk tomorrow."

"Well, if I must make such a sacrifice, so be it."

"Try to find a way to console yourself."

After Nadia dropped me off, I made my way to the desk, drawing more than a few suspicious looks for my less than reputable appearance, and retrieved my key. The Chinese dumplings I ate were a rapidly fading memory, and I considered the epicurean delights that lay within the palatial hotel. I also knew a certain redhead I might convince to join me.

Now, if only the thrice-damned telephone would say silent for just one night, I prayed.

As it turned out, my prayers were answered. The answer, unfortunately, was *No*.

Chapter Thirty:

I was enjoying a wallow in the tub of my room, but to my regret, telephones were included in the amenities, as well, and mine clanged unendingly for attention until I braved forth, clad only in a towel to pull the head off the mechanical beast.

When the operator connected us, Nadia Ravenwood said, "We've had a bite on our bait. Oscar called and said that Henry and his Mr. Baker are leaving the house tonight and have given all the serving staff the evening off."

"Why would that sneaky excuse of a butler tell you that?"

"Hopefully, because I lit a fire of insecurity under him."

"Sounds like a wonderful trap you've just been invited to, you know."

"Doesn't it just?"

I sighed. "We're going anyway, aren't we."

"I'll be along soon." She hung up.

At the least, I would have provided the Medical Examiner with a freshly washed body should worse come to absolute flaming hell worse. I quickly dried off and dressed, almost capriciously choosing full evening wear with top hat. If one was going to be a burglar, one might as well do it in style. Instead, I chose my well worn, comfortable clothes with cloth cap and old trench coat.

I loitered under the awning, letting the liveried Waldorf Astoria doormen give me *get-thither* looks until Nadia's little red roadster roared up. I barely got my door shut when she thrust us into traffic with a warning blare of her horn.

"Do we have something that resembles a...what do you call it again... Oh. A plan?"

"We'll get in. Poke around. Get out."

"Ah. Three clear and concise steps. Well done."

"I could throw you out at the corner."

"And miss my opportunity to say I told you so? Nothing doing."

Nadia was far more circumspect than her attitude conveyed, as we drove around the block twice, looking carefully for anything out of the ordinary near the Bowen manor. "I can't see a reason to hesitate," I said. "And God knows I've been looking."

"All right. Let's go."

We left Nadia's car a ways down the block, and as we strolled up the sidewalk, we kept our eyes out for traffic and movements at windows. She came dressed for the occasion. In her long black coat and black bell-brimmed cloche hat, she'd be near invisible in the shadows. Through the garden gate we went, stealing up to a back door, where Nadia went to work with skeleton keys. I held the bag of tools, glad to have the .45 close at hand. She unlatched the lock, and soon we were within a darkened hall. Nadia pointed upwards, and I followed after her, flashlight at the ready but left off.

We came to a back set of stairs next to a dumbwaiter, the servants' access to the upper floors, and crept along. The upstairs hallway led us to a variety of bed chambers until we reached the front of the house and came to Henry Bowen's study. We listened intently, but other than the slight creaking produced by every large house, there was nothing to alert us to the presence of another person.

Nadia tested the door and found it locked, so then

produced Mary Bowen's pass key. We opened the door, but slowly, taking in the scent of fresh varnish from the recent bullet hole repairs. Nadia slipped in, and I followed, seeing her point to the open curtains; a flash of light from this room would be easily seen from the street. "Stay by the door," she whispered.

I watched as she carefully eased her way around the study, using only the wan glow of the streetlights outside for illumination. Henry's wide desk had been cleared of all papers, but Nadia waved for attention and pointed to the corner of the room.

There was a safe.

I caught the flash of her teeth as she briefly smiled and reached to take the bag of tools from me. From then on, I divided my attention between listening outside the room and keeping an eye on Nadia. I heard the dull *thunk* of the safe's handle being turned, and soon heard the slight rustling of papers as Nadia lifted them up to catch the light from the street.

The telephone began to ring.

Through the shadows, Nadia and I looked to each other for a moment, then she motioned for me to go and answer. I picked up the receiver. "Hello?"

The operator was on the line. "I have a call for Henry Bowen."

"Go ahead, operator."

There was the clicking of connections being made, and then I heard a desperate voice, "Henry?"

"Yes?"

"Henry, for God sakes, why haven't you sent the money?"

It was Richard. Now that I had him on the line, I tried to think of a way to reel him in. "Where are you?"

"Where am I? Wait. Who is this?"

While I was thinking of an answer, Nadia had stalked up to me, moving quietly as a ghost. She took the receiver from my hand. "Richard? This is Nadia Ravenwood. I know you're in a desperate situation. Let me help you. Because if you're counting on Henry, I wouldn't. It looks like things are completely out of his control."

That's when I heard the squeaking of brakes as a car came to a halt directly outside the Bowen mansion.

"Richard? I need an answer."

"You can't help me." He broke the connection.

Nadia rapidly clicked the telephone handle. "Operator? Operator? Can you give me the numbers of that last call? Yes? Thank you."

I replaced the telephone as Nadia rushed to close the safe and return to me. We moved with speed and were halfway down the steps when we heard the front door open and saw the flash of light from the foyer chandelier and also heard an angry male voice echoing through the house.

"I still say it's a mistake not to make certain he stays quiet."

Chapter Thirty One:

Nadia Ravenwood and I were as still as statues, barely breathing, straining to hear the words that echoed from down the hall, words that became more faint as the speakers ascended the stairs.

"But he's my brother."

"He can't be allowed to talk. Granted he doesn't know the big..."

We'd lost our vantage. Clearly, Henry and the voice who sounded like the smug tones of Mr. Baker were discussing Richard Bowen's very life, or death, and even in the shadows I could see the fraught emotion playing across Nadia's face, doubtlessly deciding to either get closer and overhear more, or knowing her, possibly confront these knaves in their very den. Sadly, the law would take a rather dim view of how we came to be here. "Shhh...we've been lucky so far," I whispered.

She nodded once, emphatically, and we carefully exited out the back door to the garden. It was well we did not abandon our stealthy retreat, as when we came to the iron gate, we spotted a stocky man in a leather coat and cap, loitering across the street...the same one we saw in the company of the man with the eye patch at this very house when we eavesdropped on their dining room conversation the night before.

I heard the faint *click* that came from Nadia's pocket, the sound of her releasing the safety of the Browning pistol.

My revolver was as ready as ever, but if I was going to bring my Colt .45 into play, I'd make a racket hauling back the slide to load a round in the chamber. It's a sound anyone with any familiarity with guns would instantly recognize.

We watched as the man lit a cigar with a match, and in the flare of light I saw he was missing two fingers from his left hand. I wasn't certain how long Nadia and I were to be caught betwixt and between enemies, until I heard a short, sharp whistle, and the man looked up and walked quickly down Park Avenue, where soon we heard the sound of a motor being engaged and a vehicle driving off.

I exhaled in relief. "The guards are gone. Shall we take this opportunity to make our escape?"

"Or, we can now approach the front door and see if we can rattle anything loose from anyone inside."

Nadia Ravenwood was not the type to let a chance go untested. A phrase which would probably be engraved on my tombstone someday. We slipped out from behind the garden gate and took a stroll up Park Avenue and around to the front of the mansion. Repeated pulls of the bell finally brought a rather haggard Henry Bowen to answer the door himself. "You! What in God's name do you want?"

"Servant's night off?" Nadia said blithely. "So sorry to disturb you. Have you heard from Richard?"

"What? No. And I wouldn't tell you if I had. Go away, or I'll call Detective Broderick."

"Very well, if you insist. Though I thought I'd tell you that I have heard from Richard myself."

Henry Bowen's throat constricted so hard he coughed in a spasm. When he caught his breath, he wheezed out, "What did he say?"

"That he needs money from you. If you would like, I'll be happy to convey it to him, keeping the police

Michael Siverling

uninvolved."

Henry paled, shaking his head. "Mr. Baker is going to take care of everything," he said as if in a trance. "I don't...I don't need you."

And with that he shut the door.

We made our way back to Nadia's car without delay. "I don't like the sound of that at all," she said.

"But you got the telephone number from the operator, yes? We can track down the location of the place Richard called from."

"Not until tomorrow morning when our friendly shift supervisor comes to work, and hopefully tomorrow won't be her day off. Until then, the best we can do is call the number ourselves, but I don't want to tip our hand."

"The police could trace it."

"I know. And that decision is tearing me apart. Never mind, you're right. We have no choice. Richard's life is at stake."

Nadia fired up the Packard and aimed it south, honking her horn and yelling foreign curses at the vehicles and pedestrians who dared to share the same street, until we came to a jarring halt in front of the cream-colored four-story building that was the New York Police 5th Precinct in Chinatown, drawing the attention of a few uniformed officers lounging by their patrol cars.

Nadia slipped the card bearing the Commissioner's courtesy note under the bulbous nose of the desk sergeant and made a demand to see Detective McDonough most immediately. That resulted in a wait of over half an hour as he was tracked down to report back to the station. "Come by for dessert?" he said as he eyed us.

Nadia stepped right up to him, looking upward, as he had a head's worth advantage in height. "I have a deal for you. I will need your promise you will agree to my terms."

"What terms?"

"Allow my associate and I to accompany you, and I'll tell you how to find Richard Bowen."

Detective McDonough's wintry eyebrows rose in amusement. "I have twenty eight jail cells here. Twelve of them are reserved just for women. How about you come along quietly and we'll find you the very best one."

"On what grounds?"

I wasn't sure how this argument was going to play out. All I knew, three other policemen were slowly closing in around us, hefting their nightsticks in anticipation of us resisting arrest.

Chapter Thirty Two:

Nadia Ravenwood and Detective McDonough were practically nose to nose, or actually her nose to his chin, as they glared at each other. "I can have you locked up for obstructing my investigation," McDonough said through gritted teeth."

"I'm not obstructing, I'm offering to help."

"By withholding information?"

"For looking out for my client. Cooperate with me, and you'll have your arrest, and I'll have the satisfaction that my client is safely taken into custody. Or, you can lock us up, and when the newspapers get hold of me, I'll tell them all about how I tried to help, but you didn't let me."

"You wouldn't dare."

"Oh, she would, I assure you," I interjected. "Miss Ravenwood has never been known to bluff. It's just not in her nature."

McDonough took a step back. "Just what are you going to do if bullets start flying when we show up? You going to risk getting shot?"

"Nonsense," Nadia cooed. "I'll have you and your big strong policemen to protect me."

That was it. McDonough started to laugh. "Damn, woman. All right. You and your boy here can come along, and God help us all. Now, where is Richard Bowen hiding?"

"I don't know. What I have is a telephone number he called from less than an hour ago."

"Well, give it here."

Nadia recited the prefix word and four numbers, and McDonough repeated it back and then rushed out of the station lobby, leaving us with a somewhat bemused bunch of policemen for company. He was back in a matter of minutes. "It's from the Laux Hotel on Bleeker Street. You three men come with me. Richard Bowen is about five-foot-ten with blond hair. Running shouldn't be a problem as he's got a wooden leg. Let's move in quietly."

"With whom shall we ride?" Nadia asked.

"Find your own way there."

The race was on. Or, actually, it wasn't, as Nadia's Packard Roadster with its ninety horses under the hood simply leapt away down Elizabeth Street over the rain slicked road. "The good detective is bound to be a bit cross if we get there too far ahead of him," I said as Nadia darted along.

"Honestly, I wanted to drive off the moment he blurted out the address. So I think I showed considerable restraint."

"I'll be sure to have your attorney mention that at your trial for obstructing the law. What do we do if we find Richard first?"

"We won't know that until we do."

"I was afraid you'd say that."

Our lead was short lived, as we could hear the police sirens from behind as Detective McDonough and his men ordered the traffic to give way. "That's cheating," Nadia complained.

Nonetheless, after a couple of miles of dare-devil driving that doubtlessly shortened my life considerably, Nadia attained the goal first, as the police had prudently shut off their sirens a ways back so as not to spook their quarry.

The Laux Hotel was a four-story affair fronted in

grimy red brick with a general store serving as the first level. Nadia and I rushed toward the grey-whiskered night manager, where she slapped down a ten dollar bill. "Blond man with a false leg...which room?"

The man's eyes never left the money. "207".

Nadia and I took the creaking stairs under the dim hallway lighting until we found our target. We listened at the door, only hearing incessant coughing and scratchy strains of a phonograph emanating from nearby rooms. Nadia rapped sharply. "Richard. Open the door. Now."

We heard a pair of dull thumping sounds, then the door was violently wrenched open to reveal a haggard Richard, leaning on a crutch. "What are you doing here? Are you trying to get me killed?"

"The police are on their way to arrest you. Do you know anyone in this hotel?"

"The police? What?"

"Do you know anyone else?"

Half stupefied, he pointed across the hall. "There's a couple of girls there..."

Nadia spun about and stepped to the opposite side of the hall, then softly knocked until a disheveled peroxide blonde opened the door halfway. "What do you want?"

"I'll give you twenty dollars to hide my friend from the police for five minutes."

The blonde was not born yesterday. "Money first."

Neither was Nadia, who held up a twenty dollar note and tore it straight in half before handing one part to the woman, who nodded. I shoved Richard out the door. Nadia grabbed his coat and hat and tossed them into the blonde's room. Once Richard was behind a closed door, we returned to 207. I rushed to the window and lifted it open, quietly as I could, as even now I heard the heavy stomping tread of policemen charging up the stairs. I took a long step away from the window.

Detective McDonough barged in, pistol in hand and eyes darting everywhere at once. "Where is he?"

Nadia shrugged. "Gone. I wonder if he didn't hear your sirens and make a break for it out the fire escape."

"The fire escape?" McDonough bellowed. "On one leg?"

I chuckled. "You can't underestimate people, detective. Why, just today Miss Ravenwood and I followed a man with no legs, and we had quite the time keeping up with him, I tell you."

McDonough turned to his men. "Start questioning the manager, check the neighbors, and find out who's working the beat here and get them out looking for Bowen."

Nadia and I drifted out to the hall and stationed ourselves at the far end while officers knocked on doors but gathered nothing for their trouble, especially from a now rather perky peroxide blonde who answered their questions with wide-eyed innocence while lying shamelessly to their faces.

Chapter Thirty Three:

After all the excitement of racing to beat the police to find Richard Bowen, there came a period of tense quiet as we holed up in the apartment of our new partner in crime, an aspiring showgirl named Maude who was content to smoke my cigarettes while she silently admired both halves of the twenty dollar bill, which she held up to the dull ceiling lamp.

Richard wouldn't shut up, just kept nattering on. "How did the police find me?"

"They're the police," Nadia said. "It's what they do."

"But how did you find me first?"

"Because I do what the police do, only better. Now hush. I'm trying to hear what's going on outside."

We let things lie a good half hour, then decided to make our escape. After trading my cap and trench coat for Richard's cashmere overcoat and homburg, along with his crutch, I walked with a stiff-legged limp, descended the stairs, hobbled past the concierge, and out to the street. There, I tottered around a bit, hoping to fool any lingering coppers on the lookout for a one-legged man. Having not been apprehended, I banged the crutch against a streetlight three times, garnering odd looks from some passersby, as a signal for Nadia to bring Richard down. Before long, we were racing northward up Manhattan Isle, with me crouched in the damned rumble seat again.

Fortunately, I received an early reprieve when Nadia dropped me off at the lobby entrance to the Waldorf Astoria. I strode around to her side of the car. "Aren't you coming in?"

"I'm going to take Richard to my home tonight. Tomorrow, we may as well move out of here, so pack your things."

I looked up to the towering height of the grand hotel. "So I'm to stay one last night? Well, if sacrifices must be made."

"Come to my place early." She drove away, leaving me in a cloud of exhaust.

As I watched her go, I wondered if it wasn't too late to arrange a rendezvous with a certain redhead I knew and hurried inside to my room.

The next day saw me arrive at the Ravenwood Brownstone in the morning, if not exactly at a time considered early. I greeted Mr. Ivanov as he answered the door, and when I saw him bend to take my travel bag from the porch, I noticed the long-barreled Smith and Wesson .44 revolver under his formal jacket. "I see we're on a war footing."

He looked carefully along the street then closed the door. "Yes." His tone was flat as if this happened every day. "Are you suitably prepared?"

I showed him my own Smith and Wesson, and he sniffed with disdain. "That is not a gun. That is a toy."

"Yeah? Well, I've got a bigger toy around here somewhere, if Nadia brought our bag of trouble in from the car last night."

Mr. Ivanov jerked a thumb at the coat closet before walking deeper into the house, leaving me to my own devices. He only played the part of a butler in front of company, the rest of the time he was more like a guard dog except with less manners. As I hung up my coat and hat, I saw our little black leather bag and confirmed my Colt was still within.

I found Nadia and her company in the Reading Room, where Richard and Mary Bowen sat sharing the sofa, and Nadia lounged on one of the oversized chairs. Mary and Richard had dressed for the day, but Nadia was still in her kimono with the Persian slippers on the floor, as her feet were tucked up underneath her. I saw the remnants of breakfast on numerous tiny dishes set across the nearby table. Mr. Li had gone all-out and prepared a plethora of dainty, exotic nibbles that I missed. It surprised me that Nadia had brought out her precious Swiss chocolates for the guests. That was unprecedented.

In the clear light of day, the ravages on Richard's face were evident: black-rimmed eye sockets, sickly pale complexion. In contrast, Mary looked like she'd matured overnight, with her long light-brown hair done up in a sophisticated coif reminiscent of Nadia's wavy, bobbed locks. But Mary's childlike enthusiasm bubbled up when she saw me. "Stephen." She sprang off the couch. "You helped bring Richard back to me." She gave me a hug. "Thank you."

"You're welcome, O' Princess." I patted her back. "Richard, how are you feeling?"

He showed me a wan smile, for Mary's sake, I was sure, but he could not shed the haunted look in his eyes. "I'm as best as can be expected. I know there's a lot of trouble ahead for me soon. But for now, and for the chance to see Mary, I'm grateful."

"Mary," Nadia said. "It's time for us to discuss some things with your brother. Will you excuse us?"

Mary narrowed her eyes and pursed her lips in preparation for an argument, but when she saw the stern look on Nadia's face, the girl showed good judgment to concede. "All right. But I'm not a child, you know."

"I'll fill you in later."

Mary bent to her brother and gave him a hug, then straightened to give us a little bob of a curtsy. When she shut the door behind her, Nadia gave Richard the hooded-eyes look. "Now is the time for you to tell us everything."

"I doubt you'd believe me, even though it's the truth."

Nadia reached behind her and, with a sudden move, tossed him a book, which landed squarely in his lap. I saw it was the tome of Nordic Mythology she'd gotten from the library, the one that matched the book in Richard Bowen's room.

"Then tell me a story," Nadia said with a dark smile.

Chapter Thirty Four:

Richard Bowen stared at the book. "How do you know about this?"

"You told us, in a way," Nadia said. "We found this same book in your room. You were especially attracted to the legend of the god Tyr. Why?"

Richard kept his eyes on the book. "If you read the story, then you know about Tyr's sacrifice, how he alone, of all the gods, was brave enough to risk his limbs to bind the Fenris Wolf in an attempt to keep him from devouring the world."

"A sacrifice you felt a kinship with?"

Richard looked up with defiance in his glare. "Yes. There are many of us, a legion of men who fought in the War and came back...broken." He looked at me. "Although some of us were lucky."

"Don't expect me to apologize for my good fortune."

"No. Of course not. Forgive me."

"Done," I said. And I meant it. *There but for the grace of God and Nicholas Ravenwood go I.*

"So tell us how the god Tyr is so important to you now?"

"It's hard to explain, to those who just aren't..."

"Wounded?"

"As it turns out, there's a band of us. Men like me. Men who feel we still have more to give, if the cause is just. Men who feel like we've just been discarded."

"And what do you call yourselves, you and this band?" Nadia asked.

Richard drew himself up a bit straighter. "We are the Companions of Tyr. And we've taken an oath. And part of that oath is loyalty to each other."

With a look of quiet pride, Richard recited: "Hail to the One-Handed God. Hail to Him whose name is Honor. And whose Word is iron, who alone never shirks the thankless task." He looked at me. "It is to men like these that I am pledged."

Nodding, I understood that allegiance between veterans, wounded or otherwise.

Nadia steered clear of any emotional reaction. "I see...So, when Stephen and I went to collect you from that opium den, it was one of your Companions who attacked us?"

Richard had the grace to look glum. "I have no memory of that."

"No, you were drugged pretty thoroughly, that was for certain. Nevertheless, there was a man with a white eye patch who tried to keep us from taking you home, and a faux platinum blonde. Neither of them appeared to be under the sway of opium. Who were they?"

"I cannot tell you."

"So the woman is a member of the Companions of Tyr?"

"She's considered a sister...of sorts."

"And the All Night Mission down by the Bowery?"

Stubbornness showed in Richard's scowl. "I don't know what you mean."

Nadia and I shared a brief glance. Looked like Richard was determined to keep some secrets. "Let's get to your immediate problem," she said. "There's an arrest warrant out for you because the police think you murdered May Scott."

Anguish twisted his face. "No, I can't believe it. I

would never hurt her. Never."

"The police must have evidence you did. Is there anything you know that you're not telling us?"

"No. Nothing."

"What did you and May argue over that night?"

He sighed. "I tried to tell her that I may be called on to do something dangerous, and I didn't want her waiting for me if worse came to worse. I couldn't do that to her. Not again."

"Dangerous? Like what?"

He shook his head. "I can't say. I took an oath."

Nadia sighed. "Richard, May Scott was killed by a long, thin double edged blade with a reinforcing spine. Do you own such a weapon?"

For a moment, Richard Bowen forgot how to breathe. "Yes," he finally whispered.

"That walking stick you said you were missing. That was a sword cane?"

"Yes."

"So there you have it. Either you murdered May Scott, or someone else did it with your sword cane."

Richard lifted himself up, grasping the arm of the sofa, anger stamped on his face. "How many times do I have to say it? I didn't kill May."

"You certainly couldn't have done it in the condition we found you in. You were so doped up you couldn't walk, not even with a cane. That, and the fact that the most probable murder weapon is missing tells me that someone is keeping your sword cane to use as leverage over you. And it looks like your Companions of Tyr are the most likely suspects."

Richard sank back down. "But, I don't understand. We had a plan, a mission."

"And what was that?"

Richard hung his head. "There are enemies of this country, people who move in the shadows. They're the real threat. And if these people manage to make their moves, then what happened over in Russia and what started in China last year will happen here, at home."

I asked, "Are you speaking of revolution?"

He looked up. "Hard to believe, isn't it? Until you look and see how the agitators are moving in, stirring everyone up."

"And you and your Companions of Tyr are trying to stand against them?"

"Yes. By using their own methods. They move in secret, and so do we."

Nadia again: "You said you were celebrating the night we found you at the opium den. What was the occasion?"

"My ascension within the ranks." Richard sobbed. "I was to be a full member of the Companions, and be given my first command. But it all went to hell that night."

I didn't know how to act, seeing a grown man cry. He hadn't only lost a leg in the War, he lost his place, his calling, and now his dignity and possibly his freedom.

"You know, the police are going to nab you eventually."

He sniffled. "You think I don't know that?"

"We'll arrange for the best lawyer possible, but now is the time to face this head on. No more running."

He sighed. "I'm grateful to have had this chance to stop a while, catch my breath, and for how you're looking after my sister."

My turn: "How does Henry figure in the Companions of Tyr?"

"Henry knows nothing about it. I've never told him anything. All I wanted from him was enough money to hide out 'til they found May's killer. But he never came through."

Nadia didn't look at me, nor I her, as I was certain she remembered seeing the man with the white eye patch giving Henry Bowen stern words in his own house. I let her take it from there.

"Richard, tell me, the man with the white eye patch in Chinatown...who is he?"

"He's my... my Commanding Officer."

"Did he help hide you from the police?"

"No. The woman did."

Mr. Ivanov rushed into the room. "The police are here."

Chapter Thirty Five:

This was bad.

Nadia Ravenwood, being caught in the company of a man she helped escape from the clutches of the Law was a situation that not even the entreaties of a Guggenheim or Morgan or any other influential member of high society who owed Nadia a favor or five could affect. Our goose would be well and thoroughly cooked to be caught with accused murderer Richard Bowen in her house.

Fortunately, this wasn't our first time hiding people. Nadia took command. "Richard, go with Mr. Ivanov, and for God's sake keep absolutely quiet. Stephen, get Mary and bring her back here. Go."

I found Mary downstairs in the aromatic kitchen, watching the diminutive Mr. Li as he swiftly manipulated dough into ascetically pleasing shapes with hands that could also break a man's bones. "Mary, come along. We've got coppers on the doorstep and need to help keep your brother out of sight."

Her bright gray eyes popped open, then took on a sly look well beyond her years. "What do you need me to do?"

"Make yourself scarce, and if the police ask, you haven't seen Richard. Okay?"

She nodded. "Can I play the phonograph?"

"All you want."

Once I got Mary installed in the Reading Room, I went to the parlor, where Miss Nadia Ravenwood was lounging on her throne as she received her guests: one I knew, the other I didn't. "Ah, Stephen. Please join us. You know Detective Broderick, of course, and this other gentleman comes all the way from Washington, D.C."

The man was tall with a solid build, had dark thinning hair and a clean-shaven face. A pair of dark eyes took direct aim at me. He wore a plain woolen suit and held up an open wallet that displayed a golden shield. "I'm Agent Paul Reynolds from the Bureau of Investigation."

"Stephen Locke from Chicago. What's the BOI doing here?"

From the Reading Room next door, strains of a Bessie Smith recording reverberated through the wall. I recognized the opening notes of *Young Woman's Blues*. It sounded like Mary was getting quite the musical education.

"I've been sent here to assist the local police with a matter that may have National implications."

"National implications?" Nadia echoed. "Ah, like the bombing of Wall Street, what, six, seven years ago? Tell me, who was responsible for that? I heard it was Anarchists."

Johnny Broderick's handsome face twitched at the corner of his mouth as he witnessed Nadia needling the man from Washington.

"No one has been arrested for that yet, ma'am."

"Really? Unsolved? After all this time? Interesting. Anyway, tell me how you're going help our fine detective here solve this case?"

Johnny spoke up. "Henry Bowen has made a complaint that you are harassing him, Miss Ravenwood, and since he is assisting us in an ongoing investigation, I'll have to ask you to stop."

Nadia scoffed. "You brought a BOI Fed in here to tell me that?"

"National implications," Reynolds said.

"Well, seeing how his brother Richard is a client of mine, I don't see how I can avoid Henry."

"Yeah, about that," Broderick said, "I got a call from McDonough down at the 5th Precinct. He says you took him on a wild goose chase last night."

"I gave him a very good lead. It's not my fault he was too slow to take advantage of it."

Broderick looked at me.

I nodded. "It was solid, detective."

His face grew a tight smile. "Look, Miss Ravenwood, I'm giving you fair warning...you two back away from this. The Feds are involved, and it's unhealthy to poke around Henry Bowen or his business. Get me?"

Nadia looked to Agent Reynolds. "And just why is Washington interested in my client?"

"I can't tell you that, ma'am."

Nadia gazed at him like a vulture over dead meat. "Hmm, let me see. Your Bureau of Investigation has a new leader as of a couple years ago, yes? What was his name, Hooper? Heever?"

"It's Director Hoover, ma'am."

"Tell me, is it true that he fired all the women investigators in the Bureau?"

"Women are unsuited for the job, ma'am."

Johnny Broderick looked away, as if to admire the exquisite parlor.

Nadia sneered. "Interesting viewpoint Washington has. Quite unlike the New York police, who employ women such as Detective Isabella Goodwin and Mary Sullivan, wouldn't you say, Detective Broderick?"

"Miss Ravenwood, getting back to the point, steer clear of Henry Bowen."

"It's clear he's cooperating with you in some manner. What is he helping you with?"

Agent Paul Reynolds glowered at Detective Broderick as if to say: 'Are you letting her walk all over you?'

Broderick caved. "It's police business, now Washington's, as well. And definitely not yours."

The gentlemen took their leave as Nadia scowled at their backs. When I heard that Mr. Ivanov had safely escorted them outside, I exhaled. "Well, that was a bust. Let's help Richard Bowen turn himself in without delay."

"You're right." She sighed. "We'll be no good to anyone if we're arrested for harboring a fugitive. Mary's going to hate us for this."

I retrieved Richard from behind the false wall in the basement we call 'The Unwanted Guest's Room' and assisted him back to my quarters. Having had some time to himself, he'd arrived at the conclusion that it was better to turn himself in to the police rather than be captured at gunpoint by itchy-fingered cops.

When he was ready to go, Nadia, dressed in her riding apparel, brought Mary down to the vestibule, where we gave brother and sister privacy to say their goodbyes. Ultimately, as a teary-eyed Mary hurried back upstairs, Richard stood up straight and wheeled around on his one leg to face the door. "Once more into the beech."

Nadia and I walked down the front steps on either side of Richard, taking the time he required with his crutch, which allowed the car that rolled past the Brownstone all the time needed for the driver to fire several shots at us.

Chapter Thirty Six:

It was a ridiculously strange moment.

The gunshots were rapid, though unimpressive, less loud than an automobile backfire and raised no warning to us. Rather, it was the cracking ricochets from the brickwork that sent the alarm to our nerves. I had a strange, stuttering glimpse, like when a motion picture gets stuck in the cogs of the projector, where I clearly saw Walter Reeves at the driver's side window of his green Chrysler Imperial, lips skinned back from his teeth as he rolled past, gave the car some gas and clashed the gears as he rolled away.

"Oh, my." That came from Richard as he looked down to a tiny hole in his cashmere overcoat. "Oh, my."

I felt his weight increase on my arm as I slowly lowered him to the sidewalk.

"I'm so sorry," he muttered.

I heard Nadia shout out for Mr. Ivanov as I unbuttoned Richard's coat and pulled the lapels aside, along with his jacket underneath to see a red stain ooze out from a matching hole in his shirt. "Don't worry, old man." I pressed down on the leak. "Such a tiny thing, you'll be up and about in no time." I realized I was babbling.

Gasping, Richard attempted to catch his breath while muttering apologies over and over...

Mr. Li physically hauled me away as Miss Murphy knelt on the other side with the medical bag she kept for emergencies.

"Richard!" It was Mary, throwing herself down the

front steps.

Nadia intercepted her in her arms.

Mr. Ivanov shouted from the open door. "The ambulance is on its way."

Soon, we had a bizarre tableau on the sidewalk in front of the Brownstone, with Richard being attended by Mr. Li and Miss Murphy while Mary knelt and held his hand and Mr. Ivanov fended off the gathering group of curious, ghoulish spectators drawn to the sight of tragedy.

After I returned from washing the blood off my hands, I made myself useful, lighting one of Nadia Ravenwood's Turkish cigarettes for her, and set fire to one of my own as we sat on the top steps. She took in the smoke and slowly released it, then closed her eyes. "Could we have possibly done any worse?"

"It was Walter Reeves. He must have been stalking our place, hoping to see Richard."

"I gave him my card." Nadia blew smoke.

"We didn't know he was crazy."

She looked at me, the pools of her dark eyes steady. "Is he crazy? So far, the police think Richard killed May Scott. And if Richard dies, do you think they'd keep looking for another suspect? For all we know, this is Walter's way of getting away with murdering May."

"That's...diabolical."

"It's a theory. Certainly Walter Reeves stands a good chance of getting away with shooting Richard Bowen by playing the part of the avenging angel. What jury would convict him?"

When the ambulance arrived, Nadia Ravenwood ordered everyone to their tasks: Miss Murphy and Mary to accompany Richard while Mr. Li and Mr. Ivanov were to follow to keep an eye on everyone. As for me, Nadia said, "Now you and I go to see Detective McDonough and try to not get ourselves arrested."

Mid-morning Manhattan traffic, being the worst of anyplace in the world, impeded us in our race against time to the 5th Precinct in Chinatown. Ultimately, we made it without incurring an automobile accident only to find Detective McDonough was out and about already, and we'd have to wait for him to check in with the desk sergeant. He came strolling in less than an hour later, and Nadia Ravenwood popped up from the bench we'd been sharing with assorted ne'er do wells. "Detective, I've got Richard Bowen."

He looked like she'd slapped him. "What? Where?"

"Saint Luke's Hospital."

"Hospital? What's he doing there?"

"He was shot. Just this morning."

Detective McDonough's face froze. "What did you do?"

"Probably saved his life. Though I haven't seen him since the ambulance arrived and have no idea if he's still alive or not." Before McDonough had a chance to think, Nadia added, "My car is just outside. Shall we go?"

Naturally, I was stuck in the rumble seat again. I was glad we were heading to the hospital as I was certain I'd develop advanced galloping pneumonia by the time we arrived, as I was buffeted by icy winds and pelted by near-frozen raindrops. The moment Nadia pulled into the receiving area of St. Luke's, Detective McDonough leapt out of the car and came around at me. "You. Tell me now, and don't look at her." He pointed at Nadia. "Just how did Richard Bowen come to be with you last night?"

"Damndest t-thing." My teeth were chattering. "He just showed up, and Miss Ravenwood convinced him to go straight to you this morning. That's where we were headed."

"Who shot him?"

"We don't know. A car drove by. It happened so fast."

Detective McDonough scowled, then turned about and stomped into the hospital as I massaged my frozen ear, rendered painfully tender by pressing up against the rear windshield so I could overhear what Nadia told the good detective so as to make our stories match.

Chapter Thirty Seven:

I garnered a smile from Nadia for being just clever enough to avoid getting tripped up by Detective McDonough as she took my arm and followed the detective inside the hospital. After negotiating the twists and turns of the antiseptic hallways, we found our party: Mary Bowen was bookended by Mr. Li and Mr. Ivanov as she sat next to Miss Murphy. The Crown Jewels could not be safer. But what was wonderful to see was the smile on Mary's face as she came running up to us. "The doctor got the bullet out. They say Richard should be all right."

"There, detective," Nadia said. "I release Mr. Bowen into your custody."

"You're not empowered to do anything for anyone." McDonough grumbled. "But you're right enough. He's mine now. Where's the doctor?"

It took a while to round up the surgeon, a Dr. Pratt by name, a mature man of confident bearing, just the type of doctor you'd want working on you. He was less than pleased to have to take the time to talk to the police, however. "What do you want?"

"When can I talk to him?" McDonough asked.

"Talk to him? You do realize I just removed a bullet from the man, do you not?"

"Yes. Now when will he be able to talk?"

The doctor shook his head. "He'll regain consciousness when his body is good and ready. Other than his missing leg, he appears to be in good health. Barring a chance of infection, I don't foresee any complications, but as to speaking with him? Well, that's going to be entirely up to the patient. If there's nothing else?"

Nadia spoke up. "Dr. Pratt? I was wondering if I may consult with you?"

"Consult with me?"

"Yes." Nadia unbuttoned her black velour overcoat and suede vest, opening it to reveal her left side, and the wide stain of rust colored blood that soaked through her blouse. "It appears that I didn't get away quite unscathed myself."

Dr. Pratt stared wide eyed for a moment before shouting, "Nurse," leaving Detective McDonough and I to rush to Nadia's side as she held up her right hand, warding us off. "I've made it this far, let's not fuss now."

In a few moments, Nadia was placed in a wheelchair and rushed out of the room as Dr. Pratt shouted orders on ahead. I turned back, only to see all eyes on me: Mary, Ivanov, Li and Murphy, staring with the most accusatory glares possible. "I didn't know she was hurt."

McDonough shook his head as he ambled off. "I've got to arrange for a police guard on Richard Bowen. You, boy, are on your own."

The suspense, long as it seemed at the time, was relatively short lived. Nadia Ravenwood walked out under her own power, explaining to all of us gathered to greet her, "A bullet grazed a rib, might have cracked it, nothing to be done about it."

"Rest comes to mind," Miss Murphy stated.

"And so I shall...as soon as I get some time. Stephen? Would you be so kind as to bring the car around? The rest of you go back home."

Mary said, "I want to stay here in case Richard wakes up."

"I'm sure the doctor will call, dear." Nadia winced.

"For now, I need you to do as I ask. Let us take care of you."

"Like you took care of Richard?" Mary sounded accusatory as only a teenager could.

Nadia favored her with one of her best, implacable looks. "I'll tolerate no mutiny. You'll see Richard as soon as it's possible. That I promise. In the meanwhile, I want you to take care of yourself, and my people."

"Your people?"

Nadia reached over and gently turned Mary about, facing Miss Murphy, Mr. Li and Mr. Ivanov. "My people...as you are now a member of our household, you are responsible to and for each other. Understand?"

Mary nodded, too overwhelmed to say another word. Almost the same way I felt. "You're letting me drive?"

"Just for now. I'm wrapped up like one of Carter's mummies under my coat, and it's inconvenient to move much."

I did as I was told, wary of the little car as I carefully engaged the motor and got the feel of the clutch, only stalling out a pair of times. I came around to assist Nadia in getting into the cab of the coupe, but she just rebuffed me with a look. Once we were set, I asked, "Where to?"

Nadia held up a card. "Mr. Walter Reeves was kind enough to give us his calling card. Therefore, we should make a call on him, wouldn't you say?"

"I was actually wondering why you didn't tell Detective McDonough that it was jolly old Wally who shot at us."

"I want first crack at him. He made me angry."

And just that quick, I felt sorry for the poor, doomed man.

The card Walter gave us had the address to his business, the tall, tiered Heckscher Building, where he managed insurance for shipping companies. It was a grand structure, clad in ornate panels and a tall crown mast that caught the sun like beaten gold. Nicholas Ravenwood and I once attended to a matter here where we took the case of an illicit love affair gone tragically wrong and transformed it into a story of a bungled burglary and homicide, burying the truth along with a body but protecting a woman's reputation.

Nadia had me drive down Fifth Avenue to Saks and Company, where I was sent to fetch her a new overcoat. I rushed in and found a wool velour fur-trimmed number in black, and upon my return received the high praise that my choice was *adequate*.

Rounding back to the Heckscher, one of the attendants in the arched elevator lobby informed us that the offices of Reeves Nautical was up on the 21st floor, but when the operator delivered us there, we found the office door locked. It was dark behind the frosted glass.

I grumped. "Odd to be closed before four o'clock on a weekday."

"Well, Mr. Reeves was out of the office this morning, this we know."

I volunteered to go and fetch some burglar tools from the car.

"Don't wander off," she said as I departed.

By the time got back, Nadia was gone.

Chapter Thirty Eight:

I tried the door, finding it now unlocked, and stepped through with my hand on my revolver. The richly wood-paneled office was unmanned, offering nothing but a wide vista of the city beyond the tall windows. As I turned back, a glint of light on the carpeting caught my eye, and I retrieved yet another abandoned .25 cartridge, the result of Walter Reeves' poor gun handling.

I raced out across the tiled floor to the elevator lobby, taking the first one that opened. "Emergency," I said to the operator as I pressed a twenty dollar bill into his hand. "I need to get to the street."

The operator's eyebrows tried to disappear beneath his cap when he saw the bill, then he announced to the others in the car: "Express to the first floor, going down."

There were complaints of 'I've got an appointment' along with some 'what does this mean?' which were ignored as I felt my stomach flutter with a mixture of fear and falling until we reached the bottom, and I shoved my way out ahead of anyone else.

I ran through the arched opulence of the elevator lobby and into the wide, marble-faced space of the entrance, turning this way and that as I looked for Nadia. I was about to run outside when I caught that ever-present black feather of her cloche hat moving above the crowd. I backed into the doorway of a Western Union office to observe Walter Reeves walking with one hand holding Nadia's elbow and the other buried in the pocket of his long fur coat, presumably holding a concealed pistol. If he wanted to shoot her without setting himself ablaze, he'd have to pull his hand completely free of his pocket and fire across his own body.

The man had absolutely no idea what he was doing.

As they passed by, I saw Nadia Ravenwood's lips moving, speaking rapidly as Walter's eyes were practically bugged out of his puffy face. I slipped out of the doorway and fell in step behind them as they wound their way through the visitors in the lobby heading for the doors. I could see Nadia had this situation going her way, despite how it looked. Then I saw her raise her free hand to her hat, the signal to take Wally out.

I waited until we cleared the lobby and reached the crowded Fifth Avenue sidewalk where I stepped up and shoved my hand into Walter's pocket to get a grip on the pistol, and I used my other hand to lever his elbow forward, causing him to point the gun at a rather tender part of his own body.

Nadia spun and slipped her hand under his overcoat, but not before I caught the shiny glint off the blade of her push dagger.

As for Walter, he stiffened and froze.

People walked around us.

"Go ahead and shoot," I said into his ear.

Walter couldn't speak, he just made odd, squeaking sounds as Nadia said warmly, "Now, Walter, let's try this again, shall we? Why don't we go back up to your lovely, comfortable and very empty office and have a discussion, yes?"

I gave the back of his elbow a pop and pulled out the pistol, which I shoved into my own pocket. "You can always call for a cop. Of course, then you'd be arrested for attempting to kill us this morning." To Nadia, I said, "How'd you get yourself into this predicament?"

"I made noise walking away from Walter's office, then crept back to see if I had lured him out. He opened the door as if to be sure the coast was clear. Talk about being surprised when he saw me, I thought he'd shoot me again. I figured to let him think he was making a break for it and walk me around as his human shield, at least until you caught up with us or I got tired of playing nice."

The three of us reversed course, with Nadia and I holding up a sweating Walter Reeves on each side. We got back to his business offices and simply dropped him down to sit on a chair in his waiting room as Nadia locked the door and I looked over the pistol I took from him. It was one of Colt's little monsters, advertised as a 'vest pocket' model. I slid out the magazine and counted out four cartridges, then racked the last one out of the chamber. I put the pistol and loose ammunition into my left overcoat pocket then pulled out my revolver, casually pointing it at nothing as I kept it in plain view.

Nadia had her back to the door as she consulted a small black leather book. "You kept some very detailed notes here, Walter."

He looked up at her, then slapped his pockets. "My diary. How did you..."

Nadia shrugged. Clearly, she'd lifted it out of his coat at some point during our recent walk together. "It's interesting that you've removed some pages. Why did you do that?"

He frowned. "What do you mean?"

"The day May Scott died is missing, as is the day after. Your notes pick up with your attempts to find Richard Bowen, including waiting outside my house this morning. Why did you choose today for that?"

Walter Reeves was looking in any direction except Nadia's. "I don't want to talk about it."

Michael Siverling

She sighed, then unbuttoned her new overcoat. "Look at me, Walter." Nadia shed her coat and vest, putting the dried, rust colored blood of her blouse on full display over her bandaged ribs. She then leaned in close, crowding her face to his. "You shot me today, Walter. You could have killed me. So as of now, I'm trying to decide why I shouldn't return the favor."

Nadia held up the sharp, double-edged blade of her push dagger, letting the reflected light flash into Walter's eyes.

Chapter Thirty Nine.

I wasn't certain if Walter wet himself before he fainted, or after. It really didn't matter, I supposed. Nadia backed up with alacrity, spitting a curse in Russian. "What the hell?"

"They don't make ruthless assassins like they used to."

With slightly more than gentle slaps, we roused Walter. He groaned and began moving his limbs as if trying them out for the first time while mumbling incoherently. Once his eyes focused on us, he tried to crab away. "What happened?"

"Do you have a washroom?" I asked.

His smelly predicament dawned on him. "Oh, I need a change of clothes, yes. Please."

It turned out that Walter's accommodations in the Heckscher Building spared no expense; not only was there a fully appointed washroom, but a closet with two sets of clothes, including one for formal evenings, as well as all the accoutrements. There was even a back room that held an ornately upholstered couch and selection of wines, the perfect little rapscallion's hideaway.

When Walter had put himself back together, I looked around at the unattended desks. "Where is everyone?"

"The office is closed...for my mourning period."

Miss Ravenwood had made herself at home behind Walter's expansive mahogany desk, causally perusing and tossing his papers about. "Sit down, Walter."

Before he could protest, I gave him a slight kick

behind his knee and pulled down on his shoulder to drop him into a visitor's chair.

"What...what are you going to do to me?"

"Considering how you shot me, I'd say the question is, what are you going to do for me?"

"What do you want?"

"Information. Start with what's on the missing pages of your diary."

Walter looked confused. "I don't know why those pages are gone. My diary hasn't been out of my sight."

Nadia waved it. "Au contraire, I took it right out of your pocket and you didn't notice."

Walter put his eyebrows together, looking like he was trying to give birth to a thought. "That woman..."

"What woman?"

Walter suddenly looked like a kid who got caught with his hand in the cookie jar, or maybe his whole head, as he flushed and fumbled until Nadia asked again, forcefully, "What woman?"

"I met her shortly after I saw you two outside Richard Bowen's house."

"We'd sent you home."

"I know, she followed me."

"This woman, a blonde...with brown eyes?"

"Blonde, yes, but her eyes are a rather lovely green."

Nadia shot me a look, as this sounded like the woman who was with Richard at the opium den. "Tell me everything that happened with her."

"She told me that she was a friend of May's and she knew May would be far better off with me than Richard. I agreed, of course, and told her because I was worried about her, that I had followed May into Chinatown the night she died."

"Wait, you were following May Scott that night? For

how long?"

He squirmed a bit. "I was waiting for May and Richard outside the restaurant that night, but only because I was sure that scoundrel Richard was up to no good. I saw May get in a cab then he took one himself. I followed her in my car, and later I saw her cab pull over, and then she got out..."

"Then what?"

"I had to park, get out of my car to follow her. I saw where she went and wrote down the address."

"In your diary, on the pages that are missing?"

"Well, yes. But I remember the place was on Doyers Street."

"Okay? So what did you do?"

Walter looked out the window to the skyline. "I went home."

"You left her there?"

"I didn't like the looks of the neighborhood. There were, um, people about, staring at me."

I wanted to punch him. "So you left May Scott in a neighborhood where you felt unsafe? That's the most cowardly act I've ever heard."

"But the very next day I went to her house to check on her, but she didn't come home. Later, I heard she'd been killed. Murdered. And I knew it was Richard's fault."

I had to look away from Walter Reeves, bury my feelings over a man who could abandon the woman he loved...made me contemplate doing some bad things to him.

Nadia's deep, dark eyes were cool as ice as she stared at him. "So tell me exactly what you and this mystery woman discussed."

Walter took a breath. "After you sent me away from Richard's house, she came up to me on the street before I got inside my house. As I said, she told me she was a friend of May's, and that she was sorry for my loss."

"What was this woman's name?"

"Hella, not Helen, as I thought at first."

My education in the classics didn't fail me here, for 'Hella', or sometimes simply 'Hel', was the Goddess of the Underworld in Norse mythology. "What else did you talk about?"

"She agreed with me that it must have been Richard who killed my May, the proof of his guilt being how he ran from the police. So she and I swore an oath that if there was anything we could do to get justice, we would."

"And shooting Richard Bowen today was you getting justice?"

"Only a coward shoots a one-legged man," I added.

Walter inflated his chest. "It was no less than he deserved."

Nadia scowled. "But how did you know Richard was at my home this morning?"

He blinked. "Hella told me."

Chapter Forty:

Here was an eye opener, our newest enemy, whose 'Nom de Guerre' was the Queen of the Nordic Underworld, managed to take blustering, bumbling Wally Reeves and send him out to actually shoot people, Nadia and myself included. Walter's eyes kept bouncing from Nadia to me. "What are you going to do with me?"

The answer was simple: Nadia Ravenwood and I had best wrap Walter up like a Christmas present and deliver him to Detective McDonough in order to mollify him enough to maybe not arrest us for harboring Richard Bowen. I was about to voice this, but the sly look in Nadia's eyes made me hesitate.

"First things first, Walter. I see you have a Dictaphone. Let's get your story down, shall we? This will be your chance to tell your side of it, about how this was a matter of justice."

Walter fell for it at once, not seeing that he was actually providing us with a full confession of his shooting Richard Bowen and Nadia Ravenwood. A recording of Walter along with his pistol to match with the bullet recovered from Richard should have his whole goose neatly tied up.

We gave the Dictaphone a quick test, and then after helping Walter get his lines straight, let him record his statement. Once done to Miss Ravenwood's satisfaction, she said, "All right, let's get our coats and get out of here. You won't give us any more trouble, will you, Walter?"

"No. I promise."

Michael Siverling

And he was true to his word, for less than the minute it took us to step outside his office. That's where a short, stocky man with a long-barreled pistol intercepted us.

"What took you so long?" Walter said in a rush. "They were going to take me to the police."

The thug motioned with his gun for us to go back inside.

Nadia was quick to retreat, moving all the way to the back to Walter's office, as we were now confronted by not only the man with the pistol, but Hella, the green eyed minx herself, who appeared behind him. The blonde, now dressed to fit in with the Fifth Avenue crowd, complete with a mink wrap, reached a velvet-gloved hand to pet Walter's face. "Relax, my brave man. Surely, you didn't think I'd let anything happen to you."

Nadia stood at the corner of Walter's desk while the man with the gun accosted me. "You are armed, yes?" He spoke with a soft Germanic accent.

I held up my hands. "What can I say? It's a dangerous city." I was getting my first good look at him. The low slung cap shaded pale blue eyes, while the man's face was round and marked like the moon. The weapon he held looked like a skinny rifle, then I saw it was a long-barreled Lugar pistol with a shoulder stock on one end and a silencer on the other. It was the sort of weapon that could make those long, quiet shots into Henry Bowen's study from a hundred yards. Afterwards, it could be broken down and hidden beneath his scuffed leather coat.

"Put your pistol on the table."

I slowly dropped Walter's .25 pistol with its loose ammunition alongside my Smith and Wesson.

"What about you?" He pointed at Nadia.

"She carries a knife, of all things," Walter said.

Nadia shrugged. "You'll have to kill me to get it."

~160~

"Very well. You stay on your side of the room over there, and we will get along fine."

The platinum blonde detached herself from Walter and came my way, eyes fixed on the desk. "Ooh, that's a pretty thing." She picked up my revolver.

I carry a shiny, nickel-plated model, not out of any sense of vanity, but to make the gun easier for people to see, thinking, if they see it in my hand, they'll know I mean business, and I'll be less likely to have to shoot them with it.

Hella held it up to the light. "Mama like," she purred, then whipped around and pointed it at my face, giggling like a kid getting a pony ride.

I showed her my best I-dare-you look. "Careful. It's loaded."

"We have to leave," Walter said.

"Wait," the German replied. "You and I need to have a few words together."

Walter blanched. "A few words? What for?"

"What did you tell these people?"

Walter looked at Hella. "Just what you told me to say."

"Nothing else?" the man demanded with narrowed eyes.

"No. Nothing. I swear."

The man looked to Nadia and me. "You people would not mind letting us know what Mr. Reeves has been discussing with you, yes?"

"We have his recorded confession for shooting Richard Bowen," Nadia said. "He claims to have done it for revenge against Richard for murdering May Scott."

"Recorded?"

Nadia held up the wax cylinder. "Here, listen to it yourself." She placed it into the dictograph and set the speaking tube.

Walter's voice issued forth: "My name is Walter Reeves, and this is my statement for the New York Police."

Nadia lifted the needle off the cylinder. "Need you hear more?"

The German rushed up, waving her back with his gun, then he wrenched the cylinder off the machine and stamped it flat underfoot. He then went straight to Walter, pushing him back with the barrel of his gun toward the tall windows.

Walter stumbled and pleaded, "I took all the heat..."

I heard a crash of glass and a screeching scream that diminished as fast as the body fell.

An icy wind swept through the office, scattering papers like autumn leaves.

Chapter Forty One:

Hella laughed.

The thick-shouldered man stormed toward us, holding his gun straight out. "Stay as you are for a few minutes. Do not follow us."

Hella blew me a kiss and ran after him out the door. "Wait for me, Captain."

As soon as they disappeared, Nadia and I were at the broken window where the cold, wet wind slapped my face. I didn't know if it was the chill of the air, or the horrible realization that Walter Reeves, dim witted, gullible Walter Reeves, was callously shoved to his death that froze me to my soul. Looking down, I saw that Walter must have hit the first tier of the Heckscher Building. Thankfully he hadn't fallen all the way down to the street to land among innocent pedestrians.

"Come on," Nadia said. "We need to get to Detective McDonough."

"To turn ourselves in?"

"No. To tell him what we know about Walter Reeves, and to give him the wax recording."

"The one that our German Captain just flattened?"

"That was the test cylinder I had Walter start to make sure the Dictaphone worked. I've still got the recording of the full confession. I switched them as soon as our new friends forced us back into the office."

It was sleight of hand Nadia's father couldn't have done better.

"Shouldn't we wait for the police to arrive?"

"You want to stand around answering questions, or do you want to get these bastards?"

"Let's go."

We made it out of the building as the sirens from the police cars were heard coming down Fifth Avenue. I made a point to exchange my Colt .45 for a pocket full of burglary tools from our bag of trouble, along with the loaded spare magazine. Nadia insisted on driving us down to Lower Manhattan to Detective McDonough's 5th Precinct, claiming I drove her car like it was a milk wagon. As it turned out, McDonough wasn't quick enough to avoid our arrival. "What do you want?" he spat when he came down to the police station lobby.

Nadia held out the sealed wax cylinder like a gift. "For you, Detective. A recorded confession of Walter Reeves, admitting that he shot Richard Bowen and me this morning in front of my home."

"Walter Reeves? Who's that?"

"Former romantic rival of Richard Bowen for the affections of May Scott. Seems he shot Richard in revenge, although it's possible he actually murdered May and then tried to kill Richard to cover his tracks."

McDonough shook his head. "Where do I find Reeves? I need to question him."

I was cold, tired, hungry and still recovering from the shock of the recent murders. "It'd be a one-sided conversation."

He glared at Nadia. "What's he talking about?"

"Walter Reeves flew out the window of his 21st floor office in the Heckscher Building."

Detective McDonough looked from Nadia, to me, and back again. He closed his eyes for a moment, then opened them. "I have Richard Bowen under guard at the hospital. You say this is a confession of the man who shot him. A man who is now dead. Now, since you've made a great noise about having Richard Bowen as your client, is it too much for me to believe that you were the ones who helped this Reeves guy out the window?"

"We didn't but someone did. And when we find out the name and location of that person, rest assured we will let you know."

Detective McDonough started to speak, thought better of it, and simply told us, "Go away."

We did not need to be asked twice. We drove down the rivers of streets that cut through the canyons of Manhattan. I let the ride go along in silence until, "I see we're keeping information from the police again, as usual. Now what?"

"Now I really wish Walter had been truthful with us. Clearly, he'd been fed a plate of lies by the peroxide-haired Hella. Sounds like they used him to do away with Richard Bowen, only Walter bungled it with that ridiculous toy pistol of his."

"So first, Richard's Companions of Tyr hide him from the cops, and then they try to have him killed?"

"Yes. Because Richard may have spilled something they wanted kept secret, possibly just the fact of their very existence, or their anti-anarchist stance."

"Okay," I said slowly. "So, if the Companions of Tyr are against the anarchists, and Detective Johnny Broderick and Agent Reynolds are working along with Henry Bowen on some kind of anti-anarchist case, then where are the actual anarchists?"

"Remember Johnny Broderick let it be known that they were after gangsters who may have been aligned with the anarchists?"

"Right." Then it dawned on me. "Oh, no! You're not suggesting we go and look up your pet mobster Owney

Madden again, are you?"

Nadia shrugged. "We have nowhere else to turn. Both May Scott's death and Richard Bowen's freedom are entangled with whatever this Companions of Tyr plot is. Owney said he may have a lead when we showed him the Companion of Tyr's symbol."

"Or we could follow the lead Walter Reeves gave us when he said he followed May Scott to a place on Doyers Street."

"Yes, but which exact address was it? Granted, the street is near Columbus Park where May Scott's body was found, but we'll need much more to go on before assailing that neighborhood."

"So, Owney Madden?" I asked.

Nadia just nodded.

But first, Nadia drove us to the Ravenwood residence. I was cheered at the thought of at least getting a final, exquisite meal from the hands of Mr. Li before Nadia took me out to be killed by gangsters.

I felt it was a reasonable last request.

Chapter Forty Two:

Mr. Li did not disappoint. Despite the fact that Nadia and I arrived too late for dinner, Mr. Li made us sandwiches, although calling the lightly grilled, thinly sliced roast beef and seasoned cheese creations by the pedestrian name of 'sandwich' smacks of sacrilege. We also had the company of Mary as we dined at the kitchen table. Mr. Li whipped up a parfait for her to enjoy. She was looking forward to seeing Richard at the hospital tomorrow and was disappointed that Nadia and I would be going out later.

"May I come with you?" she asked with bright eyes.

Picturing this young innocent girl in the speakeasy nightclub made me choke.

"Not this trip, dear," Nadia said.

Mary put on a pout. "This is one of those *when I'm older* things, isn't it?"

I agreed. "Some time around the turn of the next century."

After our supper, Mary went back to the Reading Room to wear out some more of Nadia's jazz recordings as she and I separated to change for the night out. When we reconvened in the vestibule, she was wearing a gold sequined turban style hat with a blood red gem in the center and her signature black feather to the side. Her dress was concealed by a night-black wrapped cape that sported ebony feathering all along the edges.

Stepping outside the Brownstone, I got my next surprise: Mr. Ivanov at the door of a beautiful midnight blue Rolls Royce limousine. "What the hell is that?"

"That is a Silver Ghost, the result of cashing in on a favor owed. Mr. Ivanov was kind enough to volunteer to drive us tonight."

"Clearly, whoever loaned you this beauty didn't hear about what happened to your Rickenbacker."

The fact we now had a chauffeur and bodyguard rolled up into one cheered me a bit. It was a pleasure to ride in the comfortably upholstered back seats, as Mr. Ivanov, looking more like a Prussian military officer than a chauffeur, took the helm and ferried us toward midtown. All too soon, Owney Madden's Hotel Harding came into view, and Nadia Ravenwood and I descended the basement steps to the *Club Intime* and paid an exorbitant $25 apiece just to clear the doorway. But the price of admission was worth it when the bent-nosed doorman informed Miss Ravenwood that Madden wasn't in attendance this evening.

"Aw, too bad," I said over the fast-tempo jazz music. "Looks like we'll have to come back and risk getting killed some other night."

But Nadia got that certain look in her deep, dark eyes, the one you don't want to be in front of. "I didn't get all dressed up for nothing." She then plunged into the frenetic crowd. I was left at the doorway as Nadia didn't even remove her cape, but it wasn't long before I spotted that black feather in her cap winging its way back to me. "I told one of the bouncers I needed to see Owney for a special job he promised me and my twin sister. For that, I got a leer and the word that Madden was with his 'Uptown Sweetie' tonight."

"Uptown Sweetie? Who's that?"

Nadia looked sly. "Not a *who* but a *what*, and it's the *Cotton Club*, by name. Come on, let's go."

The *Cotton Club* was all the way up in Harlem, while

we started from the opposite side of Central Park in the Times Square district. Just last spring, Charles Lindbergh made his daring flight over the Atlantic Ocean to Paris in something over thirty hours. I didn't think we were going to beat his time. Regardless, we eventually made it to the unassuming entrance on Lennox Avenue, oddly made to look like the side of a log cabin.

The *Cotton Club* used to be a supper club owned by Jack Johnson, the heavyweight boxing champion, until Owney Madden forced himself in. And while the entertainment was superb, the venue, with its small floor, crowded tables and overabundant jungle-like foliage, was a bit claustrophobic. Madden also made it a clearly segregated operation, with all the performers on one side of the showroom and the strictly Caucasian audience on the other. But what else could you expect from a low-life gangster like Owney Madden? Frankly, it was an inferior nightclub when compared to a place like the *Savoy Ballroom*, practically next door, with its mirrored walls, crystal chandeliers and marble staircase. Also, everyone was welcome there, especially if you could dance.

We left Mr. Ivanov at our getaway vehicle and made for the crowded door, where Miss Ravenwood's card got us admittance. Once inside, I assisted with her unveiling, revealing her attired in a flowing gown of beaded gold, cascading from her shoulders with images of moons and stars cunningly worked in, looking like she stepped out of the pages of H. Ryder Haggard's *She*.

We no sooner turned around when I saw dead-eyed Owney Madden staring at us. "I got a call you were coming. How do you like my place?"

Nadia offered her hand. "It's okay. It'd be better if you got someone like Duke Ellington to head up your orchestra. Were you ever able to find out about the symbol

I showed you? The arrow pointing upward?"

His lips flinched in what may have been an attempt at a smile. "It's just all business with you, isn't it. Yeah. One of the boys knew what you were talking about. Let me get him over here."

Owney Madden raised a hand, and a tall man with a long, serious face strode over, moving gracefully through the packed room. "Let me introduce you to Jack Diamond. Some of the guys call him 'Legs'.

Chapter Forty Three:

T he four of us were seated at a round table while a subset of the house orchestra softly played music during the dinner hour. Madden and Diamond were monopolizing Nadia Ravenwood, making me feel like an unseen ghost, which was fine by me where murderous gangsters were concerned.

As for Nadia, she couldn't have looked more at home. Granted, she had a pretty shady past over in Europe, and it made me wonder how the criminal elements in London and Paris stacked up against the ones in New York. Madden had champagne brought over, Nadia took the tiniest sip, and I watched the three of them go at it, felt like I was sitting front-row at a Broadway play.

Jack Diamond said, "The guy you really want to talk to is Little Augie."

"What's a 'Little Augie' when he's out and about?" Nadia asked.

"Jacob Orgen."

Nadia didn't look at me, nor I her, when the name *Orgen* was spoken. That was the odd name Detective Johnny Broderick dropped on us as a sliver of a clue. "What's he got to do with anything?"

"Little Augie's the man who looks after the labor rackets, arranging who strikes when, and what company, and so on. He's got a sweet operation going. Anyways, I heard they caught a guy snooping around one of the warehouses at the docks. He was marking up some crates, scratching that arrow sign into 'em. Augie's boys had a hard time getting him to talk, 'specially as he tried to fake not knowing English."

"Really? What was his native tongue?"

"He was a Jerry, you know, a German."

Nadia waited for Diamond to light a cigarette, then: "This man they caught, he have any missing limbs?"

Diamond's eyes narrowed. "Limbs? Nah. I heard his face was messed up. Some of the boys said it looked like it was burned in a fire or something once. You know who this guy was?"

"By the word *was*, are you saying he's no longer among the living?"

Diamond and Madden shrugged in unison.

"What if he is?" Diamond asked. "That mean anything to you?"

"It's one less man I can get answers from."

Diamond and Madden shared a look of respect for Nadia's ice-cold demeanor. "Told ya," Madden said out of the side of his mouth to Diamond.

"What was in the crates?" Nadia asked.

Diamond's long face went still. "That's no one's business."

"Well, let's see," Nadia mused aloud. "Crates could be alcohol, but you boys have all that sown up, and they'd be way larger than you'd need to smuggle narcotics, so I'm going to go ahead and say *guns*."

"She's been called a witch before," I added as the boys at the table just stared.

"Who's got them now?" Nadia pressed.

Madden turned to Diamond, who looked down, shaking his head. "I'm saying I don't know. But there's been a lot of talk that maybe someone wants to ransom them back."

"Who?"

"Don't know that either. Don't care. All I know is that there's some serious heat coming off those things, and the cops are sniffing around hard."

"Cops like Johnny Broderick?" Nadia asked.

"Broderick?" Diamond snorted. "He's a mug. I could take the likes of him anytime I wanted. Nah, the problem lately is there's some Federal boys moving in."

Madden said, "Word is there's a guy named Reynolds come to town. We know him from when he was a Prohibition cop. And he knows us."

"So what?" Diamond said. "All these cops are fumbling around in the dark. They don't know anything."

"But you're saying Augie Orgen has the dirt on this group with the gun shipment?"

"Yeah. That's fair to say."

"And you can arrange a meeting?"

Diamond's face split into a grin. "It'll cost you."

"What?"

Diamond stood, holding out his hand. "How about a dance?"

Nadia accepted; Madden and I watched the two of them proceed to the floor while the four-piece band played a slow, bluesy instrumental of *Moonlight and Roses*.

"So where do you fit in?" Madden asked out the side of his mouth, not taking his eyes off Nadia and Diamond as they swayed across the floor.

"I'm the guy who'll do whatever it takes to keep Miss Ravenwood safe."

"Tough job. But I'll give you this for free...don't trust Legs Diamond."

"Any particular reason?"

"Other than he's a two-timing, back-stabbing snake? No. Not at all."

I looked over at Owney Madden, wondering if I

should appreciate a newly displayed sense of humor or just plain honesty.

"The guy can dance, I'll give him that," Madden said.

The song went on for far too long in my estimation, but eventually it ceased and Diamond escorted Nadia Ravenwood, looking like a golden goddess come to earth, back to the table. "Mr. Diamond has agreed to arrange an introduction with Mr. Orgen," Nadia announced. "Now, if you gentlemen will excuse me, I have work to attend to. You have my card, Mr. Diamond."

"You can't leave so soon," Diamond said with an edge to his voice.

"Sit down, Legs," Madden said. "The lady has places to go."

I stood along with the others, and then Nadia and I departed, not without longing looks cast in her wake. "You really need a better class of boyfriend," I said as I assisted her with her cloak.

"Say what you want, we got another puzzle piece to work on."

"Yes, and all the gangsters in New York as dance partners."

"Come on, let's go home, shall we?"

"May as well. We only got shot at once today."

Mr. Ivanov assisted in getting Nadia bundled into the cab of the Rolls Royce, and soon we were on our way back to the Ravenwood Brownstone. But it wasn't long before Ivanov announced, "We are being followed."

I stiffened. "Are you certain?"

The stony silence affirmed Mr. Ivanov's opinion on the matter.

"You just had to jinx us, didn't you," Nadia said to me.

I reached under the seat for our bag of trouble and

retrieved Nadia's Browning and my Colt, knowing Mr. Ivanov had at least one .44 caliber revolver of his own at hand.

"We're coming up on Central Park," Nadia said. "Let's take the first entrance off Douglas Circle."

It wasn't lost on me that we were now very close to St. Luke's Hospital where Richard Bowen was recovering, and I wondered if we'd be joining him as patients ourselves in the immediate future.

Mr. Ivanov maneuvered the long, heavy automobile expertly, and we were soon among the shadows cast by the trees of the park when the car behind us honked its horn repeatedly. Mr. Ivanov spun us about until we were blocking the road as a black late Model-T screeched to a halt.

"Just what do you think you're doing?" Detective Johnny Broderick yelled.

Chapter Forty Four:

I
t was an odd spot for a conference. Mr. Ivanov stayed back with the Rolls as Detective Broderick and Agent Paul Reynolds stood with Nadia and me. The wind whispered through the trees in our little oasis, where the towering, glowing heights of New York's buildings loomed around us. "Consorting with bad company, Miss Ravenwood?" Broderick asked with a grin.

"Getting answers, Detective. How about you and your friend here? Any progress of your own?"

Reynolds asked, "Who did you meet with and what did you discuss tonight?"

"Sorry, I thought your Director Heever said women were unsuited for investigations, so why do you think I'd know anything?"

"It's Hoover, ma'am. And I just asked a question."

"Let's try the Socratic Method," I said. "What is your interest in Little Augie Orgen?"

Broderick shrugged. "I see you figured out who the name belongs to. He's a gangster, runs the labor racketeering that fits right in with Communists and anarchist agitators. It's like adding one and one."

"Yes..." Nadia said, "only, in this instance, you might add up to three. There may be other *tangents in the field.*"

"Like who?" Reynolds asked.

Nadia shrugged in the confines of her cape. "I'm not sure."

"You're avoiding the question," Broderick stated. "Who'd you see tonight? Owney Madden?"

"He does own the club, you know."

On an impulse, I decided to throw out the name of a guy I really didn't like, despite the fact I'd probably catch hell from Nadia for doing so. "There was also a man named Diamond. Some call him *Legs*."

"Legs Diamond?" Broderick said. "What's he have to do with anything?"

"He just wanted to dance," Nadia said.

"And to tell us that you're a mug, Detective, and that he could take you any time he wanted."

Johnny Broderick's pleasant face remained calm under the illumination of the amber streetlamps. "Oh he did, did he?"

I didn't dare look at Nadia, but I'd swear I felt the heat of displeasure from her dark-eyed gaze upon me.

"Ma'am, tell us what was said back in that club."

"I'm sorry, Agent Reynolds. But until you manage to drag me and my army of expensive and highly efficient lawyers into a courtroom, I shall have to respectfully decline. For now."

"When was the last time you heard from your father?"

There are sounds you hear that can make the world stop in its tracks; the hammer of a gun being cocked, screams of pain and imminent death. And in this case, it was the words that made up that particular question that could ignite a bonfire of anger within Nadia Ravenwood.

I was holding my breath.

"Whatever do you mean?"

"Simple question, ma'am. Your father, Nicholas Ravenwood, left the country in September of '25. Have you heard from him since that time?"

"No."

"Do you know where he went?"

"No."

"Would it surprise you to know he went to Russia?"

"Quit playing games, Agent Reynolds. If you have information to confirm, or accusations to level, come right out with it."

He shrugged. "Very well, ma'am. The government knows Nicholas Ravenwood went into Russia two years ago. Information gets somewhat muddled after that. There've been rumors he was arrested and shot trying to escape. There's also been some talk that he was attempting to overthrow the Bolshevik government, while others say, instead, he was actually working for them."

"That's ridiculous," I blurted out. "Nicholas Ravenwood was one of the people who damn near pulled off a counter revolution in Russia back in '18. I know. I was with him." What I didn't mention was that all his efforts came to ruin because of the failed assassination attempt of Vladimir Lenin and the resulting Red Terror reprisals that followed.

"See? My father would no sooner work for Communists than you would, Agent Reynolds."

Johnny Broderick must've read Nadia Ravenwood's dark mood. "Come on, Paul. Let's go."

We watched as the lawmen angled their car around and puttered off back to the streets of the city. I kept my eye on Nadia, as well as Mr. Ivanov for the silent trip home. Ivanov fought against the Reds in the Russian Civil War under General Wrangel, the *Black Baron*, in Crimea. After the defeat of Wrangel's Imperial Russian Army, Nicholas Ravenwood helped Mr. Ivanov escape to Istanbul and recruited him into his service. I'm sure all the talk tonight about Russia stirred up deep feelings within Mr. Ivanov, as well. After we got home, I assisted Nadia from the Rolls then Mr. Ivanov left to return the limousine to its owner, and we were met by Miss Murphy who informed us all was well within the household.

After we bid Miss Murphy a good night, Nadia turned to me. "Stephen, do you still keep a bottle of whisky in your room?"

"Yes. Ballentine's. The genuine stuff."

"Bring it to the Reading Room, if you please."

"But you don't drink."

"I'm not drinking," she said softly. "Tonight, I'm having some medicine."

Chapter Forty Five:

B y the time I rounded up the bottle and a pair of glasses, Nadia was sprawled across the sofa. She'd shed her golden plumage and was wrapped in her kimono with stocking-clad feet on display. "Doctor Locke reporting, ma'am. Where and how do you want your medicine?"

"Call me *ma'am* like that *merdeux* Reynolds and I shall get up off this sofa, and you don't want that. Pour me a measure. I'm just trying to treat the pain in my side."

"Aye, aye." I gave her a single finger and poured one for myself. She tossed it back and grimaced. "Ugh. Cigarette, please."

I arranged the standing brass ash tray for her convenience and helped her light one of her Turkish firecrackers, setting fire to one of my own Chesterfields, then I took the nearest chair. Nadia stared at the ceiling, casually drawing smoke and sending it upward as she pulled one of her ebony locks straight, then let it go to curl up again, something I've seen her do in the past when troubled. She then turned her large, lovely eyes to me. "Stephen, do you have any idea why my father would go to Russia?"

"No. I doubt what Reynolds said is even true. Last time Nicholas and I were in Russia, we barely got out with our lives."

Nadia watched smoke rise to the ceiling. "I've been jealous of you, you know. You got to know the man better than I. He's been a ghost to me my whole life."

"I'd never be so bold as to claim I knew Nicholas Ravenwood. The man was the consummate chameleon. With military men, he'd act like the very model of the modern major general, when out among commoners, you'd swear he'd been spawned in a ghetto."

"And when he was with women?"

As I failed to respond, Nadia sighed. "Never mind. I can imagine. What I didn't tell you about my upbringing was that every so often, when Father didn't come to see me, a woman would show up instead. It was always the same, though it was never the same woman twice, but they'd all say that they were a 'special friend' of my fathers. Made me wonder why I wasn't 'special' myself."

"I can't speak to that, but I do know he was proud of you, especially when you were out running wild and breaking the law, or escaping the custody of those expensive boarding schools. To hear him speak, you'd think you were the Joan of Arc of the criminal delinquent set."

"Just to hear him speak was all I wanted of him. What you said is just more proof you know him far better than I do."

I shook my head. "First of all, claiming to know Nicholas Ravenwood is a ridiculous notion on the face of it, starting with the fact that I'm pretty sure you know him better than you let on."

She sent another plume of smoke upward. "Maybe. But go on."

"See? I can't even get a straight answer out of you. I still have no idea why he picked me out of that crowd of shivering Army recruits at Arkhangelsk, Russia. All I know is that my commanding officer called me in and introduced me to 'Captain Ravenwood', though he wasn't wearing a uniform, and tells me I've been seconded to him. The next thing I know, I'm in civilian clothes on a train to Moscow."

"Why did you stay with him?"

I shrugged. "Well, he did save my life."

"After risking it."

"Granted. But after everything blew up in Moscow and the Bolsheviks were raiding the British and American Consulates and just about everyone we'd been secretly working with was arrested, shot, or both, Nicholas got word to me along with forged travel papers and enough rubles to bribe my way out. He could have just left me for the wolves, and he would have had a far easier time of it himself if he had, seeing that I didn't even speak Russian, but he chose to take me out with him."

Nadia pondered for a bit, then: "Right before I came here to New York to take over the business, Father wrote to me in Paris, suggesting that I should keep the 'bright young man' he had taken on as an assistant, saying that your only weakness was a tendency toward being soft on enemies." Her eyes narrowed. "Though, I noticed a bit of ruthlessness in you tonight when you intentionally aimed Johnny Broderick at Mr. Jack Diamond."

"Hey, you heard Diamond. He said he can take Broderick anytime. I hope I get a ringside seat to that event."

"Me too." All was quiet between us for a bit, and then she sighed. "Well, I'm off to bed."

"So, are we still pursuing this case now that the Feds are involved?"

"I think May Scott deserves justice, and if Richard is innocent, then that is what she would want to see proven were she still with us. Besides, this is Mary Bowen's brother we're talking about. For her sake, we should see if we can help both Richard and Henry, whether Henry deserves it or not."

"How philanthropic of us."

"Oh, believe me, someone is going to pay for all this. See if they don't. Now, would you be so kind as to make sure I don't fall down the stairs on my way to my room?"

I saw her up and got a glance at the lady's boudoir: it was a mix of a four-poster bed along with a French armoire and triple mirrored vanity, with gowns and dresses draped here and there amidst a cluttering of shoes on the carpeting and an atmosphere tinged by jasmine incense. For a moment, Nadia lingered by her door as she stared up into my eyes, looking for what, I did not know. Time stood still, until:

"Miss Nadia, I can't sleep."

The spell was broken by the appearance of Mary Bowen, wrapped in a new pink-satin robe embroidered with roses. Nadia gave me an indecipherable smile with her eyes as she turned to Mary. "Tell you what, young lady, why don't you stay in my room tonight?"

And with that dismissal, I gave the ladies my best courtly bow and removed myself from the hall to collect my 'medicine' from the Reading Room, as it appeared sleep would be elusive for more than one of us this night.

Chapter Forty Six:

Breakfast was always a wonderful event at the Ravenwood Brownstone. You could expect no less from Mr. Li. In his youth, he was a member of the *Righteous Harmonious Fists*, trained in the mysterious ways of what we in the West call *Chinese Boxing*. Nicholas Ravenwood found him a few years after the Boxer Rebellion, living in destitution in Manchu, China, where Nicholas was working as a spy for the Japanese military against the Russians during the battle and subsequent siege of Port Arthur. As a reward for Mr. Li's service, Nicholas sent him away to Paris to the school of *Le Cordon Bleu*, where he trained to become a Master Chef, a profession that allowed him to serve as Nicholas's eyes and ears aboard luxury ships and exclusive hotels around the world, until Nicholas summoned him to New York.

But all I knew that morning was the anticipation of an exquisite breakfast in my immediate future, an anticipation that was shattered by the sight of Miss Murphy, still in a flannel dressing gown with her rust colored hair escaping her night bonnet, burning the toast in Mr. Li's kitchen. "What are you doing here?"

"Well, hello and how do you do, too. You want an egg?"

"I want a breakfast that'll stay where I put it."

"And I want to be Queen Maeve. So what's your point?"

"Where's Mr. Li?"

"The Miss sent him off on an errand. I'm sure it was

nothing simple since she didn't send you. Now, what do you want for your breakfast?"

"Whatever is handy."

She brought me tea and buttered toasted bread with a fried egg dropped into the middle of it. As I sat at the kitchen table where Miss Ravenwood and her staff usually shared their meals, I asked, "Where is everyone?"

"The Miss and Miss Mary already breakfasted in Miss Ravenwood's room. Mr. Ivanov and I already ate. You're the tail end of the beast."

I gave my meal the scant time it deserved and was soon on my way upstairs. The strains of music drew me to the Reading Room, where I found Nadia and Mary amidst a snowdrift's worth of newspapers with the tune *Big Butter and Egg Man* rolling out of the phonograph. They, like Miss Murphy, were still in kimono and dressing gown, leaving me the only one dressed for the day. "Ahoy," I called from the doorway.

Mary waved from her perch on the arm of a chair nearest the phonograph as Nadia shuffled the pages of the Herald Tribune and the Times to the side of the sofa. "Welcome, Stephen. Sleep well?"

"Not as well as some. What's our plan for today?"

"First, we're taking Mary to see Richard at the hospital as soon as visiting hours come round, then, you and I may have some business in Lower Manhattan."

I was wondering if 'Lower Manhattan' meant Chinatown, and if that had anything to do with Mr. Li's *errand*. I helped myself to some of the morning's newspapers to see if the rest of the world was in as bad a shape as usual. That's when I noticed that some of the papers were old and dated last August with the reports of the execution of the convicted anarchists Sacco and Vanzetti in Massachusetts. I held up the page and caught

Nadia's eye, careful not to disturb Mary's enjoyment of the ragtime jazz.

Nadia simply arched an eyebrow. "Lot of that kind of thing going around these days."

I nodded in agreement, remembering Richard Bowen's grave concern about the growing anarchist threats to our country, and although there appeared to be some doubt as to the guilt of the two Italian gentleman, they were nonetheless made to keep their appointments with the electric chair.

But the slow morning gave way to a flurry of activity as the women disappeared from the Reading Room to dress, leaving me to exercise one of the skills of my profession: the waiting. Eventually, Nadia came down attired in her riding gear, vest, jodhpurs and boots, a sure sign she was expecting action, while Mary appeared to have matured overnight with a layered day dress of rose pink with gold threaded designs worked in and her hair done up in an approximation of Nadia's waved bob. My appreciation lasted as long as it took for me to realize I was doomed to the rumble seat of the roadster again. Fortunately, the drive to St. Luke's was short and traffic less crowded today with the sky clear of clouds for once, though it rendered the air bitterly chilled.

We arrived at the destination and I got an unprecedented view of the place, looking like a French Chateau wedded to a domed cathedral. But the stringent smell of the hallways was the same for hospitals everywhere. Richard Bowen's private room was a few floors up and easily found by the signpost of the uniformed police officer sitting in a wooden chair just outside his door.

Only the policeman wasn't moving and Richard wasn't in his room.

Chapter Forty Seven:

As Mary ran to the hall, screaming for a doctor, Nadia checked the young policeman, pointing to the small trickle of blood from a tiny puncture in his neck. "Drugged," Nadia snapped. "They must be using a wheelchair or something to move Richard. Keep Mary with you."

Those boots of Nadia's must have been custom fit, for she ran like a gazelle. I spotted a nurse coming toward us, alarm written across her face as I pointed to the policeman. "He's been drugged. Get a doctor." I took Mary's hand and raced with her back to the elevators.

"Where's my brother?" Mary cried.

"Alive, or they would have left him in the room." I hoped the girl took some kind of solace in my ramblings. The problem was, the hospital was impossibly huge, with potential escape routes everywhere. I needed to think: Nadia said they'd use a wheelchair for Richard as his missing leg prevented mobility. My best bet was to get outside and try to spot the getaway vehicle, most likely a large automobile or enclosed truck.

But as the world's slowest elevator finally delivered Mary and me to the ground floor, I heard the sounds of screams echoing through the hallways. I took Mary's hand and we pushed our way past the congregating hospital staff until we broke through into a ring of astounded witnesses looking at Nadia Ravenwood as she stood, panting and catching her breath, one booted foot on a pistol on the floor, standing over a bloody faced man in a hospital orderly's garb as she held onto a covered gurney.

I could hear a policeman's whistle echoing through the hallways as Mary and I went to Nadia, who threw back the white sheet that was concealing Richard Bowen. "He's breathing...but I'm guessing he got...a dose of whatever laid out...the policeman upstairs," Nadia said between deep breaths.

Mary was at Richards side, pleading with his unconscious form as I took a gander at the man at Nadia's feet. He was mumbling incoherently through a mouthful of broken teeth, courtesy of Nadia's knuckleduster, no doubt. "Well, good luck getting this one to talk," I said in an aside to her.

Nadia shrugged. "I was going for our blonde friend, Hella. She's all dressed up in a nurse's uniform, which is how she got close enough to give the copper upstairs the needle. She looked back and saw me coming up behind her, so she sent her friend here to stop me. When she saw me punch his face, she decided she didn't want the same treatment and ran for it, leaving Richard behind."

"How'd you catch up with them?"

Nadia shrugged as we made our way out of the crowd around the gurney; a doctor had arrived and was taking charge. "I just wondered...how would I get a covered body out of a hospital?"

Nadia then pointed up to an arrowed sign that directed one to the *Pathology Building*. "Little Hella didn't know the shortcuts around here, thank God, but I'm betting they parked either an ambulance or maybe a hearse out by the bay where bodies are delivered, thinking they could just wheel Richard right out of here."

"So, in essence, you simply thought like a criminal?"

"I've had practice. Come on, let's check on Richard and get Mary out of here."

The Ravenwood Conspiracy

We were soon surrounded by police as we waited around to hear that both Richard and the young policeman would recover from the administration of narcotics. The thug whom Nadia left holding a small handful of his own teeth was given a cursory examination and then shuffled off to incarceration, since he was unable to answer questions even if he wanted. Nadia showed her courtesy card from the Police Commissioner to one and all and blithely informed anyone who asked that all inquiries should be directed to Detective McDonough of the 5th Precinct. Once Mary had her assurances of her brother's care and recovery, she said to us, "But what about Henry? Why isn't he here for Richard?"

"I don't know, dear. Why don't we go and see him?"

Mary was all for that; me, with the rumble seat in my future, not so much. But I wasn't about to let Mary or Nadia go to that gilded snake's nest without me. I walked ahead to Nadia's Packard and got my Colt out of the bag, slipped it into my waistband then took my perch for the drive down Park Avenue with my pistol digging uncomfortably into my hip.

The portal to the Bowen mansion was once again guarded by Oscar, who actually appeared to be almost pleased to see us as Mary pushed past. "Where's Henry? And why hasn't he been to see Richard in the hospital?"

"Mr. Henry Bowen is in his study, not to be disturbed."

Mary darted past him.

"Wait. Miss Mary."

She was halfway up the winding staircase with Nadia in close pursuit. I grabbed Oscar by his shoulder, preventing him from stopping them. "You really don't want to do that, Oscar. Miss Ravenwood's already knocked a few teeth out today. Don't give her the chance to make a necklace."

Oscar looked upward. "I confess I've been worried, but Mr. Henry left strict instructions last night he was not to be disturbed. I haven't heard from him since."

Mary's scream echoed through the house.

I charged up the steps until I reached the study. Nadia and Mary stood on each side of the doorway, affording me a view of Henry Bowen seated in his chair and slumped forward across his desk; one side of his head a broken, red ruin.

Nadia took Mary by the shoulders and spun her about to take her down the stairs. "Look it over and put together what happened. I'll call the police."

I stepped into the study and closed the door, leaving me alone to find answers with a man who'd never speak again.

Chapter Forty Eight:

There's a trick that happens between my body and my mind, where the two of them become disconnected. I discovered this in the War and on a few occasions in the service of Nicholas Ravenwood. At times, when I'm confronted by a horrific or dangerous situation, it's like my nerves go dead, my hands don't shake, my voice doesn't falter, and I can carry on with whatever it is I have to do. So far, this condition has lasted me long enough to get by with whatever task is at hand. The shakes came afterwards.

Before I moved, I took a breath; the air in the room told me Henry had been dead for hours, but no more than that. The curtains had been drawn, but the green glass shaded lamp on the desk remained lit, and the telephone receiver still lay on the hook. I looked around the room; nothing was out of place that I could see. I made my way to the desk, walking slowly in a wide circle, noting the safe was closed and locked. Looking down at Henry's body, I saw a shiny nickel-plated revolver close to his right hand. My very own Smith and Wesson.

For an arranged suicide scene, it was rather good.

I crouched down low and looked under the desk where I found a small scattering of pieces of down feathers, some that looked scorched. It's an assassin's trick to muffle the sound of a gunshot by jamming the barrel into a pillow, and I was willing to bet good money that there would be a small cushion missing from somewhere in the house. Looking at the entry wound on Henry's head, I saw it was lacking the gunpowder burns that accompany a close up shot like this.

Far more likely was the idea that Henry was shot at his desk by someone who stood over him on his right side and used the muffled revolver so the house wasn't alerted by the noise, and then the killer picked up as much blown-out feathering as he could before escaping.

The situation came down to this: The setup didn't fool me, and certainly wouldn't have fooled even a half-drunk homicide detective. But it might be just enough to frame the owner of the revolver, namely me, on a charge of suspicion. And that became a scary thought indeed.

"What'd you find?"

Nadia's voice from the doorway almost made me jump out of my skin. "How's Mary?"

"Holding herself together. I don't want to leave her long. The police are on their way. What do you have?"

"Everything's arranged to give the impression of a staged suicide. And the killer used my gun."

"Ah. Interesting."

"Yes, considering how this could land me in a jail cell for the foreseeable future."

Her dark, lovely eyes gave me a look of sympathy. "We'll burn that bridge when we come to it." Then she approached the desk, pointing, "What's that under his hand?"

I looked, and now saw that the spray of gore from the gunshot left a small square clean spot just under the hand that held the gun. Getting closer, I saw a scrap of paper beneath the heel of Henry's hand. Gingerly pinching his sleeve, I gently lifted his arm up a bit, revealing a torn paper edge with the words 'what happened to my family should nev-'. Evidently, someone removed whatever Henry had written after the shooting.

Nadia nodded as I reported my findings, then she knelt down by the safe and twisted the dial.

"What are you doing?"

"Checking to see if anything's different since we came here last." She opened the safe. "Ah." It was completely empty.

"What was in there before?"

"I'll tell you later. Let's get downstairs."

We descended to find Mary, along with Oscar and a few of the staff, in the library. Mary's face bore a look I'd seen before. Some people, when they go through the fire of extreme adversity, will give in to it, have it overwhelm them. But there are others who brave the flames and come out like tempered steel. Mary's face bore the trails of her tears, but there was now a quiet, fierce determination burning in her eyes.

Nadia took Oscar by the arm and drew him into a corner, telling me with her eyes to follow. "Where's Mr. Baker?"

"I haven't seen him since last evening."

"Oscar, now would be a good time to tell us about the men your Mr. Henry involved himself with. Start with the man with the eye patch."

He looked like she'd stabbed him. "The man... His name is Godwin, or so he said. No one was supposed to know when he comes here, especially Mr. Richard. I don't know why, I just did as Mr. Henry told me."

"Oh, but Oscar, you heard more than that, didn't you?" Nadia purred. "You were curious, of course, and were worried about the family. So tell me, what did you find out?"

Oscar seemed to collapse within himself. "It was all about saving the family. The Bowen fortunes had been in decline for some time. Mr. Godwin told Mr. Henry that he had a way for him to make a lot of money."

"Doing what?"

"Investing in certain companies. Mr. Godwin wanted Mr. Henry to be the one making the stock purchases. I don't know why."

"And were these stock purchases made from companies that manufactured armaments?"

Oscar's lips trembled. "Yes. Of course."

"Why *of course*?" I asked.

"That was the original basis of the Bowen fortunes. And the reason for the family's tragedy."

Nadia's dark eyes narrowed. "Tragedy? You mean when Henry, Richard and Mary's father died on the Lusitania when the Germans sank it?"

Oscar nodded.

"It's rumored that the ship was secretly carrying war materials to England, and was therefore a legitimate target for the German U Boats, despite it having civilian passengers onboard." Nadia breathed a curse in German. "If word of that got out, then the Bowen family would have been ruined."

Oscar sighed. "And that's why Mr. Henry did what he felt he had to do."

Nadia took a breath to ask another question when a wide-eyed maid rushed in. "The police are here."

Chapter Forty Nine:

The library was getting crowded.

The first police to arrive hailed from the 15th Precinct and were well aware of how to treat the upper class citizens who inhabited the land of the rich and powerful, actually making their approach via the delivery entrance. We answered their questions and advised we were there in our capacity as Richard Bowen's advocates and Mary Bowen's *Guardians Ad Hoc*. Everything was going swimmingly until the arrival of Detective Johnny Broderick and Agent Paul Reynolds, neither of whom looked happy to see us. But that was nothing compared to the blatant scowl we received upon the arrival of Detective McDonough. Word must have spread like the proverbial wildfire.

Nadia and I were separated from Mary and the house staff and brought to the Reception Room off the vestibule where the three Officers of the Law sat us down and loomed over us.

I asked, "Would now be a good time to say just how much we enjoy working with all of you?"

McDonough just blew out his cheeks and rolled his eyes as Broderick and Reynolds stared.

"Cut to the chase," Broderick said. "And none of your usual runaround. Who killed Henry Bowen?"

"I take it you're not falling for the suicide gag," I said. "Just as well, you're going to find out that the gun in Henry's hand is mine."

That got McDonough's attention. "Care to explain

that one a bit more, my lad?"

"I lost it. Just yesterday, as a matter fact."

"Where?"

Nadia jumped in. "You're asking the wrong questions. I'd want to know who murdered Henry Bowen and why? Does his death have anything to do with the work he was performing on your behalf, Detective Broderick?"

Johnny kept his face deadpan calm.

Agent Reynolds cleared his throat. "You two need to tell us everything you know about this. Now. Or I'll have Broderick run you in."

Nadia took turns staring at Broderick and Reynolds, as if they were two cuts of beef she was trying to decide between. "No, I don't think you will. You've reached a dead end, unfortunately, in this case with poor Henry. You need Stephen and I out and about to stir things up for you. Detective McDonough will vouch for the fact that we arranged for him to not only arrest Richard Bowen and get a high profile murder case under control, but also provided him the identity of the man who attempted to kill Richard Bowen."

"I'm not convinced that man wasn't actually aiming at you," McDonough said under his moustache.

Reynolds reddened with anger. "I said, you have to tell us what you know. Now."

Nadia stood. "No we don't. Stephen and I are going to walk out of here and take Mary Bowen with us. Any attempt to stop us will be treated as an attempted false arrest. And that will go hard against you. Very hard indeed. Although my lawyers will no doubt be overjoyed."

"How do you explain the gun used to kill Henry Bowen?" Broderick demanded.

"I don't," Nadia replied blithely. "As you're so fond of telling me, that's a matter for the police."

With a last haughty look, Nadia Ravenwood walked out like royalty, leaving me to shrug and give the assembled coppers my best what-can-you-do look, then I followed her out. We collected Mary along with our hats and coats and made our escape via the back garden and a long walk around to Nadia's Packard, keeping a wary eye on the reporters who'd been gathering like a flock of carrion birds along Park Avenue. For once, I happily took to the rumble seat as we made our getaway.

We drove directly back to the Brownstone, allowing me a longing glimpse at the Waldorf Astoria as we passed, especially as my runny egg on a slice of burnt toast seemed ages ago. Although upon our arrival, we were informed by Miss Murphy that Mr. Li was still out and that there was a telephone message for Miss Ravenwood from a man who described himself as her *dancing partner from last night*. Nadia went upstairs to return the call, and suddenly I found myself alone with Mary Bowen. "What can I do for you?" I took her coat.

She simply stared at nothing, slowly shaking her head, until she murmured, "How could this happen?"

"For what it's worth, I think that your brother Henry was trying to do what he thought best for his family. For you. And for some reason, that cost him his life."

She looked at me. Something fierce was alight behind her gray eyes. "Will you catch whoever did this?"

"I don't know. What I do know is that Nadia and I will try."

"And what will you do when you find them?"

"Nadia Ravenwood believes people should get what they deserve."

Mary nodded once. "I want to be alone for a while." Then she climbed the stairs.

She met Nadia coming back down, and the two of

them conversed in low whispers, until Nadia squeezed Mary's arm and they continued their separate paths. "We have a date," Nadia announced.

"A luncheon date?" I was hopeful.

"No, but perhaps we'll find a street vendor along the way."

"Where are we going?"

"Madison Square Garden. Our Mr. Diamond wants to meet somewhere public."

"He can't be *Our Mr. Diamond* as he's sure as hell is not *My Mr. Diamond.*"

"Well, park your feelings somewhere else. He said he's going to arrange a meeting with the mysterious Jacob Orgen."

"Little Augie himself, eh?"

"Yes. Let's not antagonize anyone from the start for a change, shall we?"

"Your wish is my command."

Chapter Fifty:

It was a pleasure to be riding inside the cab of the Packard for a change. Our departure had been slightly delayed as we awaited the arrival of Aunty Kit, whom I barely recognized when she rang for admittance. I was the one to answer, and I saw her dressed in simple, somber black with a modicum of makeup. "I'm here to see Mary."

"You?"

"Listen, I've buried a husband, a father and a brother in my time. I'm here to help Mary with the arrangements and anything else she may need."

I ushered her in, marveling that the brash, bold woman I knew had been replaced by this quietly serious person. She and Nadia exchanged a few hushed words, and then Nadia and I left for our engagement.

Mind you, Madison Square Garden isn't the same one since being rebuilt a couple of years ago and isn't even anywhere near Madison Square. But as Rome had its Coliseum, we had the Garden for our modern sporting events. And though I didn't find any food vendors on the corner, I had the opportunity to quickly consume a grilled cheese and malted milkshake at the Liggett's next door to the main box office. Afterwards, Nadia and I loitered about near the marquee that advertised the coming of a Rodeo to be held here next week. I'd just lit a cigarette when Nadia touched my arm and nodded. "Here he comes."

Jack Diamond swaggered down Eighth Street like he owned it. He wore a long overcoat with fur-lined lapels and cuffs and a broad Panama-style hat. He gave Nadia a charming smile and me a sideways glance. "Hello, there. No room at the kennel for your pet?"

"Hello, Mr. Diamond," Nadia said. "You have some information for me?"

He chuckled. "Madden said you were all business, though I thought differently out there on the dance floor. But yeah, I've got something."

"Is it about the shipment of guns?"

Diamond looked about, but the traffic and pedestrians were few so early in the afternoon. "If you represent a serious buyer for the merchandise, I can get you a meeting with Little Augie."

"Of course. Are there any other bidders?"

As Nadia and I didn't represent any kind of illegal armaments buyer, this was a problem. Not that anyone could tell by Nadia's straight face.

Jack Diamond's dark, drooping eyes narrowed. "Yeah, as a matter of fact. One for sure."

"What sort of armaments are we bidding on?"

"Real hodgepodge. Almost like a salesman's sample case; a little of everything, like automatic rifles, machine guns, grenades. Little Augie has all the numbers and the what's what."

"Where do we meet with Mr. Orgen?"

"Corner of Delancey and Norfolk. Tomorrow night, eight o'clock."

"And the merchandise is nearby for our inspection?"

Diamond was about to respond, but suddenly his eyes grew large as he stared over our shoulders and started backing away.

Detective Johnny Broderick walked up behind us... "Hello, Legs, I hear you think you can take me," and moved in on a rapidly retreating Jack Diamond. There was a flash of movement, a dull *crack*, and Diamond spun halfway around, and without breaking stride, Broderick grabbed him and hefted him up and drove him headfirst into a sidewalk wastebasket, causing it to tip over on its side.

Johnny Broderick turned about, tipped the brim of his hat to Nadia, and walked on. We watched as he swiftly stepped to the street where a car with a grinning Agent Reynolds was waiting. With a last jaunty wave, the pair of lawmen drove off.

As for Jack Diamond, he was attracting a crowd as he moaned and rolled back and forth, like a turtle trying to escape its shell.

"Well, I doubt we'll get any more use out of him today."

I was befuddled. "How did he know we'd be here?"

Nadia's dark eyes resembled a gathering storm. "I arranged this meeting on my telephone today. That's how Detective Broderick knew. Come on."

Nadia's driving back to the Brownstone was even more reckless than usual, until she reached a block away, and then she slowed to the pace of a walking pony. She alternated looking at the road and leaning out her side of the car staring up at the telephone lines that were strung along the streets until she pulled in behind a dark gray delivery truck parked just three homes down from hers.

I followed her as she got out of the Packard and pointed up to the nearest pole where I spotted the wire that trailed down to the box of the truck.

Nadia stepped to a rear tire then struck it hard with her push dagger, creating a hiss as the truck tire sank flat. There came a slamming of a door as a man looking like a slightly smaller version of Agent Paul Reynolds appeared, coatless, with an automatic pistol strapped to a shoulder holster. He fumbled a gold shield out of a wallet. "Federal

Agent."

Nadia stood with her arms crossed. "So?"

The Agent looked like he'd been hit with a bucket of iced water. "I said, I'm a Federal Agent."

"Get back into your dirty little truck and listen to me telephone newspapermen from the Herald Tribune, the Times, and whoever else I can interest in a government spy in action."

The man paled. "You can't."

Nadia smiled. It was the kind of smile I could picture on a queen who'd just ordered the beheading of an enemy rival. "So what are you going to tell me to convince me to keep quiet?"

Chapter Fifty One:

Agent Marcus Robertson, as the young man came to be known, was sitting stock still in Nadia's exotic parlor, only his eyes were darting about here and there as we awaited the arrival of Agent Paul Reynolds and Detective Broderick.

I'd not been idle, and after my brief labors sat with him. I smoked, he declined. "So, are your parents proud of what you do?"

He didn't respond, acting like he was held prisoner. Finally, Nadia came up, leading Broderick and Reynolds. Agent Robertson stood as if launched out of his chair. "I'm sorry—"

"Go wait for the repair truck," Reynolds told him. "When the tire's fixed, take our truck back to headquarters."

"Do I unhook the wire, sir?"

Nadia simply grinned.

Reynolds sighed. "Yes. Unhook the wire. Wrap it all up. Now."

The young Agent departed in all haste as Nadia ascended to her throne. "Illegal wire tap, Mr. Reynolds? What do you have to say for yourself?"

"I'm going to ask you to overlook this in the interest of the country."

She let out a small laugh, glanced at Broderick, then me. I could see her movements weren't as quick as usual and surmised her damaged ribs were causing her pain, not surprising given all the running and punching she performed today. "So, what are you prepared to offer in return for my silence?"

Reynolds looked confused. "I told you, this is a matter of national importance."

Nadia helped herself to one of her Turkish cigarettes from the sandalwood box, lighting it and taking a long draw, before expelling the smoke. "Let me spell it out for the slow ones in the class. I have numerous associates in the news industry. Mr. Locke here, as we were awaiting your arrival, photographed the inside of your truck and all the equipment you use to spy on American citizens. I will have him turn over the yet undeveloped film to you in return for your telling us everything you know about the Bowen family and their troubles."

"This is blackmail...against the government."

"No, it's blackmail against incompetent agents of the government. If you hadn't tipped your hand by showing up at our meeting with Mr. Jack Diamond, I'd have never known you were listening in on my telephone calls."

Broderick answered, "I've been trying to keep you out of this business ever since you butted in."

"Well, congratulations Detective. Now I'll never know what Mr. Diamond was going to say."

I kept my expression still at that complete lie.

Reynolds' face twisted in anguish. "You can't blow this operation."

Nadia took another draw, sending the cloud toward Reynolds. "What I do now is up to you."

Broderick placed a hand on Reynolds' arm. "Tell her."

"Okay. Here's the deal. I'll let you in, and you don't mess anything up, because if you do, I swear to God, I will arrest you myself."

"Agreed."

I took a roll of film out of my pocket and tossed it to Agent Reynolds. "Here you go."

He looked down at the film in his hand. "Well, all right, then. Come on, Broderick. We got what we want."

"So you'd leave without holding up your end of the bargain?" Nadia asked.

Reynolds looked defiant. "It's for the good of the country."

"It's also not the roll of film you want," I said. "If you look again, you'll see it's not even exposed yet. The actual film is safe and out of your reach. I just wanted to see who we were dealing with."

Nadia fixed Reynolds with her most imperious look. "Agent Reynolds, you may go. We'll speak only with Detective Broderick from here on."

Reynolds spun about and marched out, slamming our front door in the process. Johnny Broderick shrugged. "What can I say? I have to work with the guy."

"Please have a seat, Detective Broderick," Nadia said. "And let's get to it."

"Okay, Miss Ravenwood, but why you're still involved, it's all beyond me. There's nothing good to come out of this."

"Start from the top. What was Henry Bowen doing for you?"

"Mr. Bowen came to us a while ago, saying he'd tumbled onto some shady characters who were trying to buy up military weapons, and in bulk."

"He ever tell you who these people were, specifically?"

"No, only that they referred to each other with code names. Henry was positive that these people were anarchists, working on behalf of Russia, and were planning something big. We were going to nab this gang when they went to pick up the weapons, only the guns got hijacked before the anarchists could get their hands on them. That's when someone sent a message to Henry Bowen by shooting up his house. He must have been suspected of being the leak."

"And these anarchists, do they have a specific name for themselves? Like *The Galleanists* do?"

"Yeah, Henry said they called themselves the *Companions of Tyr*."

"And they are plotting against the United States?"

"From what Henry said, it's some deep, secret society stuff, and they were using him to acquire the weapons."

Nadia and I traded looks of dread.

For myself, all I could wonder was how every answer made our case so much darker.

Chapter Fifty Two:

W e let Johnny Broderick go with the actual roll of film. I wasn't certain how the photographs would have turned out anyway, as the inside of the Bureau of Investigation's truck was singularly uninteresting; there were some tools and spools of wire with a small table and an electric receiver set and headphones along with a stenographer's notebook, and that was it.

I showed Johnny Broderick out. "Nice job on Legs Diamond, by the way." After he drove off, I returned to the parlor where Nadia was slumped in her chair, looking as weary as I'd ever seen her. "Now, what can I do for you?"

She patted the cigarette box next to her. "Remind me, who was the detective in the stories who smoked to solve problems?"

"Sherlock Holmes. Everyone knows that."

"Oh. Well, growing up I was reading all about Arsene Lupin and Raffles instead."

"Glamorized thieves. How unsurprising."

"Says the man who likes Robin Hood." She gave her cigarette box a final pat. "I was just wondering what to do to try to make some sense out of all this. At this rate, I'm wondering if smoking opium wouldn't help."

"Again I ask, what can I do?"

She sighed and sat up taller. "Let's review. Henry Bowen tells the police that he's involved in a plot to arm anarchists, and these anarchists are called the Companions of Tyr."

"Correct."

"Richard Bowen tells us he's been inducted into the ranks of the Companions of Tyr, and that they are actually a secret anti Anarchist society."

"Also correct. Clearly, some families don't communicate well."

"Both Henry and Richard are involved with the same people. There's Mr. Godwin, he of the white eye patch sect, who not only tells Henry what to do but who also is Richard's Commanding Officer in the Companions of Tyr."

"And let's not forget their associates, the short man with the long gun and the crazy blonde vamp, both as murderous as Jack the Ripper and Lucrezia Borgia."

"I always felt Lucrezia may have been maligned, however, Miss Peroxide gives vampires a bad name. Also, let's not forget the mysterious Mr. Baker who conveniently vanished after Henry's staged suicide."

"Right. So now we add an actual shipment of weapons, intended for the Companions of Tyr, that gets stolen by local gangsters and offered up to the highest bidder. But who paid for the guns in the first place?"

"I have a theory," Nadia said slyly.

"Do tell."

"Remember when Jack Diamond said the weapons looked like a salesman's sample kit? What if that's exactly what it was?"

"What do you mean?"

"When I got into Henry's safe in his study, I saw a stack of stock certificates from companies like Colt, Browning, Springfield and Thompson. All of them American armaments manufacturers. Being a chief shareholder in these companies might allow someone to have special access to the merchandise."

I thought this over. "That's conceivable."

"Yes, especially if the stockholders are a private consortium under an umbrella corporation."

"What corporation?"

"An entity called *The Fenris Group*."

"Fenris? As in the mythological giant wolf? The one who bit off Tyr's hand?"

"The same. It's also the name of the holding company on all those stock certificates I found in Henry's safe."

"And you're just telling me about this now?"

She shrugged. "It hadn't come up in conversation until this moment."

I spent a little time lighting a cigarette to keep myself from talking. Nicholas Ravenwood would occasionally do the same thing to me, not tell me an important piece of information until it became absolutely necessary for me to know. And here was Nadia echoing her father's actions. It was times like these where her parentage was certainly not in doubt, as far as I was concerned. "All right, so given all this, where does it leave us?"

"It leaves us going to speak with Richard Bowen again. Now that the people he trusted drugged him and attempted to kidnap him out of the hospital, I believe he may be more inclined to tell us the truth."

I watched Nadia as she slowly stood and gingerly stretched. "You move like you've been thrown from a horse, and then had the beast perform the *Black Bottom* on you."

She looked down at her riding attire. "Well, at least people will think that's a plausible story. Let's go."

Night was falling and my hunger was rising as we drove to St. Luke's, where we now found two uniformed guards who argued against allowing Nadia and I admittance until Richard himself heard us and ordered the police to let us pass.

"I understand I am to thank you for preventing my abduction?"

Nadia waved his gratitude away. "If you're in a giving mood, then why not give us everything you've been holding back on your Companions of Tyr?"

Richard's pale face, almost a match for the hospital sheets, looked away. "It is true, isn't it? Hella came and tried to kidnap me? And now Henry's dead?"

"It's worse than that. Your Mr. Godwin had been conspiring with your brother Henry without your knowledge. Godwin was playing you both."

"Not just me," Richard said bitterly. "All the men we gathered, all the men who took the oath to fight against the anarchists. But for God's sake, why?"

"That is what we're trying to find out. Richard, there is clearly some deeper, more sinister purpose at work here. Now tell me...what was it you and the Companions of Tyr were supposed to do?"

He sighed. "Godwin said the time was coming when we'd have to arm ourselves and strike a blow against the enemy, and once that was done, they and their plans would be laid bare, and the whole country would rally behind us. And not just America, but the rest of the world. But we had to wait until we caught the enemy in an act of sedition. Godwin promised the time was coming soon."

"You and your Companions have meetings, yes? When is the next one scheduled?"

Richard looked up. "Tonight."

Chapter Fifty Three:

Nadia was looking at the street as she drove us back to the Brownstone. I was looking at her. In the shifts of reflected light, her face was as pale as the occasional glimpses of moonlight that strayed in. "We don't have to do this, you know."

"You don't. I do."

"Your father made me swear an oath to protect you."

"Liar. Father would do no such thing."

"How would you know?"

The moaning of the motor along with the changing of the gears was all I heard as I buried myself in the silence of regret for letting those words escape my lips. "I'm sorry. That was uncalled for."

She shrugged. "As you say. But I'm going out tonight. You may come with me, or not."

"I'm with."

She turned and flashed a smile. "Good. I'm glad. Now, let's get properly dressed for the occasion."

"And have a last meal?"

"Of course."

The sandwich Miss Murphy prepared was worse than the breakfast, and I took a solemn vow to take myself out to dinner at the Chalet Suisse, or Voisin, or Adolph's... something of that caliber should I survive the evening. At least I was comfortably attired in my old clothes, without a stiff collar, and my reliable trench coat and cap. Nadia appeared in a long-sleeved black tunic with matching knickers, and stockings that looked like ballet slippers.

These, along with her black velour coat and cloche hat, made her dressed in the appropriate color for my funeral.

As I helped her into her coat, I noticed an odd scent over her Egyptian perfume. "What's that I smell?"

"Horse liniment. Miss Murphy swears by it for my ribs. I had her wrap me up again."

"She must have had it still on her hands when she made my sandwich. Did I hear you on the telephone earlier?"

"I've arranged for a little local support in the Bowery. Also, I heard from Mr. Li."

"Ah. Has his errand met with success?"

"We'll have to see."

"And that errand was?"

"Patience."

"It's almost as if you don't trust me."

"Tell me, how was your date with that redhead? What was her name again?"

"Oh, will you look at the time? We must be off."

Nadia smiled. "Indeed."

She drove us down to Lower Manhattan. Our destination was the All Night Mission where we'd seen Hella. Richard reluctantly confirmed that a room upstairs was the primary meeting place for the Companions of Tyr. I had no idea how we were going to infiltrate a place like that, especially after we tipped our hand with the smoke bomb trick, but Nadia Ravenwood was determined to try.

The Bowery itself was alive this Friday night, with people out and about to the music halls and speakeasies. She parked us a good block away, and we strolled along with the sidewalk crowds, my pockets heavy with my .45 and spare magazine along with some selected burglary tools and a flashlight. I'm surprised the local beat cop didn't hear me rattling along.

The Ravenwood Conspiracy

As we approached a pool hall, shadows detached themselves from the surroundings and materialized into three ragged youths, the grime on their faces substituting for the beards they were unable to yet grow. I recognize Anthony, our local smoke bomber, from our earlier encounter as he touched the bill of his cap. "Miss Romano. Nice to see you gain."

I noticed Nadia was prudently using her *Anna Romano* alias with the local boys. "Hello, Anthony. I'm glad you got my message. Ready for some work?"

Anthony looked back at his lieutenants. "Just one thing, Miss Romano. The boys need to know if you're going up against any Italians or Irish?"

Nadia nodded. "Not to worry, my good man. There are no *Black Hand* or *White Hand* problems tonight. But the people we're after are dangerous, and you'll need to keep your distance."

"Especially," I added, "if you see a short, tough looking guy in a leather coat who calls himself Captain. He's a bad man with a big gun."

"Okay." Anthony nodded. "So what do you need?"

"To get as close to the All Night Mission's second floor as we can."

"Okay. Me and my guys will get a look. Be right back, Miss."

I lit a cigarette as Anthony and his cohorts wove their way through the crowd and out of sight. It wasn't long before one of Anthony's boys came running back. "You got ten bucks?"

Nadia produced a folded bill, and the redheaded street denizen ran back.

"I hope he was really part of the gang," I said out of the side of my mouth. Before we knew it, the same youngster came back and waved at us to follow. We came up next to Anthony as he leaned against the stained brick wall. "Okay. There's a shoe shop right next to the Mission. The owner lives upstairs. I gave him the money and told him to take his wife and kids out for an hour and to keep his trap shut. Good enough?"

"Well done," Nadia replied.

"We'll keep an eye out," Anthony said. "You hear banging on the pipes, you get gone, okay?"

I looked up at the All Night Mission and its cross, wondering what we'd find within.

Chapter Fifty Four:

Nadia slipped Anthony some folded bills and we made our way over to the shop, where the sign proclaimed the names of *Endicott and Johnson* as the proprietors. Nadia asked me for the double-headed skeleton keys, and I blocked her from view as she went to work behind me. I heard a lock *click*, then: "Let's go."

We set a bell to tinkling as we entered, but the store, with its rich aroma of tanned leather, was dark. We found a set of stairs behind a curtain at the back where the inventory was kept and ascended. Nadia unlocked the door at the top and we found ourselves inside a warm, unlighted kitchen, with the scent of spices lingering in the air.

We moved to the room at the front of the apartment, where we found worn furnishings and the lights of the marquees across the street glowing through the thin curtains. But just outside the window was our avenue: the fire escape shared with the building that housed the Mission. We opened the window and deftly slipped out to the iron railings, and through the street noises from below I heard Nadia's sharp intake of breath; she must have felt some pain from her prior injuries as she moved.

We crouched beneath the window of the Mission, noting it was dark within. I attempted to lift the sash and found it locked. Nadia went to work on the glass with the diamond tip drill bit, which made a grating sound as she worked. Soon she'd cut deep enough to tap out a small piece of glass just large enough to reach inside and undo the latch.

I kept my hand on my pistol as we crawled over the sill, not knowing if we'd alerted anyone inside. Once within, with the window pulled back down, all was quiet except for the street noises coming in through the small hole she'd made. As my eyes adjusted to the gloom, my ears began to hear a droning of voices coming from below, and I recognized a slurred rendition of a Gospel Hymn being sung.

The room was set up like a classroom, with chairs in rows facing a blackboard that showed a heavy powdering of chalk but no discernible words. Nadia and I slowly crept forward, alert for the slightest squeaks from the wooden floors. I could see a dim light glowing from under the door that led inward, and when we reached it, the voices were still faint.

While we listened, there came an irregular thumping sound that grew louder until it stopped, and we clearly heard a male voice, "Damn it," and then we heard the odd footsteps retreat. I saw Nadia's scowl, and then she opened the door just enough to get a glimpse out and swiftly closed it, then leaned to my ear. "There's a sign on the door...an arrow pointing down. I'm betting it means the meeting's been cancelled."

"So now we can leave?" Me being hopeful again.

"No. The door across the hall is marked Private. I'm going to see what's on the other side."

It was no time nor place to argue with her, no matter how much I wanted to talk her out of it. We crouched on the inside of our door, listening for any potential sound of danger, then Nadia swiftly opened up and stepped into the hall and across. That door, of course, was also locked.

I watched as she knelt down and worked on the lock, deftly probing with the skeleton keys for what felt like hours. She tried three different key shapes until there finally came the sound of the latch being turned. We practically knocked each other over in our haste to get out of the hallway.

Inside was windowless and black as pitch, so I risked the flashlight. Now we could see this place was sparsely furnished with a plain table, a desk lamp, and six wooden chairs. The airless room held a stuffy chemical smell, and as we approached the table, we saw the reason: On the floor was a metal bucket, half-filled with ashes. Clearly, the enemy was covering their tracks.

With the glee of a child on a sandy beach, Nadia dug into the ashes, but the resulting treasure hunt only produced scraps of scorched paper, of which the only legible uncommon words were *Chariot* and *Ram*, and the pieces of photographs; puzzle bits that showed parts of a large motorboat with a name on the bow that began with the letters *MO*.

Suddenly the door opened up and a male voice said, "Hello?"

Fast as a blink, Nadia turned on the desk lamp and aimed it at the door, revealing a ragged looking man with the wrinkled scars of a mustard gas attack on his face. "Get out," Nadia shouted. "And stay out."

The man at the door shielded his eyes from the glare. "Miss Hella? Is that you?"

"Yes," Nadia said in a hushed tone. "Now go."

"Sorry. Someone below said they heard footsteps up here."

As he retreated, I slowly let out a breath and lowered the heavy gun I had trained on him, hidden behind the light. I was grateful I didn't have to shoot. "I think our luck's run its course," I whispered.

"Agreed."

We gathered our bits and pieces in my handkerchief

and spent a few moments at the door, trying to judge the best time to cross the hall, then made our break for it. We'd just opened the window to the fire escape when there came from below a sound like a thundering herd clomping up the stairs. "Must have realized Hella wasn't up here," Nadia said quickly. "Let's go."

We made a mad dash across the fire escape back to the apartment and scrambled down to the store, no sooner arriving when we heard pounding on the front entrance and an angry voice demanding, "Open up."

"Aw, don't waste your time," came a voice that I recognized as Anthony's. "Old man Endicott went out and ain't been back."

"You sure, kid?"

"Yeah. Spare a smoke?"

Then there came a space of relative silence save for the street noises, until I heard a gentle rapping at the window, the *all clear* signal. Nadia and I slipped out to see Anthony's grinning face. She walked up and planted a kiss on his cheek before we hurried away, and I swear I saw that boy blush. As we reached her Packard, I said, "Well, too bad tonight was a bit of a failure."

"Not altogether." She gently patted her bundled burnt offering of clues.

Chapter Fifty Five:

Nadia concealed her treasure just as I noticed she was leading us away from where we'd parked the Packard.

"Something about this getaway you're not letting me in on?" I asked.

"We need to find our Mr. Li and bring him home. I sent him down here to dig up some information."

"My stomach wants him home, as well. Where is he?"

Nadia simply pointed away toward Mott Street...and Chinatown.

"Aw, hell. You do realize this is all enemy territory, right? And we just stirred up a hornet's nest of trouble."

"Yes. Which is why I want to take Mr. Li out with us, rather than having him risk getting cornered on the subway or elevated trains around here."

We made our way with a brisk pace, turning into the other world in the span of a block. With the appearance of the strung red Chinese lanterns, it was like suddenly arriving in Hong Kong, with the exceptions of all the cars and New Yorkers out and about on a Friday night. Nadia led me to a building where the marquee proclaimed one had found the *Port Arthur Chinese Restaurant* with its red pagoda-style roofing and green and gold facing with dragons embossed thereon. I was struck by the name of the restaurant, remembering that it was the actual Port Arthur in Manchu where Nicholas Ravenwood managed to deal a blow to the Russians in their war with Japan over twenty years ago.

The restaurant was one flight up over an Import Export store, and when we reached the public dining area, with its mix of Western chairs and tables amidst Eastern designs of red and gold painted pillars and exotic oriental displays, the enticing aromas sparked a strong desire to stay and dine. Nadia Ravenwood spoke a few quiet words to a waiter in Western evening wear, and a short time later we saw Mr. Li approaching from the kitchen area, pulling on his overcoat and bowler hat. Clearly, Nadia had sent him down to mix with the people who worked in the restaurant businesses and gather information, just as he used to for Nicholas Ravenwood.

"It's good to see you, Mr. Li."

"And you, Miss. I have something to report."

"Later. We need to leave now."

Mr. Li was a short, slender man, with gray strands in his Western-style hair, but somehow this little gentleman walked at a pace where I practically had to break into a run to keep up with him. I trailed behind a bit as we wound through the Friday night sidewalk crowds. It was because I had a particular vantage behind them that I saw a pair of shadows detach themselves from the doorway of a closed barber's shop and walk swiftly toward Nadia. I was about to shout a warning, but immediately saw there was no need.

As the rough-looking men moved to attack, Mr. Li suddenly spun about and, with a flurry of fists and kicks too fast for the eye to follow, rapidly reduced the thugs to a pair of moaning, writhing lumps on the ground. The activity happened so fast that the people around us barely had time to notice as Nadia and Mr. Li walked on toward the Packard. My contribution to the fight consisted of kicking a fallen blackjack into the street as I passed by. When we reached Nadia's car, I saw young Anthony nearby, staring back the way we came, his face an expression of surprise and admiration as he opened the door for Nadia.

I got the rumble seat, as usual.

Eventually, we made it back to the Brownstone, where Nadia, Mr. Li and I gathered in his kitchen, sipping Jasmin tea, and in my case, holding my cup and waiting for my hands to warm up to be able to feel again.

"I'm sorry we didn't have time to question those gentlemen who attempted to stop us on our way out," Nadia said.

"They looked like first-line foot soldiers," I said. "Probably left to watch that ridiculous red Packard we've been seen driving. That was quite the pugilistic display, Mr. Li."

The gentleman simply nodded. "I had some difficulty getting the people to speak with me. Mostly, they are all from the Southern Provinces, and I am from the North. But I have learned of a few open secrets."

"Open secrets?"

"Things that are known, but not to be spoken. For instance, there are indeed tunnels that are still in use under the streets of Chinatown. One in particular is now guarded, leading from Doyers Street to the mansion on Chatham Square."

"That mansion..." I said, "as you call it, is where some very polite Hatchet Men with British accents threatened us."

Mr. Li nodded. "Indeed. There are men who have come here, some months ago, who are neither Leong Tong nor Hip Sing Tong. It is said they have come here from Shanghai to promote the business of the *Righteous Sons of Guan Yu*."

"Who?"

"Guan Yu. A mighty general who was elevated to

godhood, a God of War and a God of Honor."

"Sounds hauntingly familiar." Nadia sighed. "The Eastern match for the Companions of Tyr. And what is the business of these Sons of Guan Yu?"

"Opium. Though there have been whispers that the money they make is for the buying of guns."

"You said they're from Shanghai. There was a huge Communist purge there a few months ago. The international press is already calling it *The Massacre of Shanghai*. I wonder if this is connected?"

I huffed. "Are we back to Communists and anarchists again?"

"Maybe. China right now is in a war for reunification, only the Russian Bolsheviks are supporting one side and the Empire of Japan the other, so it's not just an internal conflict."

"And here we are again," I said. "Stuck pulling at threads that lead nowhere."

"They're not threads," Nadia put in. "They're the strands of a spider's web. And they're all connected somehow. And every time we look, it gets larger and more frightening."

Mr. Ivanov appeared in the doorway. "There's a message. A Mr. Godwin says he wants to meet alone with Mr. Locke."

"Godwin? You're joking. What for?"

"He says he wants to parley."

Chapter Fifty Six:

There's a restaurant in Central Park that's been around a while, a sprawling structure that looks like someone melded various styles of architecture together. Since its refurbishment, it's become the place where Mayor Jimmy Walker has his unofficial headquarters and where he spends the majority of his time in a hideaway office. I thought it an odd spot for a clandestine rendezvous. I was advised to dress appropriately and had donned my evening wear and top hat while I awaited my host just outside the main entrance. I confess I spent my time not so much admiring the soaring, glowing skyscrapers surrounding the Park as much as I was looking for lurking assassins.

Nadia was dead set against this meeting. "Are you insane?"

"If I am, it's from long association with the Ravenwood family. The mysterious Mr. Godwin said he wants to talk. I figure the least we can do is hear him out. He wants to meet me at the Casino in Central Park."

Nadia's dark eyes glared. I swear, I could have lit a cigarette off the heat of her gaze. "And you want to do this alone?"

"That's what he said. Look at this possibility...perhaps he wants to come over to our side."

"Or they plan to grab you and squeeze out what you know, or use you as a hostage."

"Well, only one way to find out."

"And for this, he wants you in evening wear?"

"What can I say? He sounds like a snob."

So, after a grudging concession, I was allowed to take a taxicab to make my appointment. That's when Godwin nearly killed me by startling me to death.

"So glad you came."

I swear, it was like he popped out of thin air right behind me. After I let out my breath, I turned to see the man himself, dressed as I was, looking like a Stage Door Johnny ready to prowl the chorus girls' dressing rooms of Broadway. Only instead of an eye patch he now wore a monocle. "Do you perform any other magic tricks, Mr. Godwin?"

He had an easy laugh. "I am serious. I'm glad you're here. I think between the two of us we can come to an understanding and avoid a lot of literal bloodshed. And do please call me James."

I pointed to his monocle. "So, you're not the wounded veteran, after all?"

"I simply keep up appearances. They're important, you know."

"Are we to go in?"

"No. We've enough privacy out here."

"So why did I get dressed?"

"Men are less inclined to go rolling around in the gutter in their Sunday best, don't you think?"

"Well, if you think that'd stop me..." I left the phrase unfinished.

"Oh, I'm not here for a rematch. But please don't think I wouldn't accommodate you if you wanted to take a swing. But I really do want to discuss business first."

I gave an after-you gesture.

He lit a cigarette. "You and that girl you work for are

really out of your depth, you know. You two are just the ones rich people call for a clean up, or a cover up. Only now you've blundered into matters far above your station and into the realm of governments."

"Funny you put it that way. The man I used to work for thought nothing of shaking up governments. Ask the Germans. Or the British. Or the Japanese. Or the Russians."

"But the daughter is just a woman who meddles."

"We must be doing something that gets to you, otherwise why are we speaking?"

He regarded me through his lens. "You really must think highly of yourself. Make no mistake, you're a nuisance, nothing more. You see, I know all about you. Your failed academic career, your brief, undistinguished military service. And how you now spend your days as a pimp to the rich and sinfully stupid."

He paused to allow a group of revelers to depart the restaurant and make a hunt out of locating their cars. Finally: "Let's cut to it, shall we? What is it you and your Miss Ravenwood want? What is it that would make you give all this up and go away?"

"Answers. For instance, who murdered May Scott?"

Godwin paused to crush out his cigarette. "Ah. That was an unfortunate accident. Someone made a foolishly impulsive move."

His word impulsive brought to mind the green-eyed woman who couldn't help but giggle at the sight of death. "You mean Hella?"

"I'll only say this...it is very hard to get reliable help these days."

A horrid picture sprang to my imagination of the wild-eyed blonde gripping the long slender blade of the sword cane with the same awful, childlike glee she showed when she picked up my gun. "And you keep a creature like her around, why?"

"Foot soldiers are required in every war."

"War? What war?"

He shook his head. "War is always coming, sir, always lurking around the corner. The world is a bale of dry tinder, only waiting for a match to set it all on fire."

"And what of Henry Bowen? What was he...a casualty of your *War*?"

"Henry got what he deserved. He knew the risks, and he tried to double-cross us."

"Really? So why am I here? You want me to join you?"

He laughed. "Oh, hell no. All this is...is some good advice and a friendly warning. We'd like you and your charming little girlfriend to stay out of the firing line. If you like, I'll see if I can throw in Hella and the sword cane we were keeping to use as leverage against Richard Bowen, and you can make the murder charge against him go away."

"And if I say no to this?"

Godwin raised his hand, and when he did the headlights of a car across the way ignited, blinding me. There came the roar of an engine and a squeal of tires, and when I could see through the glare, I saw the very polite Chinese gentleman leaning out the open door of a sedan and pointing an enormous revolver right at my face.

Chapter Fifty Seven:

I felt a sharp prick at my back over my left kidney. "Get in the car, old boy, and don't make a fuss. Behave as a gentleman and you may live out the night."

"I'd do as he says, Locke," Godwin advised. "Mr. Baker here worked as a policeman in the roughest parts of Shanghai, and you don't want to test him."

I stepped away and turned, then saw a dagger in the man called Baker's gloved hand, followed by the ratcheting sound of a pistol hammer being cocked inside the car. "Well, seeing as how you're so insistent." I was glad to hear my voice came out far more steady than I felt.

I doffed my hat and stepped over to the dark green Lincoln limousine, where I was obliged to open the door and climb into the spacious interior. The man who wanted me to believe his name was 'James Godwin' smoothly entered behind me as the driver kept me covered with an old fashioned Colt .45 six shooter, the mechanical grandfather of the pistol I'd left at the Brownstone.

Baker settled alongside the Chinese gentleman. "Really, Chang, must you cart that monstrosity around?"

The man I now knew as Chang nodded. "Good evening, Mr. Locke. And yes, Baker, I find it to be a very effective tool for when the occasion calls for it."

"I blame the American movie industry. Chang is simply enthralled by all those cowboy pictures."

"And your pursuits are more enlightening?" Chang

shot back.

Then came a surprising and rapid exchange in Chinese between the two of them. What they were saying, I had absolutely no idea. Godwin ordered, "Enough," and the two in the front seat exchanged last scowls, and as Chang engaged the gears, Baker drew his own pistol from under his coat, a small automatic that he held pointed at me over the front seatback.

"Gentleman," I said. "While I could certainly listen to you argue all day, I'd like to inquire as to where you're taking me?"

"You said you wanted answers," Godwin replied. "Now you're going to get them."

Chang drove us up the East Drive of Central Park until we reached the majestic Metropolitan Museum, where he stopped the car.

"Get out," Godwin said. "And visit the Obelisk. You may find it educational."

Not being one to argue with men with guns, I did as told, looking about the nearby trees for any more surprises as I made my way up the steps and toward the towering Cleopatra's Needle, thousands of years old and dragged thousands of miles away from its home in Egypt. I saw a shadowy figure appear from behind the Obelisk, as a hauntingly familiar voice called out, "Hello, Stephen."

Nicholas Ravenwood.

I confess. It was as if the earth turned under my feet. "Aren't you supposed to be dead?"

"Many times over, my friend. How have you been?"

"As of this moment...confused."

"I see."

I watched as Nicholas Ravenwood walked toward me out of the darkness. He stopped short, clad in a black coat and hat, just out of reach, and it was just as well as I would have been tempted to try to touch him to see if he was truly there.

"And how is my Nadia?"

"Stubborn, irascible, irritating. No doubt your daughter."

I saw him nod, his face still concealed behind a veil of shadow. "Good. And now you must go to her and convince her to stop interfering in matters that do not concern her."

"Nicholas, tell me what this is all about."

There was silence, then the whisper of a sigh. "No, Stephen. This is not for you, and certainly not for her. So go back, convince her to stop prying. For her sake. And because you owe me your life."

He raised his left hand, and from behind the Needle another figure appeared. This one resolved itself into a short broad man in a dark coat, holding what appeared to be a carbine in the ready to fire position as he kept me covered while walking a wide circle around me.

Nicholas Ravenwood stepped to my side and placed his hand on my shoulder. "This is the only warning, Stephen. Keep her, and yourself, safe."

Then he walked away.

As he kept me under the gun, the man I knew as the Captain said, "Take the advice, my friend. You do not want us to meet each other again."

And then I was left alone in the darkness.

It was a bit of a hike to Fifth Avenue and a telephone booth, but ultimately Nadia Ravenwood herself arrived in the red Packard to whisk me back to the Brownstone. "I'm so relieved to see you alive and well that I'm almost over being furious with you for agreeing to this idiotic escapade in the first place."

A wave of exhaustion rolled over me, making the last hour feel like a dream. "Speaking of alive and well, you and I need to convene a council of war. And it needs to be just you and me. So perhaps we best avoid the Brownstone for a bit."

"You want privacy? Well, all right then. Seeing how you're all dressed up and won't embarrass me." Nadia aimed the car north and drove us all the way up to Harlem and ultimately to Ed Small's *Paradise* nightclub. Once downstairs, one found a lavish setup with hot jazz served by Charlie Johnson's band and cold liquor delivered courtesy of a private request to our waiter. It was also one of the few places that wasn't run by a gangster and didn't have any of that segregation nonsense.

I made sure that Nadia was sitting close to the floorshow and waited for her ginger ale to arrive before I said over the cacophony of the music:

"Your father's alive."

Chapter Fifty Eight:

She sat and stared at me from across the table, silent and still as a statue. Eventually, she reached over and took up my cigarette case and lighter, fired up a smoke, and then helped herself to my drink that I'd just spiked with genuine Canadian whisky. After gulping down half the glass and drawing a puff, she leaned toward me. "What the hell happened?"

"Remember when you said this was getting to be like a web? Well, I met the King of the Spiders himself. It's your father. Nicholas Ravenwood is not only alive and in New York City, he's connected to everything we've been dealing with. And he's ordered us to get out and stay out."

Nadia roughly stubbed out the cigarette then took a draw on her own ginger ale. "Come over here next to me so we can talk."

I moved my chair around and she leaned in close, one hand on my shoulder, the same shoulder Nicolas Ravenwood touched as he gave me his orders. "Tell me everything."

I delivered a true accounting of my encounter with Nicholas, his use of Godwin, Baker and Chang, along with the Captain and added my thoughts on how the Companions of Tyr and the Sons of Guan Yu tied into his plans. "Which, by the way, he refused to tell me."

Nadia kept her eyes on the dancers on the floor and their energetic demonstrations of the Charleston with some of the entertainers adding a twist by performing on roller skates. She leaned over on my shoulder. "This changes everything. Ivanov, Li, Murphy...they all owe their lives to Father. I can't ask them to take sides."

"Take sides? What are you saying? We've got to bow out."

She looked up at me. "I'm saying we aren't done yet. Richard Bowen is still under suspicion for murder."

"I got that offer to turn in Hella and the sword cane."

"It's gone far beyond that. There's Henry Bowen's supposed suicide now. Not to mention the absolute, utter arrogance of it all. As if the murder of an innocent woman is something to be used in whatever damn conspiracy Father's cooked up. And he thinks I'll just walk away? Because he tells me to?"

Suddenly, Nadia threw her head back and laughed up a storm, grabbing hold of my arm as if to keep her from being swept away in a torrent. It was a terrifying thing to witness; a sound such as a Demon escaping Hell would make, but she ceased as the band crashed into a cacophonous finale. For at least a full minute, Nadia caught her breath, then ultimately she sighed as the band began to play a low, slow, sweet melody.

"Are you all right?" I finally dared to ask.

Her eyes were alight as she turned to me. "Don't you see? That man is desperate. Whatever it is Father's concocting, it must be at a delicate point. Why else would he risk revealing himself? And if that's true, then we must be close to something big...bigger than we realize."

"He wasn't kidding, Nadia."

She shrugged. "You know him better than I. By warning us off, is he being sentimental over his only daughter and a friend from his past? Or is killing us too much bother?"

I recognized the song the band played as the dancers cleared the floor: *Bye Bye Blackbird*. I shook my head at the timing. "Your father is the most ruthless, not to mention most cunning, man I have ever known. Everything he ever did had some deeper meaning. So he must be confident that we'll not interfere with his scheme. I think he wants to clear the board of a pair of inconvenient pawns. Namely us."

"And that's his mistake."

"Excuse me? Nicholas Ravenwood doesn't make mistakes. That sort of thing is left for mere mortals."

Nadia finished her drink. "Here is how it is for me, Stephen. I am going to pursue all avenues until I find out for myself what Father is up to as well as discover the truth about May Scott and Henry Bowen's deaths. Are you with me or not?"

"You have to ask?"

"Yes."

"If I wasn't with you all the way, I'd be taking a late train to anywhere else in the world until everything either blows up or blows over. Something I highly recommend to you."

Nadia leaned back, her midnight black eyes shining in the low light of the club. "All right then, my man. From here on out, everything changes. We need to get Mary Bowen to a place of safety and find a new place to nest. We say nothing to Mr. Li, Mr. Ivanov or Miss Murphy. Either Father has already recruited them, or they'll find their loyalties tested, and I'd rather not put them through that."

"We should also ditch that ridiculous little red car you borrowed."

"Agreed. Although I'll miss seeing your face when you ride in the rumble seat."

I gave her a scowl. "Where are we going to live?"

"We've got some goodwill over at the Waldorf Astoria. I'm betting I can get us in under assumed names."

"But my suitcase and, more importantly, my pistol are all at the Brownstone."

"We'll have to do without. We're starting now. You take a taxi to the Waldorf. Dressed as you are, you'll have the run of the place. Check with the front desk for a key for a Mr. Romano and they'll set you up."

"What will you be doing?"

Nadia's eyes were twin orbs of dark promise. "I'll be getting ready to storm Mount Olympus."

Chapter Fifty Nine:

The Waldorf Astoria was nothing if not accommodating. I'd taken a taxi and come by way of my apartment, gathering up a spare suit and accoutrements, and arrived at the hotel well after midnight in evening dress with my possessions carried in a bed linen sack. No one at the front desk batted an eye. By mid morning I'd enjoyed a late breakfast of the hotel's specialty of Eggs Benedict with coffee delivered to my room as I dressed and awaited my call to arms. When it came, I was summoned to the Empire Suite.

I found Nadia in the midst of Old World luxury with carved wood paneling and decorative furnishings in the baroque styling of Louis XIV. In contrast, she was dressed in a plain black silk day dress, otherwise unadorned. "I'm sorry, is there a herald to announce me?"

She raised her demitasse in greeting. "Enter, fellow Peasant. We have a campaign to plan."

I looked over the lavish chambers. "I keep expecting Marie Antoinette to pop out and offer me cake."

Nadia rolled her eyes. "Actually, this is supposed to evoke the surroundings of Emperor Napoleon."

"Old Nappy? You know your father was quite an admirer of his."

"It's one of the few things I do know about Father. And it warms my heart to remember the events of Waterloo. Now come, look at this."

She led me to a writing desk where she had the slightly blurry photograph of the yacht stolen from the All

Night Mission. "This is clearly important, the trouble is, we don't know why. It's imperative we identify the ship and its owner."

I took up a magnifying lens from the desk, but the name of the yacht was still indistinct, and the two-toned photograph gave no clue as to the colors of the ship. "Well, how many yachts can there be in the richest city in the world?"

"That's why I think we should ask one of the richest men, yes?"

"Really? Just like that?"

"I've already made some arrangements."

"Where?"

"Where the yachtsmen are, of course."

"Of course."

"Oh, before we go, I have something for you." She handed me a heavy rectangular package wrapped in butcher's paper.

I opened it and found myself holding a Savage .32 caliber automatic pistol with a box of fifty cartridges.

"Do you like it?"

I looked it over, testing the various mechanisms and finding it not so different from my Colt, just smaller and lighter, with a magazine able to hold ten shots. "It'll do for now."

"It's a gift from Owney Madden."

I resisted the urge to drop the gun like a hot coal. "Oh?"

"I telephoned him last night. Although I believe he may have thought this was a gift for me, and not you."

"Was this the only thing he offered?"

She laughed. "No, indeed. But I was certain we didn't need a machinegun. Not yet, anyway. Get your coat and let's go."

The Ravenwood Conspiracy

Nadia took up her black velour cape and cloche hat with the feather, and I followed her downstairs for my next surprise: In the arched driveway of the hotel I was introduced to Nadia Ravenwood's latest chariot. This was a Duesenberg Coupe, but with a far more sensible interior with a rear seat so that any additional passengers would not be left to die of exposure. The carriage was painted in glossy black. "Dare I asked where this little thing came from?"

"Not unless you want me to mention Owney Madden's name again. It's got eight cylinders, so it should be fast enough for our purposes."

With any luck, this car would get shot up like Nadia's Rickenbacker before this escapade was through. She drove us a short distance to *Clubhouse Row* and stopped at a massive baroque edifice that I now recognized as the *New York Yacht Club*, where much of the masonry of the facade was carved to look like the bow windows of sailing ships.

"This is a private little clubhouse for rich boys," I said to Nadia. "Us landlubbers definitely are not allowed."

"We're to be guests. Now, let me take your arm so I can pretend you're a gentleman and proceed through the ramparts."

As we made our way past the nautically themed entryway we were intercepted by an attendant whose uniform would have suited a Navy Admiral. Nadia spoke to him in low tones and handed him her card. The man gave us one last dubious look and then departed.

While waiting for something to happen, I looked about the opulent reception area and saw the club's motto displayed. Translated from Latin, it read: *We Go With Swelling Sails*, a far departure from the Ravenwood motto of *Mundo Nulla Fides*, or *Put No Faith in the World*. I then heard a masculine voice call out, "Miss Ravenwood?"

We turned to see a man deftly descending the long staircase toward us. He was dark of hair and eye and moved with an athletic grace. As he approached, Nadia said, "Please forgive us for calling on you on such a short notice."

He laughed her concern away. "Think nothing of it. According to my family, we still owe your father quite a debt over that matter with the German assassin years ago."

She turned to me. "Stephen, this is Mr. Junius Morgan. Mr. Morgan, may I present Mr. Stephen Locke."

I didn't have to consult *Who's Who* for this one. I was now shaking hands with Junius Morgan the Third, to be exact, heir to the vast fortunes of the J.P. Morgan dynasty. Nadia was pulling out all the stops; we don't generally cash in on the grace and favor of the ruling class unless absolutely necessary.

Nadia produced a large plain envelope and handed it to Morgan. "I'm trying to identify the motor yacht in this picture. Do you know of anyone who might help?"

Morgan examined the pieces of scorched edged photograph bits, looking bemused. "Well, you certainly don't like to make things easy, do you." He held up the fragments, one at a time. "My father served as Commodore at the club here, so he might know...oh, hello. I recognize this one. It's the *Moana*, Billy Leeds's yacht."

Nadia's face paled at the news. "You're absolutely certain?"

"I've been aboard her myself."

Under her breath, Nadia Ravenwood uttered either a curse, or a prayer, or possibly both.

Chapter Sixty:

Nadia said nothing during the short drive back to the Waldorf Astoria, but she was as tense as I had ever seen her. Once we pulled into the carriageway of the hotel, she surrendered the keys to an attendant.

"Stephen, call my suite in an hour. Go have some luncheon, or whatever you choose."

I was about to protest, but she vanished like a ghost at dawn. I availed myself of the Gentlemen's Café and had an order of salmon in Maximilian sauce with a French coffee, and then wandered over to the reading room, but I could not keep my attention on the newspapers. So instead I fretted and smoked and wondered how this potential collision between Nadia Ravenwood and her father was going to play out. We were handicapped in this battle, that much was certain. We were not only cut off from any potential aid that Mr. Li and Ivanov and Miss Murphy could render, but almost everyone in our entire spy network listed in our little black books, as well. They were, for the most part, agents originally cultivated by Nicholas, and therefore now suspect. Eventually the time came round for me to call on Nadia. Naturally, she surprised me again.

"We're going to Oyster Bay. I'll meet you in the lobby."

And just like that, we were driving across the Queensborough Bridge to the Long Island Railroad Terminal and thence on a train to Oyster Bay. Our pilgrimage proceeded silently, save for the clattering of the tracks and occasional sounding of the train's horn, until I watched the landscape out my window turn from urban to countryside. "Why am I here?" I asked her.

"You said you were with me."

"I will gladly follow you blindly. But now I'm following deaf and dumb, as well." I looked around at the few passengers on this leg of the journey. "I believe we are unobserved. Won't you tell me something about this errand?"

Nadia sighed. "Very well. I am hoping I'm wrong."

"About what?"

"That's just it, I can't explain yet."

"Are you able to tell me why?"

"Last summer I took on a matter of the utmost secrecy. I didn't bring you in on it as I had to keep as few people privy as possible."

"Your father used to do the same thing. I understand the nature of secrecy. So why am I here now?"

She shrugged. "As I said, I'm hoping my supposition is wrong. But if it isn't, then I may need to break confidentiality and ask for your help. Are you willing to accompany me under these circumstances?"

"Yes."

She searched my eyes, then nodded once. "Good. Let's hope we have made a long trip for nothing."

My first surprise was when we found a pearl-white Rolls Royce Phantom, with an extended chassis, waiting for us at the station. As the young chauffeur with a very military bearing assisted Nadia into the coach, I said, "Well, now I'll get to compare this with the Silver Ghost." The young man didn't even twitch an eye.

The second surprise was when we were conveyed to the long driveway of a sprawling mansion estate that brought to mind a visit to royalty. And that led to the biggest surprise of all.

Before we could depart from the Rolls, a woman came running out of the massive mansion's doors. She'd thrown a fur-trimmed camel coat over her blouse and riding breeches, and her hair was a mass of raven black curls tied down with a white kerchief. "Nadia!"

"Xenia!"

The two collided, laughing and hugging as they exchanged European-style kisses. All I could do was stand there and stare. This woman could have been Nadia Ravenwood's twin sister.

Nadia brought her to me. "Xenia, this is Stephen Locke. My associate."

Xenia, with mischief in her eyes, said a quick aside in Russian to Nadia, who simply replied, "Nyet," Russian for *no*.

"Stephen, may I present Mrs. Xenia Leeds, wife of Mr. William Leeds."

Xenia held out her hand to me.

That explained the mansion. William Leeds was actually a junior; his father made the family fortune as the *Tin Plate King*. I took her hand. "How do you do?"

"She is also Princes Xenia Georgievna of Russia."

I was suddenly stricken with indecision, not knowing if I was expected to kiss her hand, bow, or drop to all fours. My expression set the two of them off laughing again.

"How do you do, Mr. Locke. Any friend of Nadia's is family to me."

Such a charming accent.

"Please, come inside."

Nadia and the Princess linked arms as I trailed behind. Once inside the mansion, I was captured by the expensive grandeur of it all, in stark contrast to the downright easygoing, chummy behavior of the ladies. I followed them into a book-lined study with grandly overstuffed furniture and a portrait on the wall of the Princess as a younger woman, with long, lustrous hair. It could have been a painting of a teenaged Nadia Ravenwood.

As we were bid to make ourselves at home and the Princess called for tea, Nadia said to her, "Forgive me for coming to you like this. Where is your husband today?"

"Bill is away playing with his boat this afternoon. He said he'd be home in time for supper."

"He's aboard the *Moana*?"

"Yes. Why? Is there something wrong?"

Nadia reached out and took Xenia's hand. "I am worried, and I need to know...what did you do with the information I provided to you last August?"

Princess Xenia's face became a mask of concern, and she sat up straighter. "What is going on?"

"I fear for the fate of the last of the Romanovs."

Chapter Sixty One:

P rincess Xenia stood up and swiftly walked over to the tall curtained window. Without turning back, she said, "This is not a matter to discuss with outsiders."

"Mr. Locke was there. In Russia," Nadia said quietly. "With my father."

The Princess turned to face me, her eyes so much like Nadia's, threatening a storm. "This is true?"

"I came to Archangel with the British and American soldiers, then Nicolas Ravenwood took me on. I was in Russia after Lenin was shot and during the start of the Red Terror."

Xenia's expression turned bitter. "Arkhangelsk?" she said in the Russian manner. "By the time you and the British arrived, it was too late. The Czarina and her daughters and son, and the Czar himself, were already slaughtered. What good were you?"

Nadia uncoiled from her place on the sofa, strode to Xenia's side, and spoke softly into her ear. I could not hear what she said, and I was left to puzzle out what was going on. By all official accounts, the entire Russian royal family was killed by the Bolsheviks in 1918. But what did Nadia mean when she said she was concerned over *the last of the Romanovs*? From what I knew, the Romanov family was large, and there were many distant relatives alive and well and living out their days in exile.

But there had been strange rumors.

Eventually, Nadia led Princess Xenia back toward me. "Forgive me," she said, not meeting my eyes. "I have lost my father and my uncle to a Bolshevik firing squad. I still grieve."

I stood. "There is nothing to forgive, your Majesty."

She and Nadia exchanged a look, and then the mood was broken by brittle laughter.

"The proper title, Stephen, is *Your Highness*."

"Please forgive a poor, uneducated American."

She held out a hand for me to resume my seat. "As you say, there is nothing to forgive." She and Nadia took their places and Xenia took a breath. "Now, please tell me what brings you out here."

"First of all," Nadia said, "please know that Mr. Locke has my every confidence. I have only left him unaware of certain matters as I had promised you complete secrecy. But now I must ask you to allow me to bring him into your circle."

The Princess stared at me, with eyes as deep and dark as Nadia Ravenwood's. "Tell me...what would you have done for the Royal Family of Russia had you not arrived too late?"

"I would have wanted to save the children."

"Not the Czar? Or the Czarina?"

"Of course, if possible. But I would have put the children first. As I believe the Czar himself would have wished."

She considered this, then nodded. "As you say." To Nadia: "What is it you want of me?"

"Are you proceeding with the plans you spoke of last August?"

"Yes. But I am not allowed to speak of them again, even to you, dear *kuzina*.

"Despite the fact I am the one who gave you your leads in the first place?"

"Even so. I have been told each must do their part in

secrecy for the plan to be met with success."

"And your husband is helping you with this?"

A small look of pride crossed the Princess's face. "Yes. In fact, I am thinking he is enjoying the adventure perhaps a little too much."

Nadia nodded. "One final question, dear. Have you heard the phrase *Companions of Tyr* spoken at all? By anyone?"

Xenia looked thoughtful. "No. What is it?"

"Something very dangerous. And if you or your husband comes into contact with these people, then I suggest you get away quickly. They are utterly ruthless."

"Are they in league with the Bolsheviks? With the Secret Police?"

"Quite possibly."

The Princess uttered a word that I'd heard Nadia use as a curse.

"I would implore you," Nadia said, "to tell me your plans, for I fear there may be a plot at work against you."

Princess Xenia stiffened at that. "You have proof?"

"I have grave suspicions. Someone in league with these *Companions of Tyr* have taken a great interest in your husband's yacht."

"His yacht? For what purpose?"

"I don't know. But if you find out anything that gives you alarm, or even a suspicion, please contact me at once, I beg you."

Xenia nodded. "Very well. Is there anything else I may do for you?"

"Other than tell me everything you haven't said so far, no."

We were bid goodbye, and Nadia remained silent until we were back on a train toward Brooklyn. I looked around to see we were unobserved. "I'm as confused as I have ever been. Just what have you and the Princess cooked up between the two of you?"

"Oh, just a little project she asked me to help with last summer."

"What was that?"

"Determining if the Russian Royal Princess Anastasia Romanov is alive, after all."

Chapter Sixty Two:

I turned to stare out at the rustic countryside rolling past our carriage. "Would you care to elaborate?"

"I'm breaking my promise to Xenia, but I feel it's best you know everything, especially now that her situation and ours may be colliding. Last summer, Xenia asked me to look into a report that the Grand Duchess Anastasia escaped being murdered with the rest of her family and was now living in Germany. I discovered this woman, calling herself Anna Tchaikovsky, had at least once attempted suicide and had been committed to an asylum. She'd also suffered numerous illnesses. From what I gathered, among some who know the Russian Royal family, there is a belief she is the Princess Anastasia, while there are others who do not agree. Discrepancies have been explained away as differences caused by the passage of time and the privations the woman has suffered."

"My God. What do you believe?"

Nadia shrugged. "I haven't met her. I could only provide Xenia with the information I was able to gather. But I do believe Xenia was planning to bring the woman here to America."

"Really? That should prove interesting."

"Imagine how the current government in Russia, the government who committed regicide, would feel about one of its royal murder victims being found alive and well and willing to testify to the whole world as an eyewitness to the deaths of the Czar and his family?"

"Ah. It hasn't quite been a decade since then, has it?

What's Princess Xenia's interest in all this?"

"She's a distant cousin. As for her husband, millionaire Billy Leeds has made quite the name for himself as a globetrotting adventurer. He may be in it just for the excitement."

"I think he'd want to please his wife."

Nadia looked away. "They've been having problems of late. I'm not at all certain that marriage is going to last."

"So what's the Princess to you?"

"What do you mean?"

"Simple question. How do you know her? She called you something back there, *kuzima*, wasn't it? What does that mean?"

"It's just a common term of endearment."

I didn't believe her. But I wasn't about to press the issue now. There were far too many other matters to worry over. "Now what?"

Nadia sighed. "Take all the puzzle pieces and see how they fit. We have the Companions of Tyr, who are either anarchists or anti anarchists, depending on whom you ask, who are also tied to the Sons of Guan Yu from China, and together they have a small army of ex American servicemen along with a gang from Shanghai. There's a stolen shipment of weapons currently in the possession of gangsters, not to mention this mysterious Fenris group who are investing heavily in military arms. Add this to someone taking an interest in the yacht of an American millionaire whose wife is in the process of bringing over a woman who may possibly be the last of the Russian Royal family. And with this, we have Richard Bowen, accused of the murder of May Scott and the supposed suicide of his brother, Henry."

"And all tied to your father."

Nadia looked out the window. "You said Godwin told

you there's a war coming, yes?"

"That's what he said."

"So all we have to do now is figure out how to stop it."

We looked to each other, then burst out laughing. We attracted some attention, as I am certain we didn't sound quite sane. When our somewhat hysterical mirth faded, I said, "Could we at least have a decent meal first?"

"You and your stomach. Very well. What would you suggest, giving we have an appointment tonight?"

"Appointment?"

"Mr. Jack Diamond is bringing Jacob Orgen to meet with us. Don't you recall? We need to ask about that wayward shipment of guns."

"Oh. That. I was rather hoping you forgot."

We retrieved Nadia's car at the station, and I suggested we stop for early dinner. As it turned out, I got my wish and almost wished I hadn't. Nadia was determined we not miss our rendezvous, so she drove us to Billy's on East 20th Street. While I enjoyed the excellent crab salad and smoked sturgeon, the place was too close to Grammercy Park and the location where Nadia's Rickenbacker coupe was shot to pieces. As it was, we were early enough to take our time and linger near the oyster bar until Nadia declared we should go.

We parked the Duesenberg between streetlights and just close enough to keep an eye on the corner of Delancey and Norfolk. This area of the Ghetto was quiet on this night of the Sabbath. We watched as a dark sedan pulled up to the curb. "Do we approach?" I whispered

"No, not yet," Nadia murmured. "I can't tell if that's Jack Diamond or Little Augie who's arrived. Let's see who shows up next."

"Fine. Although I doubt the likes of you and I will be

privileged to call Orgen *Little Augie*."

"You might not."

Another car arrived, and from it came the long, lean form of Legs Diamond. I had to concede the fact he must have had a hard head to survive the brutal beating Johnny Broderick had delivered to him. "All right," Nadia said. "Let's go get acquainted."

We exited the car, keeping the light off in the cab and moving quietly. I looked across the street to the corner and saw Diamond was walking with a shorter man, while three other trailed behind. "Looks like someone brought their own private army," I said out the side of my mouth. What happed next made me bless our natural state of caution:

There was a small flurry of movement from the three men walking behind, then there came a flash of light and sudden crack of sound as the man I presumed to be Little Augie Orgen pitched forward as if hit with a baseball bat...shot in the head.

The gunfire made Legs Diamond spin around in a blink, pulling his pistol out, but not fast enough to keep from getting gunned down to the gutter. The three men didn't hesitate; they ran back to their car and raced away, screeching around the corner and out of sight.

Before I could stop her, Nadia Ravenwood was running across the wide street. I followed as quickly as I could, nearly catching my shoe heel on the tram tracks. Diamond was clutching his gut as he rolled from side to side, but one glance told me the man on the ground next to him wasn't ever going to move again. "Get the car." Nadia tossed me the keys. "We need to get him to a hospital."

As I ran back to the Duesenberg, I heard her say to Diamond, "Don't you dare die on me. You owe me some information, Mister."

Chapter Sixty Three:

It was a night of insanity. My memory of the drive, with me behind the wheel and Nadia in the rear seat with a mumbling, cursing Legs Diamond was disjointed, as if seen as a motion picture that'd been cut up and badly reassembled. I drove us straight to Bellevue Hospital, and was relieved when personnel who knew what they were doing were summoned out to the car. Once Diamond was carried away on a stretcher, Nadia Ravenwood and I could stop and catch our breaths. But only after we drove away to avoid the police.

Once we returned to our retreat within the Waldorf Astoria, Nadia excused herself to scrub away the blood and change her clothing. I busied myself with summoning a bellhop and putting in my order for some Ballentine's. By the time Nadia emerged from her suite's private bath, she was cleaned and wrapped in her kimono whilst I was anointing my insides with expensive Scotch whiskey. "May I pour you one?"

Nadia fetched one of her Turkish cigarettes. "No. Thank you. I need to remain clearheaded."

"Whatever for?"

"To plan our next move."

"Are you quite certain we have one? We appear to have reached a, pardon the expression, dead end."

"Perhaps. But if Jack Diamond doesn't die on us, he may yet tell us something. Those guns must be integral to Father's plans."

"This is America. Anyone can get guns."

Nadia gave me that certain smile when she believed she knew something I didn't. Irritating, to say the very least. "And that's why those particular weapons must be important." She struck up a match. "There's already been considerable trouble taken over them, instead of simply getting replacements. It leads me to believe that whatever time schedule Father is working toward, it's heading for a conclusion soon. So you may want to go easy on the whisky."

"And die sober? Ghastly thought."

Nadia let herself collapse onto a curving couch and sent a plume of smoke upward. "Damn. I suppose there's no more trouble we can get into tonight, is there?"

"If there was, I wouldn't tell you."

"Very well, Stephen. Let's say goodnight."

The next morning, I found myself in both good and wretched company. I indulged in the Turkish baths at the hotel, steaming and soaking away my troubles among the alcoholically poisoned men who'd managed to survive Saturday night in Manhattan. Nadia had sent word to me that she'd have a late breakfast ready in her suite, and once I'd been steamed and cleaned, I dressed and made my way up.

I arrived to see her decked out in a silk crimson day dress with matching cloche hat, adorned with her signature black feather. The second thing I noticed was disappointment in the form of the meager offerings of what she called breakfast, a basket of Stratford rolls with strained honey and tea for me along with her dreaded Turkish coffee. "Hurry up," she said. "We have to visit an invalid today."

The traffic was light and we reached Bellevue Hospital in good order. I felt like it took us longer to navigate the antiseptic-smelling, white-washed halls and stairways of the gigantic, castle-like red-brick buildings than it did to drive here. Eventually, we were directed to a ward where Jack 'Legs' Diamond had the bed at the far end, away from less bullet-riddled patients.

There was a brunette woman in a flowered dress sitting with him, with sad, dark eyes, who looked up at our approach, glaring daggers at Nadia. "Who're you?"

"I'm Nadia Ravenwood, and this is Stephen Locke. We brought Mr. Diamond into the hospital last night."

"Oh. I'm Alice. His wife."

"We're very sorry for what happened."

The woman sighed, her shoulders sagging. "This isn't the first time Jack's been shot."

"Mrs. Diamond, may we try to have a word with your husband?"

At this point, Jack stirred on the bed and opened his eyes a bit. "S'all right," he mumbled. "This one's okay."

Alice stood, and with a last questioning look toward Nadia, took herself a small distance away. Nadia knelt down close by and said softy, "Jack, where are the guns being kept?"

"Get away from that man."

I spun around and saw Agent Paul Reynolds charging toward us at a fast trot. "I mean it, Miss Ravenwood."

As quick as a terrier on a rat, a nurse hurried up behind Reynolds. "Sir," she hissed. "This is a hospital."

In the corner of my eye, I saw Jack grab Nadia's arm and whisper in her ear. She nodded and quickly disengaged, stood up and walked toward Reynolds. "I'm sorry, Agent Reynolds, but by what right are you keeping me from visiting Mr. Diamond?"

"What did he say to you?" Reynolds demanded.

Nadia beckoned him to come closer, and she took his coat lapels in hand and pulled him down to her level then whispered in his ear.

I saw Reynolds' face flush as his eyebrows shot up. Then Nadia let him go, and he stepped back.

"Are you sorry you asked, Agent Reynolds?" Nadia curled a finger at me. "Come, Stephen."

I quickly moved to catch up, and as we marched out of the hospital ward, Nadia said out of the corner of her mouth, "When we get out the door, move fast."

"Why?"

"I've just lifted Agent Reynolds' notebook."

Chapter Sixty Four:

There was no time to admire Nadia's deft skill as a pickpocket. We quickly found an untended linen closet and squeezed in. Nadia brought out the little leather notebook and flipped through the pages while I stood guard at the door.

"Damn the man's poor handwriting," she murmured.

I kept my eye on the hallway by opening the door a bit.

Nadia occasionally muttered foreign curses under her breath. "Still clear?"

"So far." I'd checked the length of the hall. "Hopefully it stays that way."

Nadia skirted the laundry bin and came up next to me, and together we slipped out the door.

"Miss Ravenwood?"

We turned to see Detective Johnny Broderick had crossed our path. He was still smartly dressed, as usual, but his face bore an unhappy expression. "What are you doing here?"

"Looking into the condition of that man you brutally beat down on the street yesterday, one Mr. Jack Diamond."

"Yeah," I added. "Were you the one who shot him?"

Detective Broderick's face was nearly immobile. "I don't like guns. And I sure don't need one to handle a mook like Legs Diamond. But what really brings you down here? What did you want with him?"

"I recommend you ask him," Nadia said.

The detective scoffed. "He's not saying anything."

Nadia made a production of looking helpless. "Well, then, what am I to do about that? After all, as you so love to remind me, this is police business."

Johnny had enough of us and waved us to leave, but Nadia stayed put. "By the way, detective, your friend Agent Reynolds seems to have misplaced his little black book." The book in question appeared in her hand, and she gently waved it back and forth.

Johnny Broderick's eyes followed it. His face changed from a scowl to a wan smile as he reached for the book. "I'll make sure he gets it back. I'm sure he'd want to thank you for its return himself."

"No need. Just happy to be of assistance."

Johnny began to leave, then stopped as he quickly patted down his own pockets. Finding everything in order, he touched the brim of his hat in a nod to Nadia and went on his way.

Nadia smiled and waved. "Let's get the hell out of here."

"Surely. But what was that you whispered to Agent Reynolds? I thought you were going to make him faint."

Nadia kept moving as she flashed me her imitation of an innocent look. "Why, Mr. Locke, I could not possibly say out loud what I said to Agent Reynolds." Then she grinned. "But it sure kept him distracted as I went through his pockets."

We retraced our steps through the vast whitewashed maze until we passed the black iron gates and were on our way. Unfortunately, Nadia drove us down First Avenue and back the way we came last night when we had the bleeding, cursing Legs Diamond writhing about in the back of the car.

I looked back and saw no evidence that he'd ever been in the car. "The hotel staff did a good job cleaning up the back seat."

"They are quite accommodating. Makes me wonder how much the hotel staff gets paid to keep quiet on a regular basis. I know I tipped well for this little service."

"So, speaking of how things get all covered in blood, where are we going?"

Nadia smiled, looking more predatory than happy. "Our friend Mr. Diamond told me where the military guns are hidden. I suspected they'd be close to our meeting place last night, and as it turns out, they're stashed just the next street over."

Nadia drove us up Delancey Street until we came to Essex, just a block away from the murder site of Jacob, 'Little Augie' Orgen. In the cold, overcast daylight, the streets looked run down and tawdry, the Ghetto district of Lower East Side. Normally, there'd be pushcarts lining the roadways and people crowding the mobile market, but this was Sunday morning.

Nadia Ravenwood covered her crimson dress in her black velour cape, but with her bright red hat, I felt I'd be able to spot her in the distance should we become separated. More forebodingly, she stopped to put some burglary tools into her black-beaded handbag. In response, I patted my pocket holding the little .32 pistol, though I had no faith in such a small and yet untested weapon.

After a tram passed, we crossed wide Delancey Street, and as we strolled to the sidewalk, Nadia linked arms with me. "The guns are supposed to be in the basement of the flower shop on the corner."

"The one that has the sign 'Lost Our Lease'?"

"Yes."

There were people out and about, of course, as well as a traffic cop at the corner. We walked past the shop, peering through the display window as best we could while not stopping. "Closed, I see."

Nadia steered me toward the window of a store selling phonographs that was just past a small alcove marked for deliveries to the flower shop. "Think I can get us in?"

I rolled my eyes. "In broad daylight? Are you truly determined to tempt fate?"

But I realized I was speaking to thin air; Nadia was already down the three steps and at work on the lock.

I strolled casually over to block her from view then lit a cigarette. As I looked around, watching the traffic roll past and the people ambling about, I noticed a truck had parked with its motor running in front of a nearby chop suey restaurant on our side of the street. I was about to quietly ask Nadia how she was managing when from behind me came a harsh, grating noise.

"Got it," she said.

I quickly came about and joined her, seeing that she'd given up on picking the lock and had simply pried the door open with a jimmy.

"Let's go."

We stepped into an invisible cloud of floral scents, and I closed the door as best I could. "There was a new lock installed on that door recently," Nadia explained. "An expensive one. I think this means we're on the right track."

It was dark inside the narrow hallway, and from somewhere, too close by for comfort, I could hear voices.

Chapter Sixty Five:

There was the muted glow from the papered-over windows, leaving the shop a confusing maze of shadows. We didn't dare turn on a light as it would signal to anyone lurking about that they were not alone. We gave ourselves some time, getting our eyes used to the gloom, but before I was ready, Nadia crept forward. I followed close behind as she stalked past a hanging curtain. The area beyond was darker, but the voices we heard became clearer.

Then came the sound of a sharp impact, nearly causing me to jump, along with loud bantering in the tones of Chinese. We moved carefully toward the noise, found a set of wooden stairs descending sharply downward, and from below, odd flashes of light moved erratically.

Slowly, I readied my pistol and took the steps one at a time, easing my weight, crouching low to try and catch a glimpse of what was at the bottom of the stairs, when the board below me groaned.

A sharp voice called out, "Who's there?"

All at once a light burst forth from a naked bulb suspended from the ceiling, and I saw three men within a maze of crates, some open, with a ragged hole knocked out of the bricks in the wall behind them.

"Hold it," I shouted.

Naturally, they bolted in all directions.

Two of the men I glimpsed leapt back through the hole in the wall while the last one simply disappeared. I dropped from the stairway just as my ears were boxed by the sharp explosions of gunfire, and I landed clumsily behind a wooden crate. As I scrambled to my feet, I heard a voice call out, "Hold fire," and then shouted an order in Chinese.

It was Baker.

My fear was confirmed when I heard him say, "Locke? Is that you, old boy?"

"Hello, Baker. Fancy meeting up like this."

"Not really. You're a bit early, you know. About five more minutes, and we'd have been far and away."

"Am I to apologize?"

"It'd be nice."

As I was talking, I looked around for Nadia, but she was nowhere to be seen. And that scared me more than being pinned down with no way out, having no idea what she may be up to.

"Now, Locke," Baker said in a reasonable tone. "I'd advise against anymore shooting. There are enough explosives down here to blow us all to Kingdom Come."

"Seems we're at an impasse."

"Why don't you simply let us finish up here, and we'll be on our way? You're rather stuck, you know. If you try to go back up the stairs, I can pick you off in a tick."

"Same to you if you bolt for the hole."

"Yes, but remember the explosives? There must be some innocent lives around here somewhere. Or don't you care about such things?"

I sighed. I had to end this quickly, as God alone knew what Nadia Ravenwood was up to at this very moment. "Baker? Here's the deal. Take what you got, and get out. Then we both walk away."

"How unexpectedly reasonable of you, old boy. Until next time, then."

I waited for a bit, but didn't hear a sound through my

ringing ears. Until there came a bouncing, clattering noise that shot fear into my blood and made me charge up the stairs and throw myself flat to the dusty floor just as a gut-punching explosion bellowed up from below.

That bastard Baker had tossed a grenade as a parting gift.

"Are you all right?"

I looked toward the sound of Nadia's voice and saw her in the gloomy shop, only she wasn't alone. She was standing alongside a man while holding her push dagger up under his chin, causing him to hold his head back. I pulled myself to my feet and rushed to her, spotted a large revolver on the floor. Nadia Ravenwood had Chang by the throat. "He came sneaking in behind us, but I was ready for him."

From outside came the sound of a heavy truck laboring down the street.

"There go the guns," I said.

"Yes, but we have a new friend. Don't we, Mr. Chang?" Nadia stepped back, snatched Mr. Chang's pocket square, and cleaned the blood off the tip of her blade. She then handed the handkerchief back to Chang.

He dabbed it under his chin. "You've actually lost here, you know. We had already loaded the majority of the weapons."

"And you know where they are being taken."

He made an expansive shrug. "Yes, but now that they know I was nabbed, they will simply change the location of the delivery to somewhere else. So as you see, my value as a hostage is worthless."

"Well, we'll have the privilege of your charming company," Nadia said. "Come, I hear the fire brigade approaching."

There were shadows crowding the outside shop

window, *Joe Public* attempting to peer inside. The explosion had drawn attention, and we'd have to make a fast retreat...and soon. I made an 'after you' gesture to Mr. Chang, and he went to tip his hat in acknowledgement, but I jammed the barrel of his own revolver into his ribs to stop him. I took his unusually heavy bowler from off his head and saw the small, two barreled derringer affixed to the inside crown, confirming my suspicion about his hat from our first meeting.

Mr. Chang looked to Nadia and me in turn, then: "Well, you can't really blame a chap for trying."

Chapter Sixty Six:

We took the side door out to the street with Nadia in the lead and me prodding Mr. Chang along. We managed to thread our way through the crowd and the confusion of the firemen and police directing traffic, with most of the attention on the phonograph store next to the florist shop, as it now displayed a shattered main window, an unexpected consequence of the explosion in the basement. When we reached the Duesenberg, Nadia got into the back seat with Mr. Chang, and I drove, aimlessly at first, as I just wanted to get us away from the area.

From behind, I heard Nadia ask, "What do you call this gun?"

"It's a derringer," Mr. Chang responded. "And you really should be careful with it."

"Well, I'd hardly miss at this range, wouldn't I? Now, to business. I intend to turn you over to the police."

"On what charge?"

"Oh, that's a matter of negotiation. Now, if you decide to cooperate with me, then I'll simply say you're one of the anarchist Sons of Guan Yu, and the police will be happy to entertain you for a while. On the other hand, if you make me cross, then I'll tell the coppers that I suspect you of murdering May Scott."

"I did no such thing."

"Perhaps, but when you consider how Miss Scott was murdered in Chinatown, and you happen to be Chinese, well, as you see, you're liable to be severely and quite unfairly treated."

There was silence from the back seat until Chang spoke with quiet bitterness. "Clearly, you are as ruthless as your father. I believe you. What is it you want?"

"Tell me what my father is planning."

"That I would not reveal even under torture. Take me to the police instead."

Nicholas Ravenwood inspired loyalty. Or fear. Smart money would bet on fear. Though I had to wonder how far I'd go for him myself in the old days.

"Alright, then," Nadia said. "I want the evidence against Richard Bowen, namely, his sword cane that was used to kill Mary Bowen."

"That is possible," Chang said. "What do I receive in return?" He laughed.

"You're a pawn in the game, Mr. Chang. I'll be happy to just have you taken off the board. Why do you laugh?"

"Your use of the word, *pawn*. I heard an amusing story from your father once. All about how, at the end of the War, his plans to take control of the Russian government were falling apart, so he searched and found a stupid young American soldier, intending to parade him around Moscow to convince the Anti Bolsheviks that the United States was going to show up and fight for them. It didn't help, so Ravenwood had to make his escape. He brought the young American along, intending to use him as a decoy if they got caught by the Red Army. They made it across the border, and afterwards Ravenwood said he decided to keep this boy around, rather like a somewhat useful pet he had grown accustomed to having. Now, Mr. Locke, be a good boy and drive us to Doyers Street in Chinatown."

My hands were gripping the wheel hard, and I was driving faster than I should have.

Nadia touched my shoulder. "It's all right, Stephen.

Let's just get this part over with."

I turned the car about and aimed for Chinatown, forcing myself to relax and drive, although my hands were aching from their attempt to strangle the steering wheel. I drove under the elevated tracks of the Bowery until I turned into the narrow warrens of Chinatown.

"Stop in front of the theater," Chang said.

"I'll come with you."

"Miss, you do not trust me?"

"Well, look at that, you have a sense of humor, after all, Mr. Chang. Stephen, you stay here. And keep the motor running."

I opened my mouth to protest, but realized the futility of that act. Instead, I gave Mr. Chang a promising stare to which he responded with a smile and a tip of his bowler hat. I watched Nadia disappear into a side door and kept my pistol in hand, watching the local people pass by and counting by the seconds.

Suddenly, I heard the flat bark of what could have been a gunshot, followed by Nadia bursting out the door at a run. I was halfway out of the car when she shouted, "Get us out of here."

I stood aside as she dove for the Duesenberg, scrambling across the seat as I jumped in behind her, engaged the engine and glad I didn't stall the motor as I leaned on the horn to get people out of the way. I got around the corner to Pell Street and aimed the car for anywhere but here. I looked over to Nadia as she caught her breath with a confusing mix of laughter and pained groans. "Are you hurt?"

"I may have undone my stitchwork, but it was worth it." She proudly held up a black and brass-trimmed walking stick like a trophy.

"I heard a gunshot."

"I was obliged to shoot Mr. Chang in the leg."

"You what?"

"Used his own gun, too. Noisy little beast."

"But why did you shoot him?"

"I didn't like the way he spoke to you."

Speechless, I kept my eyes on the road.

"Besides...I warned him I was going to take a pawn off the board."

Chapter Sixty Seven:

We were back in Nadia's suite at the Waldorf Astoria as young doctor Eugene Cuff attended to her wounds while I waited in the parlor. The doctor emerged from the bedroom with Nadia in tow, wrapped in her kimono. "Again I must stress how important it is for you to rest and allow your wound to heal."

"Of course, doctor. And thank you so much for being so accommodating."

The doctor gave her a disbelieving look from the side of his eye. All of us present knew quite well that Doctor Cuff was at Nadia's beck and call due to the fact that she had a bit of blackmail over the physician, but regardless of that, she paid very well for his services. And we both politely pretended everything was on the up and up.

I saw the doctor out and then returned to Nadia, sprawled on the ornate sofa. "You have no intention to rest, wound or no wound, do you?"

"Stephen, please be so kind as to come give me a light and cease asking silly questions."

I joined her with my lit lighter offered, but she took hold of my hand and stared into my eyes. "I don't care what Father or anyone else says about you. You are the only one in the world that I can truly rely on. For us, nothing else matters. Do you understand?"

If pressed, I would have confessed I'd been stewing over what Mr. Chang said about me and how Nicholas Ravenwood took me in. And where I should have just let it go as a lie told by an enemy, something about his words cut right through to me. But now here was his daughter, Nadia, setting things right. I looked into eyes that a man could get lost in. "Yes," was all I could manage to say.

"Very well. Now, let's get on to more immediate matters, shall we?"

I set fire to her Turkish smoke and lit one of my less poisonous ones for me. "So now we have May Scott's murder weapon, what are we to do with it?"

"Personally, I should like to see it delivered to the police with the actual murderer attached to it. Preferably by the pointy end."

"We know who that was?"

Nadia gave me a speculating look as she sent a stream of smoke my way. "I think you and I would vote for the same person in this case."

"Hella, she of the giddy homicidal glee. But all we have is suspicion at this point. We have no evidence to examine or witnesses to question."

"Au contraire, we have the murder weapon itself. Let's take a look and see what we have."

"Shouldn't we consult, say, an actual police detective?"

She shrugged. "I was rather a bit of a criminal myself, once. It's just the opposite side of the same coin."

I fetched the cane and took it to the writing desk. The wood was black lacquered with a brass tip and ring where the handle separated from the sheath. At the boss of the cane was a brass lion's face, somewhat worn smooth by use, and while the cane itself bore nicks and marks accumulated over the years, it had been clearly rubbed down in the recent past. I gently pulled the stick apart and saw that the blade was quite a different matter. "Look at that," I breathed.

Marring the finish of the edged steel were dark, dried smears of blood. "Well, hello," she murmured.

Holding the sword up to the reading light, I could see the outlines of a fingerprint, impressed in dried blood, on the metal of the blade nearest the handle. "Someone was in a hurry. The killer didn't wipe the blade down after skewering May Scott. The sword has no guard, and it looks like whoever did the deed had to move their thumb to the flat of the blade to pull it free of May's body."

Nadia leaned back in her chair. "Now the question is, to whom does this fingerprint belong?"

"I still say it's our own blonde Lady MacBeth."

Nadia carefully returned the blade to its sheath. "Take this to the hotel safe. Then go back to your room and be dressed for dinner by seven. We are to have company and dine in the Empire Room."

I did as bid and returned to my own room. I gave myself over to resting up after the draining vicissitudes of the days past. I watched the clock spin round until the time drew near, then dressed in evening wear and wondered if I should pack along the little automatic pistol. I decided to leave it behind; if there was a gunfight in my immediate future, I was certain that Nadia would have advised me thusly. At a quarter to the hour, a bellhop arrived with a message to await the person I was to escort at the entryway to the restaurant.

I very nearly did not recognize her.

Chapter Sixty Eight:

Walking under the grand arches of the entryway and the splendid ceiling mural of *The Birth of Venus* and past a lovely bust of Marie Antoinette, came Miss Mary Bowen, transformed from a girl into a young woman. Her hair was done up like a crown, with a golden tiara woven in, while her dress was gold, as well, cascading down from her shoulders like a molten waterfall while her shoes were like an Arabian Princess's slippers. Then she gleefully broke the spell by energetically waving at me across the hall. "Mr. Locke."

I strode up to her. "Miss Bowen, may I say you are a vision tonight?"

She blushed a bit. "You may." Then her mood turned anxious. "Is there any news? About Richard?"

"Chin up, as they say, and yes, but that's for Miss Ravenwood to announce." I offered my arm. "May I?"

"Please. I almost tripped twice coming in here."

We entered the grand dining room, a blend of Grecian pillars with Old European baroque chandeliers and embellishments. Gentle music of the violin quartet wafted over hushed conversations of the aristocratically attired people. The maître 'd escorted us to Nadia's table, where the woman herself was seated, quite simply dressed in shimmering gray satin with a strand of black pearls. Then it struck me: Nadia didn't want to outshine Mary Bowen, giving her this moment to be the *Belle of the Ball*.

Once seated at the table laden with silver and crystal on snow-white linen, and, amusingly, tall bottles of ginger ale in a champagne bucket, Nadia said to Mary, "It's good to see you. Auntie Kit says you've made all arrangements for Henry?"

Mary's face became serious. "The service is this Friday. At the Little Chapel. Mrs. Krupp has really been wonderful."

"Call her Auntie Kit," I said. "I know it doesn't sound grown up, but that's what she prefers."

"But what of Richard?" Mary asked.

Nadia reached across the table and took her hand. "There has been progress. Now, I won't lie to you, the situation is still serious. But as of now Mr. Locke and I have taken steps, and our case for his innocence is much better today than it was yesterday."

Mary's breath came out all at once. "Wonderful. I've been so worried."

"It's not over yet. And now I'll have to ask you to keep the fact that you've spoken with us a secret. In matters such as these, the fewer people who know, the better."

Mary looked puzzled. "Miss Murphy asked just today when I'd last heard from you. I thought you said all the people in your home are like family."

"They are. But in my business, secrecy is of extreme importance. I'm breaking my own rules to speak with you, but I believe you deserve to know whatever I'm able to tell you and that you'll keep my confidence. I'm asking you to grow up faster than you should have to."

Mary sat up straighter with a look of determination on her young face. "You can trust me."

"I know."

I thought of the real reason we couldn't tell Mary much; the fact that, with Nicholas Ravenwood around, we couldn't be sure of our own people's loyalty.

Nadia picked up a menu. "Now, what shall we have

for dinner?"

The meal proceeded, for me at least, in a rather dream-like manner. After all the death and danger we ran through at breakneck pace, the world now had slowed and transformed into a genteel and civilized place. Within these walls, at any rate. I took full advantage of the Beluga caviar that paired fairly well with the ginger ale served in champagne flutes, as well as the half pheasant on a bed of braised romaine with an orange custard for dessert. And through it all, I could see Nadia's aim: trying to give Mary Bowen a respite from the horror of her own young life.

But our time drew to a close, and Nadia and I escorted Mary back to the lobby and called for Auntie Kit's chauffeur to come to the entrance. As I wrapped Mary in her velvet cape, Nadia and she exchanged cheek kisses. "I'll leave it to Stephen to see you the rest of the way."

Mary and I stood together and watched Nadia leave; I was looking for signs of weakness from her injury, and thought her slower than usual step was a bad sign. I then took Mary out to her waiting limousine. I waved the driver back behind the wheel and opened her door myself, assisted her in, but she stopped and gave me a quick kiss on the cheek. "I can never thank you enough," she whispered. Then she disappeared inside. I watched her drive away, leaving me suddenly feeling ten feet tall, all from the granting of a chaste accolade. All at once, I was ready to slay dragons.

I had the elevator operator take me to Nadia's floor. I wanted to check on her one last time tonight. When I knocked on the door to her suite, she took longer than expected to answer. "Oh, good. Come in. May I impose on you to help me get my shoes off?"

"Of course. What's wrong?"

Nadia made her way back to the sofa. "I've been

using a bit of laudanum here and there since I was shot, but I decided I needed to taper off. Now I'm paying the price."

"And you can't get your shoes off?"

"I can. I just really don't want to. Would you be so kind?"

I knelt by the sofa and undid the tiny buckles on the straps encircling her ankles.

"Ah. Better." She sighed.

"Anything else I can do for you?"

She cast a longing look toward her cigarettes, and I got her set up, lighting one of my own to join her. "You ever consider taking some time away from this war?"

"I would, if the other side offered a total and complete surrender. Is that too much to ask?"

"So what's the next move to be?"

"That *Fenris Group*, the company that has been buying up all the weapons stock, I thought we'd track down and find what at least passes for their public face and see if we can find out who's behind it all."

"We know who. It's your father."

Nadia looked up slyly, "Yes, but who else? Is Father in overall charge? Or is he working for someone, or some other country perhaps? Tomorrow, we start looking for answers."

And on that ominous note, I took my leave.

Chapter Sixty Nine:

Monday morning came all too soon. Although on the bright side, I was able to get a decent breakfast in the café: fried eggs and potatoes Julianne with Irish bacon. Nadia contented herself with creamed toast and a stolen slice of my bacon with her usual Turkish coffee. The meal was a rushed affair, as Nadia, dressed in a simple day frock of cascading silk, was impatient to get on our way.

Our first stop remained within the hotel itself. The Waldorf Astoria, catering to the needs of its high-roller businessmen, maintained a room with the most up to date tickertape stock feeds run by a small army of uniformed women. Here we learned that the Fenris Group was represented by an entity called *The Flint Company*, an investments management firm with an address of 120 Broadway.

Nadia surprised me by having us take a taxicab to that destination, the twin towers of The Equitable Building. The towers themselves were straight as railway lines, forty stories high, yet within the marble and bronze-faced lobby, one walks beneath Grecian arches decorated with a repeating flower motif. Here we found the building manager, a small, neat man with a fussy manner named Mr. Cleghorn. He was willing to speak to Miss Anne Romano about one of the building's business offices.

After introductions within his meticulously arranged office, where I was identified as Miss Roman's attorney, Mr. Cleghorn said, "I am at a loss, I must say. My secretary informed me you want information concerning one of our tenants?"

"Yes," Nadia said. "I am responsible for the disposition of my late husband's investments. The Flint Company comes recommended. But I feel one cannot be too careful these days."

"No. Of course not. But I hope you can appreciate that in my position, I cannot provide any sort of information regarding any of our valued tenants. It's simply not our policy."

Nadia moved in for the kill, reaching out and touching Mr. Cleghorn's arm and staring deeply with her dark eyes. "Of course, sir. A man in your extremely important and, dare I say, trusted position would be beyond any reproach. And I would never dream of doing anything that would put you in an awkward position. No, sir, I simply want to know how long the Flint Company has had their office here. For surely, you wouldn't want a widow to suffer from the unfortunate tragedy of being taken advantage of by some fly by night operation, would you?"

I made a dubious grunt. "That sort of thing would reflect poorly on the Equitable Building, surely."

Mr. Cleghorn's brain seemed to be following a rapid tennis game as he thought it over. "You just want to know how long the Flint Company has been here, yes? Nothing else?"

"Yes."

We were bid to wait in the lobby outside his office, but were summoned back in within half an hour. There were now a pair of ledgers on his desk. "Well, I must say, I have some rather disquieting facts to report."

"Oh?"

"The Flint Company has leased a space from us only since last April. Their office is currently on the corner of the thirty seventh floor. But I have no history with this company prior to that date."

Nadia nodded. "I see."

Mr. Cleghorn pursed his lips, then: "That is all I can say. Who you choose to look after your finances is, of course, solely up to you, but I will add that, as tenants of the Equitable Building, we have had no cause for complaint during the time they have been with us."

We thanked Mr. Cleghorn for his time and walked back to the lobby. "Up we go?" I asked.

Nadia simply arched an eyebrow and headed for the row of elevators for the south-most tower. After a long and uneventful upward journey, we found our way to the corner office of the thirty seventh floor, bearing the name of The Flint Company on its mahogany door. Nadia opened her handbag then handed it to me to hold. It was far heavier than usual, and I saw she was lugging around not only her father's Browning pistol, but the little two-barrel derringer she took from Chang that was now rattling around with a collection of burglary tools. I was also disquieted to see a small glass phial filled with rust-colored liquid that I guessed was laudanum.

She took out one of the double-headed skeleton keys.

I asked in a hushed voice, "We're not going to knock?"

That remark earned me a displeased glance as she went to work on the lock. Before a minute had passed, she had the door open and hurried inside.

I followed with my own pistol out but kept it under my coat as I stepped into darkness.

A light burst forth from above, and I saw Nadia had flipped the switch. I shut the door behind us and returned her handbag to her. She exchanged the skeleton key for her pistol.

The room we found ourselves in was clearly a reception area, with upholstered chairs for waiting visitors and a desk with a leather-bound but unused appointment book set next to an office telephone. Everything showed a light coating of dust.

"Looks like no one has been here for a while."

Nadia was already at the enclosed box affixed to the wall to receive letters. She opened it up and paused, until a low, light laughter escaped her lips.

"Find something amusing?"

She turned and held out a single plain white envelope.

Addressed to her.

Chapter Seventy:

Nadia Ravenwood held the envelope up to the light, then she shrugged and used her push dagger to slit it open. I gave her privacy while she read the letter, then she just handed it over to me, where I saw:

My Dearest Nadia,

This is a game you cannot win. Stop now.

The letter was unsigned, but I recognized the concise handwriting of Nicholas Ravenwood. I was about to ask her what she wanted to do now, but she simply walked past the reception desk and entered the office suite. I followed, and here we found an array of desks and chairs.

"I seriously doubt your father would have left anything of use behind."

"Do you know why he would use a place like this?"

"I'm discovering how little I knew about your father."

Nadia then took a slow walk around the room, noting the light layer of dust. There was ample light from the large, unshaded windows that provided a view to the south and east of Lower Manhattan. She walked over to the windows, softly muttering to herself. Then she stopped. "Stephen, come here."

I joined her as she pointed over the sprawling city under cloudy skies. "Over there is Chinatown, right?"

"Yes."

"And the Bowery is right next to it, of course, with the All Night Mission."

"True. So?"

Nadia looked to the enclosed corner office. "Let's see

what else is here, shall we?"

The inner office's door yielded to Nadia's burglary skills and within we found a large mahogany desk with a high-backed leather chair along with four other chairs for visitors. Opening the tall curtains revealed the same bird's eye view as the inner office, one to the south and one to the east where many wicked, bloody events occurred recently. There was a large world globe standing in one corner, along with a mounted brass telescope. The only decoration was a map of Manhattan on one wall. But the desk was both a puzzlement and a disappointment. Disappointing in that there was not one scrap of paper anywhere to be found, and puzzling as to what we did find: a bottle of Napoleon brandy with appropriate glasses and a box of Bolivar Cuban cigars, both brands highly favored by Nicholas Ravenwood.

"Looks like preparation for a celebration."

Nadia sighed, then took to pacing around the office, spinning the globe, taking in the view from the telescope, looking at the map. And stopping.

"What is it?"

She removed a glove and ran her fingertip over the lower part of the map. Then she pulled out her push dagger and slashed four cuts, removing a square and holding it up to the light. I came up to join her, and through the muted sunlight there appeared a small constellation of bright spots, tiny holes where marking pins had been removed. "Ha! Look at that."

We placed the map on the wide desk and Nadia borrowed my mechanical pencil to circle the tiny holes. "Look, two in Chinatown, one on Doyers Street, and the other on Chatham Square where we first met Mr. Chang. Here's the All Night Mission, just off Canal Street."

"Look down here," I said. "There's the docks off

South Street, perhaps where the guns were stolen out of the warehouse. And there's a spot over in Brooklyn. And what's that way over on Riverside Drive on the other side of Manhattan?"

"I've no idea." Nadia was silent, staring down, even as her father may have done once. I could picture him here, in this very room, looking out across the city like Zeus from Mount Olympus as he directed the mere mortals to do his bidding. It was an ideal location for a bit of egotistical scheming.

Nadia folded the section of map and handed it to me. "Come on. I think we've discovered all we are to find here."

We descended back down to the realm of mortals and motorized traffic and took a taxi back to the Waldorf Astoria. On the way, I noticed that Nadia seemed more tense than usual. Whether it was from her delving into the lingering presence of her father, or if she was suffering from the lack of laudanum, I could not say. When we arrived, she announced, "I want to rest a bit. Find yourself a decent luncheon."

I made a production of looking about the Waldorf's ritzy entryway. "Well, difficult as that may be... Oh-oh."

My flippant response was stopped by the sight of Detective McDonough in his baggy woolen suit. Too late for us to reverse course, he spotted us and ambled over, tipping his felt hat. "Miss Ravenwood, Mr. Locke. I trust you will not give me cause for regret."

"Regret over what?" Nadia asked.

"For not involving any uniformed officers. I am here as a courtesy. Would you be so kind as to accompany me?"

"Whatever for?"

"I am placing you under arrest on the charge of attempted murder."

Chapter Seventy One:

Nadia Ravenwood simply blinked, then said evenly, "*Attempted* murder? Are you accusing me of incompetence?"

"This is no laughing matter," Detective McDonough growled out. "I have a sworn complaint."

"And who is my accuser?"

"A Mr. John Chang."

This time, Nadia did laugh, albeit briefly. "I see. So this Mr. Chang is going to appear in a court of law and accuse me of this crime?"

"Yes. When the trial date arrives. Until then, you are to accompany me for booking, then you can arrange bail."

Nadia simply shook her head. "No, detective. I don't think so."

"Do not make the mistake of thinking I'm going to let you walk away from this, Miss Ravenwood. The only concession you're getting is I'm not going to insist on putting the cuffs on you. Yet."

Nadia made a point of looking around the entrance to the playground of the rich and influential. "And my concession to you, dear detective, is that I won't make a public fuss for your superiors to chastise you over. If you follow my lead."

"What do you mean?"

"First of all, we will proceed directly to the court. Mr. Locke will call ahead and arrange for a hearing. I believe you call it an arraignment in this country."

McDonough stroked his snow-white mustache. "Not

possible. You haven't been booked yet, so no arraignment can be scheduled."

"Oh, I believe District Attorney Banton could make the arrangements."

"Banton? Why would he do that?"

Nadia just smiled while I remembered the time D.A. Banton went after William Hamilton Anderson of the *Anti Saloon League* a few years ago. Anderson was tried and convicted of fraud and forgery charges and sentenced to Sing Sing, mainly by evidence provided by Nicholas Ravenwood. Whether that evidence was discovered or manufactured, I couldn't say. Regardless, the District Attorney owed a debt to the Ravenwood family. Only now I had to hope that Nicholas hadn't already put the fix in against his own daughter.

"So the situation is this," Nadia said. "You have a warrant for my arrest, and therefore must have witnesses and evidence to use against me. I say we appear in court today and you can present your evidence. If the judge finds it sufficient, then by all means we'll proceed. But if the judge is not swayed, then all charges get dropped and I walk free. So what do you say, detective? Ready to take a gamble?"

"If you think you're calling my bluff, don't try it, lady."

"No, detective. I think someone's using you as a pawn to try and take out the queen."

He shook his head. "I'm nobody's pawn."

"Then what do you have to lose?"

"All right. I call your bluff, but you don't leave my sight, you got that?"

Nadia playfully batted her eyes. "Really, detective?"

I'd swear he blushed. "I've got an officer from the Women's Bureau on hand."

"Oh? Very well then. And send my regards to the Bureau's Lieutenant, Mary Sullivan."

"Is there anyone you don't know?"

"The list is short."

McDonough grumbled. "All right then, let's get going, shall we?"

"If I may have a moment with my companion?"

Detective McDonough nodded, and Nadia stepped back and pulled me around so as to block McDonough's view of her. "Make that call to the District Attorney," she whispered, "or better yet, head to his office yourself. And on the way please dispose of Mr. Chang's little party favor."

I simply nodded as Nadia was busy performing a kind of pick pocketing performance in reverse, shoving her handbag up under my arm inside my coat while slipping a pair of items into my inner jacket pockets, one on each side.

"Are you ready?" McDonough asked.

"As ever, detective." Nadia ducked around me and took his arm. "Escort me away."

I stayed rooted to the spot, afraid to move, as I didn't want to chance dislodging Nadia's handbag until the pair was out of sight. Then I rushed up to my own room, keeping a grip on the bag with my free hand until I reached privacy to take inventory.

Spilling Nadia's bag on my bed, I saw both pistols, her Browning and Chang's derringer, amidst a scattering of burglary tools along with money, makeup, and her silver card case. In my coat pockets I found her 'Little Sisters', the bone-handled push dagger and the ornately engraved knuckleduster. I placed these two items back in my pockets, as I intended to return them to her sooner than the pistols.

Chang's derringer proved to be a bit of a problem, as it took me awhile to figure out how to open it up. I saw there was one unfired .41 caliber cartridge and one spent brass, the result of Nadia shooting Chang in the leg. It was a crafty move to have him swear out a warrant against Nadia. If successful, it took her out of play without having to actually harm her. It was a gambit worthy of Nicholas Ravenwood.

I closed up the little derringer, trying to decide how best to dispose of it so it couldn't be used as evidence against Nadia. I decided that a trip to the nearest river would do the trick and thought I may as well take Chang's big, clumsy cowboy style revolver to dump, as well. Unfortunately, I had orders to see the District Attorney, or get as close as I could straight away, and the Criminal Court building was right next door to Chinatown, far from any bordering river. I was racking my brain over this dilemma when the telephone rang for attention.

"Hello?"

"Stephen. It is time we speak again. Come join me in the lobby."

It was Nicholas Ravenwood.

Chapter Seventy Two:

S lamming the telephone receiver down didn't help anything, but in my state of shock, it was a reflex. My mind reeled, unable to fix on a point of action. I didn't even bother trying to figure out how Nicholas Ravenwood knew we were here in the hotel, as information was his specialty. In the end, I could think of nothing else to do but speak to the one man I'd come to fear more than anyone on earth.

My sojourn to the lobby was interrupted by the sight of Mr. Baker, who was lounging in the lobby with a newspaper. He smiled and waved as he got up and approached me. "Let's not have any silly heroics, old boy. Wouldn't do to disturb all the upper crust snobs hereabouts."

I took stock of the hotel's patrons, seeing many potential witnesses, or worse, unintended victims among them if a personal war broke out. "I'm here to converse," I replied. "But not with lackeys. Where's your master?"

"Take a stroll down Peacock Alley. You'll find him."

The *alley* Baker referred to was the main connection between the Waldorf and Astoria hotels, built when the two separate entities joined together. It had become a fashionable promenade for the rich and well-to-do to stroll to and fro on the mosaic floor between the Corinthian columns. Once within, I saw Nicholas as he stood to greet me. Seeing him now, under the crystalline lights, I got my first good look at him in over a pair of years. He was always the consummate chameleon, blending into whatever surroundings he found himself, and here he was faultlessly attired in the best of tailored suits. Although to me, he appeared to have a few silver strands in his normally coal-black hair, and his face looked a little more gaunt than I remembered. But his thin, predatory smile was the same as ever. "Come, Stephen. Sit with me."

I joined him on a plush cushioned bench, and instantly the old habit came back; Nicholas and I conversed as our eyes kept ever on the move, studying our surroundings as our lips stirred hardly at all as we spoke in tones just loud enough for the other to hear.

"You did not follow my advice," he said.

"To be precise, it was your daughter who didn't take your advice."

"And now she's paying the penalty."

"You intend to send your own daughter to prison? For shooting a rogue like Mr. Chang?"

"Mr. Chang's injury is his own fault, but I still have a use for him."

"Yes. Convicting your daughter and sending her away."

"Tell me: Do you have feelings for Nadia?"

I broke habit and turned to look at him. "Yes. But not in the way you may think."

"I see. So you fancy yourself some kind of champion for her?"

"Hardly. She doesn't need one. Rather, I am her partner, and I stand ready to support her in all decisions she makes, whatever the outcome may be."

Nicholas sighed. "I shouldn't be surprised. Your sense of loyalty was always your worst weakness. Still, I had hoped you'd have been able to keep her out of real trouble when I left her the business. Alas, I was wrong and now she will suffer the consequence of your failure."

"Nadia's in the situation because you brought her into it."

"Explain why you think that."

"It's obvious. For whatever reason, you've been playing Henry and Richard Bowen separately. Clearly, you need Richard for something. Or you did. Anyway, seeing his penchant for going on opium benders, you also needed someone to fetch him and keep him safe when he'd wander off...until you were ready to use him. Hence, you arranged for Henry to hire Nadia and me for the babysitting job. Only you didn't count on Nadia digging deeper into your business on her own."

"No matter. That situation is rendered moot. Nadia will no longer be in a position to interfere, and with her removed, you have no reason to continue." He stood abruptly. "Goodbye, Stephen."

I was surprised by his sudden departure, looked down the hallway and saw Baker and the blonde demon Hella waiting at the entrance. She boldly waved and blew me a kiss as she twirled her fox stole while Baker was now carrying a briefcase and giving me a flippant salute. They took up stations on each side of Nicholas and marched away.

A sudden, sinking feeling dropped into my gut, like a load of ice, as I rushed back to my room, only to find the place in an absolute state of disarray. I searched through all my scattered clothes and belongings only to discover that Chang's derringer and revolver, along with Nadia's Browning pistol, were gone. Stolen, no doubt, by Hella while Nicholas had me diverted downstairs.

The crushing weight of my failure fell on me. Nadia was counting on the fact that Detective McDonough wouldn't have enough evidence to hold her over for a trial. Only now, if he got Chang to testify in court, along with the weapon that he was shot with, then he'd have all he needed to lock Nadia away.

I found where the telephone wound up and spent nearly an hour haranguing the operators to connect me to the DA: *All lines are busy now. Please try your call again later*, and begging clerks over at the Criminal Courts to locate Nadia Ravenwood, only to discover she was being kept in a holding area for female defendants awaiting court appearances. My demands to speak with her amounted to naught, but a slightly familiar voice came on the line. "Mr. Locke? Is that you?"

"Yes. Who are you?"

"It's Theodore Brent, Mr. Locke."

"Brent?" Here was another shock. Theodore Brent was an attorney who'd been falsely arrested for murder last month, only Nadia and I managed to spring him from the clutches of the Law when Nadia discovered the actual murderer. "What are you doing there?"

"Miss Ravenwood had the DA call my office. I'm here to represent her at the hearing today."

"I didn't know you handled criminal matters."

"I don't, but she insisted that all she needed was, to use her words, *a mouthpiece*."

"Get back to her and tell her Chang's party favor was stolen out of my room and is headed to the prosecutor's office as evidence against her. You got that?"

I waited for what felt like an eternity until Brent came back to the phone. "All right, Mr. Locke, sorry it took so long. She was on the phone with a reporter—"

"What is she up to now?"

"She's asking for you to come down here."

"Okay."

"And bring a miracle with you."

Chapter Seventy Three:

Theodore Brent asked for a miracle. I had nothing. All I could do was get to the courthouse as fast as I was able, even if it was just to watch Nadia Ravenwood get thrown behind bars. I engaged a taxicab and asked the driver to hurry, not that my presence would do any good whatsoever.

Just past Chinatown, where all the trouble began, stood the Manhattan Criminal Courts, a red brick structure attached by way of an enclosed elevated bridge to the foreboding fortress of the City Prison, colloquially known as *The Tombs*, Nadia Ravenwood's next most likely destination. Entering the City Courts, you'd be forgiven for stopping to admire the marble walls and the bronze furnishings among the sculptures and colorful murals that just might make you forget about the cracks in the unsound structure and the history of fires in the building.

I had a bit of a mad scramble to find the particular courtroom where Nadia was to be brought before a judge, but at last, I came to the proper hallway. On one end I saw Nadia Ravenwood along with a uniformed policewoman and Theodore Trent, Attorney at Law, who was sweating too much to give anyone any reassurance. At the other end of the hall was Detective McDonough standing next to a seated Mr. Chang, who had a pair of crutches nearby. McDonough spotted me and gave me a grave nod of acknowledgement, one civilized enemy to another.

I rushed to Nadia, but the policewoman quickly intercepted me. She was a handsome specimen in her uniform that, save for the skirt, looked like the uniform of the Army Air Service. She held out her hand as if I were an oncoming motorist. "Unless you're a member of Miss Ravenwood's legal team, I must ask you to keep your distance."

I caught a glimpse of Nadia as she nodded to the other end of the hallway, indicating I should get closer to Detective McDonough and Mr. Chang. I nodded, acknowledging both Nadia and the policewoman's requests, and ambled my way toward her accuser, until I garnered a warning look from McDonough and found my seat on the nearest bench.

From my vantage point, the hallway resembled a kind of long, narrow chessboard, with Nadia the Black Queen on one end and Chang and McDonough a Knight and a Rook on the other. The clock in the hall kept ticking away the minutes, drawing ever closer to when Nadia would be called to appear before a judge. Then yet another worrisome sight came into view:

Marching down the hall, coming straight at Chang and McDonough, was the one and only Sophie Treadwell. This slender woman was one of the most fearless journalists known; she made an early reputation reporting on the War in Europe, and later tracked down and interviewed Poncho Villa while he was on the run in Mexico. She and Nadia had met while Sophie was covering the murder trial of Snyder and Gray a few months back.

Sophie Treadwell fixed her dark eyes squarely on Mr. Chang, and as Detective McDonough stood to intercept her, she shouted, "Mr. Chang? A moment of your time, sir."

McDonough started to say something, but Sophie called out, clearly and loudly, "Mr. Chang, why would your fingerprints be found on the weapon that killed May Scott?"

It was as if the whole world stopped at once; all voices ceased and all eyes were now on Mr. Chang, who sat there gulping air like a landed fish.

"Will you answer the question, sir?"

Chang grabbed his crutches and lurched for the elevators. McDonough was caught flat-footed for a moment, then he made a short run and took Chang behind the collar. It was no contest, what with Chang's leg recovering from a bullet perforation, the two of them fell on the tiles in a heap. "I made a mistake," Chang cried. "I was wrong. I must leave."

I don't know if anyone else saw it or not, but as Chang was struggling with McDonough, his eyes were locked with Nadia Ravenwood's, and he clearly got the message, remembering her prior threat to serve him up as May Scott's killer. Clearly, he bought into the bluff, especially seeing how he must have handed the sword cane to Nadia and now thought that's how we got his fingerprints. Now it made me wonder if the fingerprints Chang put on the outside of the cane would match the one we found on the blade, in blood.

There was quite a bit of confusion that ultimately resulted in Detective McDonough having a policeman take Mr. Chang away while he had to go in and explain to a judge that his prize witness just now refused to testify and would be held on filing a false police report, for starters. After thanking a wholly relieved Theodore Brent and a slyly smiling Sophie Treadwell for their help, I was finally allowed to escort Nadia out of the courthouse.

Once she and I were in the back of a taxicab, she reached over, grabbed the lapels of my coat and buried her face into my chest, smothering her repeated screams as I held on to her. Until at last, trembling, she pulled away.

The taxi driver and I exchanged looks through his

rearview mirror.

"Oh. I've smudged your collar." Nadia's voice was shaky. "Sorry."

"Are you all right?"

"I am now. But that, I admit, was close."

I'd witnessed her emotional outbursts before. Like a storm that rapidly came and went. She was right as rain when it passed. "How did you pull that off?"

"Father underestimated me."

"So what's next?"

"Clearly, we're close to blowing this case wide open, otherwise Father wouldn't have pulled this stunt to take me off the board." She drew in a breath then let it out. "We're in the endgame now."

Chapter Seventy Four:

W hen our taxicab brought us to the Waldorf Astoria, Nadia said, "I want you to call up Detectives McDonough and Broderick and invite them for dinner."

"Dinner?"

"I suppose we'll have to invite that Agent Reynolds, as well."

"Dinner?"

"No formal dress. We'll use the Astoria rooftop café. Say, seven?"

"You can't be serious."

She gave me the look.

I nodded, and Nadia took herself away, leaving me to go to the nearest telephone booth in the lobby and begin my chores. As it turned out, I could only leave messages at McDonough and Broderick's precinct houses, and I didn't even bother to try to reach Agent Reynolds, as he seemed to be attached to Johnny Broderick's hip lately. When I was done, I went to my own room, entering with my hand on my pistol, and surveyed the wreckage left by Hella's raid. I straightened up and changed shirts and gathered up Nadia's handbag and belongings.

My next stop was her room. "Here," I said as I entered, holding out her handbag.

She was in her silk kimono, and I saw the remnants of a coffee demitasse and cigarette in a tray. I waited as she looked through her bag. "Where's my card case?"

"I'm sorry. I couldn't find it. I think light-fingered

Hella made off with it along with the guns."

Nadia shot me a venomous look. "That little *prostituka* is like a magpie; she can't keep her beak off shiny things. If I get my hands on her, I'm going to take this insult out by way of her teeth."

"Well, maybe these will help." I offered up her 'little sisters', and she swooped over and snatched her weapons out of my hands. "Oh, yes. I've been feeling quite undressed without these. Thank you."

I was glad to partially assuage the loss of her silver dragon-embossed card case, still feeling it was my fault. "Speaking of getting dressed," she said as she disappeared into the suite's bedroom. "I shall return."

I settled into a chair and lit a cigarette, but before I had finished, Nadia came back, dressed in a long black-velvet tunic over black silken bloomers tucked into low, dark-leather boots. "So we are to be quite casual, I see."

"Depending on what we're able to shake out of the coppers tonight, we may be on the move right away. So eat your fill."

I escorted Nadia up to the Palm Gardens Café, high up on the roof and enclosed in glass plates that made the lights of the Manhattan skyscrapers into an orderly shaped constellation of stars. Our party was seated ahead of us and rose to greet Miss Ravenwood. Detective Broderick looked at ease, while Detective McDonough and Agent Reynolds were openly suspicious.

"Gentleman..." Nadia greeted them as I seated her. "I'm so glad you could join us."

McDonough said, "You'd be having quite a different meal if I had gotten my way today."

"No doubt. But I was set up by persons who want to stop me from looking into these matters, and I can't believe you'd want to help out a criminal like Mr. Chang, would you?"

"Of course not. As is, Chang's refusing to say another word to anyone about anything, so he'll be a guest in my precinct lockup until he changes his mind."

"Why are we here?" Reynolds demanded.

"First, we dine. Then, we speak. Gentlemen?"

Nadia went for the breast of Scotch grouse. The men were evenly split between Rhode Island Turkey and the saddle of lamb. The dinner conversation tended toward police war stories, with McDonough having some of the funniest, while Reynolds just looked glum, though it clearly had no effect on his appetite.

At the conclusion of our meal, Nadia announced, "Now, Gentlemen, I believe the time has come for some revelations."

"Of what sort?" Broderick asked.

"Of the true nature of what has been going on here."

Broderick sighed. "Miss Ravenwood, how many times must I say that these are matters strictly for the police? There is nothing we can talk about with you, even if we wanted to. Which, I assure you, we don't."

"Well, then, I suppose you can just sit there and listen to me."

"Listen to what?"

"I want to explain how much you don't know."

Chapter Seventy Five:

Nadia certainly had everyone's attention, and she made good use of it, diving right in. "First of all, Gentlemen, you have this mysterious group known as the Companions of Tyr. Which you believe to be radical anarchists, yes?"

"We have evidence," Agent Reynolds said.

"Yes, evidence provided mostly from Henry Bowen, I'd wager. And yet his very own brother, Richard, would testify that the Companions of Tyr is an anti Communist league dedicated to fighting against them. Both of these positions cannot be correct."

Reynolds and Broderick traded shrugs.

"So one is lying," Broderick stated.

"Henry was feeding you false information. Let's talk about the glass."

Reynolds looked confused. "What glass?"

"The night Henry was shot at in his study. I remember he said that he heard the gunshots break the window, but he didn't fall to the floor until a number of shots were fired. If that was true, he ought to have been lying on top of some broken glass. On the other hand, if he got to the floor first because he knew the shots were coming, then there would have been a clear spot where his body was. I saw the spot. Glass shards had made an outline of his body but no broken glass was present inside it. I believe this was a setup to fool you into thinking Henry was being threatened by your anarchists."

Reynolds and Broderick both looked uncomfortable.

"Henry also told you about a missing shipment of military weapons."

Reynolds burst out with, "How do you know all this?"

"Mr. Locke and I make it our business to know things. On the other hand, Agent Reynolds, it seems that while you are quite convinced that there is a Communist plot afoot, backed by the Russian government, you're completely in the dark as to what their ultimate goal might be. But I did see in your notebook, along with the information Henry gave you about the missing gun shipment, that you sent a subpoena to the Manhattan Savings Bank on Broadway for Henry Bowen's records."

Reynolds paled. "My notebook?"

Broderick turned to Reynolds. "You didn't tell me about any subpoena. Care to let me in on what came out of it?"

Reynolds got a stubborn look on his face. "Nothing, really. Just a report of some expenditures that didn't make sense."

"Like what?" Nadia asked.

"Like renting a boathouse when you don't own a boat. That's the kind of thing you see in smuggling cases. But how in hell did you get my notes?"

"Didn't Detective Broderick tell you? I found your notebook at Bellevue Hospital and gave it to him to return to you. I had to look inside to see who it belonged to, didn't I? Now, where is this boathouse, exactly?"

Reynolds shot to his feet. "That is enough. I should have you run in for stealing my notes. And if this rotten town wasn't full of crooked cops, by God I would."

We watched him storm out.

I said to Broderick, "You going after your partner?"

"Partner? I'm going to miss that guy like a kidney stone. Look, Miss Ravenwood, level with me. What have you got that I should know about?"

"I'll say this, Detective Broderick, the very moment I have something solid, you will be the first person I call. I will just have to trust that you'll come running."

"Just don't cry wolf."

Detective McDonough leaned forward. "Now, I've been patient, but you've got to tell me this. What do you have on that John Chang character?"

"What I have for you, my dear detective, is what I believe to be the murder weapon used on May Scott. Richard Bowen's sword cane."

McDonough frowned at her. "And that has Chang's fingerprints on it?"

"On the outside, perhaps. I knew he handled it, and that's why I had my friend Sophie make such a loud and public accusation, to spook him into making a mistake. But while Mr. Chang's fingerprints may be found on the outside of the sword cane, there is yet another I found on the blade itself, etched in blood. One that most likely belongs to the murderer."

McDonough was silent for a moment, then: "The Devil you say."

"Consider it my gift to you."

"But what if this fingerprint is the very thing that convicts Richard Bowen?"

Nadia waved the thought away. "In that case, I can only hope justice is served. But I'm betting that fingerprint belongs to someone else entirely."

"Who?"

"You said it yourself, detective. Perhaps it is the Devil."

The detectives gave up trying to crack Nadia Ravenwood, and I walked them down to the lobby, where I stopped by the concierge and had him bring me the sword cane we had in the hotel's safe.

McDonough took the weapon gingerly. "I'll get this to the fingerprint boys right away."

"On the outside, you'll find mine, along with Nadia's, Richard Bowen's and Mr. Chang's. He's the one we got it from. It was being kept in a place off Doyers Street near the theater in Chinatown. But the fingerprint, left in what I'm betting turns out to be May's blood type, is on the flat of the blade near the handle."

McDonough nodded and walked off like he was carrying a baby.

Johnny Broderick looked at me. "You think that boathouse angle may be important?"

"Could be. Miss Ravenwood and I have come across a few mentions of ships since we've been knocking around this case."

He nodded. "I'll see what I can get out of Agent Reynolds. No promises though."

I watched him leave then went up to check on Nadia. She was sprawled on her sofa with a cigarette burning already. "Are we done for the night?"

"It is so frustrating. Here I've got coppers keeping their lips sewn shut, not to mention Richard Bowen, who may or may not be holding out on us, and even Princess Xenia is keeping secrets from me. I'm certain if everyone would just open up and trust me, things would go so much better."

"Trust the woman who thinks nothing of lifting secrets out of the pockets of Federal Agents? Or breaking and entering anywhere she feels like? And they don't trust you? How utterly shocking. Despite the fact that you're holding back far more than the police. I couldn't help but notice you didn't mention the offices of the Fenris Group, or the map with the pin markings, or the photographs of

William Leeds' yacht *Moana,* or the references to the words *Ram* and *Chariot* from our little midnight sojourn at the All Night Mission, or the fact your own father may be behind it all."

Her answer was narrowed dark eyes as she blew a stream of smoke at me. "No. We are not showing our hand. And since you brought up the map, you have a choice. Do we go to the place marked in Brooklyn first, or the one on Riverside Drive?"

I just sighed and tossed a coin.

Chapter Seventy Six:

We took the Duesenberg across the Brooklyn Bridge and down to Atlantic Avenue, where we parked near the intersection of Court Street, as indicated by the tiny hole on the map. Atlantic Avenue was wide to accommodate the traffic from the docks, but the buildings of the immediate neighborhood were wholly unremarkable. Rather grimly brick-fronted structures with most business at street level and apartments above, and not many buildings over four stories tall.

At this time of night there were few people about, with most of the shops closed and all the traffic driving through to some other destination.

I huffed. "Well, this looks like an absolute dead end."

Nadia shook her head. "There must be something here. That All Night Mission was in a worse neighborhood, not to mention those places in Chinatown."

"That's rather the point. Bad places are where bad people go to blend in. This street looks a little too law-abiding for the likes of the people we deal with."

"All right then, let's take a walk, shall we?"

We strolled arm and arm under the wan streetlights, keeping our eyes moving and ears open. Until we came to an automobile garage.

"Ah-ha," I said. "Now here is one place where you could hide a truck off the street and unload it at your leisure."

"Agreed. Let's check it out."

"It may be closed, but there could be people inside

who are wide awake and waiting for a pair of rash fools to go charging in there."

As if on cue, she disengaged from my arm and hurried over to the single door next to the closed bay portals. We were out in the open as Nadia bent to examine the lock. "I think I can get it with what I've got in my bag."

I turned my back on her, covering her activity as best I could while looking around for a beat cop. Eventually, I heard the door creak open, and she rushed inside. Reluctantly, I followed and closed the door behind us. As my eyes adjusted to the gloom, I noticed the place had a heavy smell of machine oil. As we crept to the bays, we found a covered truck within.

Nadia smirked. "Tell me that's not the one we saw Mr. Baker driving as he made off with the weapons."

"Yes. Right after he pitched a grenade at me." We moved to the back of the truck and saw at once there was nothing in the bed. "Damn," Nadia breathed.

"I wonder where they moved the weapons to?"

"Let's look and see what else we can find."

Keeping my hand on my pistol, remembering that Nadia, with the exception of her 'little sisters', was unarmed, I moved cautiously. It didn't take long to cover the garage as it was one big open space, and as such, we nearly missed its hidden secret.

I was using my cigarette lighter to give us a bit of light and Nadia pointed downward. "What's that?"

The floor of the bay had an open area, where mechanics could work on the underside of vehicles. Crouching down, I saw there was broken rubble covering the floor of the concrete pit with numerous footprints evident. I handed Nadia my lighter and used the metal rungs bolted to the concrete to lower myself and found one end of the pit covered by a canvass sheet. Lifting it up, I now saw where a hole had been broken through, leading to a narrow tunnel.

Suddenly the flickering illumination above went out, and then I was nearly blinded by a bright burst of light. "I found a battery lantern," Nadia announced.

I silently cursed and hoped my heart wouldn't give out from fright as I took the lantern from her and assisted her down the ladder. Before I could utter a word of caution, she retrieved the lantern from me and ducked into the maw of the tunnel. We had to crouch for a bit as we descended until we came to yet another broken concrete wall, and it was through here we found ourselves a wonder.

We stepped out into a wide, arched tunnel made of flagstones that ran under the avenue above. "Mon Dieu!" Nadia said in a hushed voice. "Where are we?"

The half buried tracks on the ground told the tale. "It's an underground railway, no longer used. Looks like the City just sealed it off."

"Over there." Nadia rushed to a large pallet covered in canvass. Lifting up one side revealed a crate marked *Auto Ordinance Corp.*

"Ha," I said. "That be the treasure for certain."

Nadia played the light up and down the tunnel. "Left here unguarded?"

"Yes, but really well hidden."

"We're missing something."

Against all better judgment we took the time to walk around and examine the stash of crated weapons, until I spotted the wires. "Uh, oh."

Nadia and I crouched there, and I saw where a pair of braided wires disappeared into the side of a box. Gently pulling on the wires raised them from the tamped ground where they'd been buried. "I'm betting this is rigged to explode," I whispered.

Michael Siverling

"Can you make it safe?"

I ruined the edge of my penknife and cramped my hands, laboring to cut the wrapped copper wires, then we reburied them a space apart. "Now can we get the hell out?"

Nadia nodded and we made our retreat. When we got back to the garage pit, I let her climb first then took a moment to scuff over her feminine footprints in the dirt on the ground. Once back to the office, we waited until the sidewalk was clear, then slipped out, with me covering Nadia as she relocked the door. And with one final look around, we strolled back to her car.

And I was grateful my knees didn't shake until after she was driving us away.

Chapter Seventy Seven:

Bright and early the next day, Nadia Ravenwood, dressed in her riding tweeds and boots, and I were at the massive Roman Temple like Police Headquarters, waiting for Johnny Broderick to stroll in. Once the dapper detective made his appearance, his normally placid face twisted like he bit something bitter. "Why are you two haunting my station?"

Nadia rose from the hall bench we shared. "We have important news." Looking up and down the hall, she stepped closer to Johnny and whispered, "We found the guns."

Detective Broderick's eyes flashed as he whispered through clamped jaws. "Keep your mouth shut and come with me. Both of you."

He hustled us down the hallway to one of the interrogation rooms that smelled of sweat and desperation, then closed the door. "Now, out with it. Where are the guns?"

"They're hidden in an abandoned railway tunnel in Brooklyn."

Broderick threw up his hands, turned about and looked like he wanted to punch something. "How did you find them?"

"What's the problem?" Nadia asked. "We found them last night and came straight to you."

Broderick quickly turned back to us. "The problem is we already know all about the guns. We also know that those Companions of Tyr aren't going anywhere near them until tonight. And that's when we are going to catch them in the act with the goods. Unless you bumbling idiots tipped them off."

"Wait," Nadia said, "How did you find the guns?"

"Police work," Broderick spat out.

Nadia narrowed her dark eyes. "Really? Or did someone conveniently call you up and just give the information to you?"

Now it was Broderick's turn to glower. "What are you saying?"

"You still don't see you're being used?"

Broderick stared at us, dead-eyed. "Get. Out."

We followed his advice forthwith. Once outside, I asked, "Now what?"

"I believe we should begin with Henry Bowen's study."

"What for?"

"We learned last night that Henry Bowen rented a boathouse. We can't rely on Agent Reynolds sharing his information with us. And it's obvious that whatever the endgame is, it must be happening tonight to coincide with the police raid. So let's go and see if there's any stone we can turn over."

We found the Bowen residence dark and no one answered our knock, so we simply went around by way of the back garden and let ourselves in by use of Nadia's housebreaking skills. It was cold within, clearly the house staff had moved on. We ascended the back stairs and found our way to Henry's study, where once we'd found his lifeless body. Doubtless, it was my own imagination, but here felt the coldest of all. Here was also a bitter disappointment: All the drawers were open and emptied, with scarcely a scrap of paper left behind amidst the stains of blood.

"Someone had the foresight to take away any potential evidence," I murmured.

"Trouble is, we don't know if this was done by the police, or by Father's people."

"The result is the same, we have nothing."

But as we made our way out, Nadia thought to look to the mail slot, and there we found a small trove of envelopes. She swooped on these like a falcon, snatching them up and then just as quickly discarding them. "Let's see... Bereavement card... Bereavement...Ha!"

Before I could mention anything in regard to reading other people's mail, Nadia tore open a letter that contained a bill for an equipment delivery from an entity called the *Marine Park Boat Company*. Nadia waved the paper at me. "Look! A notation of the delivery address."

"That's on Riverside Drive near the Hudson, all the way across town."

"Want to bet it's at a spot pinned on the map from Father's office?"

We hurried out the back, and soon Nadia was heading the Duesenberg across the rain-slick streets, jockeying with all the other traffic in the concrete canyons of New York. Eventually, we made it to Riverside Drive and past the massive gothic towers of Mr. Schwab's residence until we reached the address of the docks that extended into the Hudson River. We parked the car and took a stroll along the pier. The wind off the river was cold, but luckily the rain had ceased as we hunted along the slips until we found the enclosed boathouse of the proper number. Unfortunately, all the windows had been blacked out, and there were hefty padlocks fastening the doors.

Nadia made a fast study of the place, muttering a mixture of German and French curses under her breath. "Can you see any way to get inside?"

"Other than jumping in the water and swimming? No. And don't give me that expectant look."

I saw her examining the locks, and then suddenly, she looked up. "Harbormaster," she said as she marched back down the pier.

We found the wood-sided office of the man on duty, a lean, gray-haired Captain Robertson by name, and Nadia Ravenwood introduced herself and produced the bill from the marine tool company. "I may have suffered a shortage in my delivery. Would you happen to know when my supplies arrived?"

He looked the paper over, then: "I'm sorry, Miss Ravenwood, is it? We really don't keep track of things like that."

"Oh. But would you know if my ship had these parts installed?"

He was surprised. "Your ship? I was under the impression that little boat was sold already and waiting for the new owner to claim it. Though who on earth would want such a thing is beyond me."

Nadia shifted to a different tact. "My Mr. Bowen may have held a few facts back from me. And I suppose you've heard he's no longer with us."

Captain Robertson nodded. "My condolences to you, ma'am."

Nadia looked up into his weathered face. "I was wondering if you could help me. I invested money with Mr. Bowen, and I fear it's been spent on whatever is inside that boathouse. Now I'm afraid I've been fooled into a bad investment. Could you tell me exactly what is inside there?"

Captain Robertson looked a shade uncomfortable. "Well, and please forgive me if I laughed just then, it's just that I'm afraid that there's no use for a boat like the Fenian

Ram these days."

Nadia blinked. "Ram?"

"Yes. I'd heard a little about it, and from what I know, it's always been a bit of a boondoggle, pardon me for saying. It was built by Holland right here in New York quite a while ago, and supposedly the Irish Republican Army was going to use it against the British, but it was just abandoned and later sold for scrap. Until it ended up here. Last I heard it's going to wind up in a museum."

"But what, exactly, is the Fenian Ram?"

Captain Robertson shrugged. "It's probably the world's smallest attack submarine."

Chapter Seventy Eight:

N adia froze for a few seconds.
"Are you alright, ma'am?" Captain Robertson inquired.

She took a breath. "Things are becoming clearer. Now, Captain, may I ask, what does the word *Chariot* suggest to you?"

"Chariot? Nothing. Why?"

"Would you happen to know anything about the motor yacht *Moana*?"

"That I do. She's moored over at the Columbia Yacht Club...just upstream from here."

With profuse thanks that left the good Captain confused, Nadia then turned about and marched out with me hurrying to keep up and hearing her mutter something about *Der Teufel*, The Devil, under her breath. "Shall we take a moment and not rush where Angels say *Hell No*?"

"It's here. It's all here. And I'm betting everything happens tonight."

"Some of it is over in Brooklyn," I said. "Where the guns are."

She waved the thought away. "Diversion. Keeping all the cops away on the other side of Manhattan while the real action happens here."

"And shouldn't we call those coppers?"

Nadia stopped in her tracks. "Who would believe us?"

I turned back and looked out over the Hudson River. Off in the hazy distance, I could see the moored, disused battleships left waiting out on the water. "Are you saying we're on our own?"

"You can walk away."

I found I had just enough nerve left to offer a quiet laugh. "Why start doing the smart thing now? So, where do we go from here?"

"Princess Xenia. I've got to convince her to tell me what she knows. Or what she thinks she knows."

It was a matter of minutes for us to move Nadia's car, and soon we were marching across the long, elevated walkway that delivered us to the tiered Columbia Yacht Club, where we were told to wait while the uniformed staff would try to find Mrs. Leeds and see if she was receiving.

We were not waiting long before Mrs. William Leeds, otherwise known as Princess Xenia of Russia, made a breathless appearance in a tailored copy of what looked like a sailor's uniform. "Nadia. How is it you are here?"

"May we speak privately?"

The Princess's eyes, so much like Nadia's, searched the other woman's face. "Da. Yes, of course. Come."

She led us around the outside balcony until we were overlooking the river. Nadia began right away. "Whatever it is you plan to do tonight, you must stop."

"Nadia. You don't know what you are asking."

"I only know that it will end in disaster. Especially if it has anything to do with my father."

The Princess pulled back a bit. "How do you know this?"

"Tell me now. Does anything that happens tonight have something to do with the Grand Duchess Anastasia?"

When the Princess pressed her lips in silence, Nadia gasped. "Oh, my God. She's here, isn't she."

Xenia looked around, alarmed. "Quiet! We were told to keep this secret."

"So you've met her? And you believe it is she? And

not an imposter?"

"I do. What is more, others believe as I, such as Duke Andrei."

"What matters is the fact that something terrible is planned for tonight. Is your husband taking his yacht out?"

"Yes. There is a private reception planned. And when the last of the Czar's immediate family is shown to be alive, then that will be the spark we need for a new Royalist uprising that will sweep the damned Bolshevik thugs away from Mother Russia for good."

"And this is what my father promised you?"

"Yes."

"And where does the *chariot* fit in?"

Xenia frowned. "How do you know...never mind. The egg is part of the price we are paying to regain our homeland."

"Egg? Oh, no. Not one of the Faberge treasures?"

"Your father has shown us the documents proving he owns interests in American weapons. Our armies will need these. It is only right that we pay for them."

My head was spinning at the size of the web Nicholas Ravenwood spun. Nadia and Xenia were now hissing at each other in Russian, leaving me in the dark, until just as quickly as they started, they stopped.

"So," Nadia said. "It is agreed. I promise not to do a thing until I am needed, yes?"

"What's going on?" I asked.

The two of them, near mirror images of the other, looked at me with the same speculative expression.

Nadia said, "You are not going to like this."

Chapter Seventy Nine:

The good ship *Moana* was lit up like a Ziegfeld Follies chorus line, with electric lights strung all up and down the masts and across the railings. It was moored in the Hudson halfway to the mothballed battleships, beyond which glowed the lights of the New Jersey shoreline. Up above, the moon was a sharp crescent that cut across the ink black clouds that rolled by. All of these were the last things I saw before I was stuffed into a narrow closet in the private study of the yacht.

Before my entombment, I was granted a rushed introduction to the husband of Princess Xenia and the master of the *Moana*, Mr. William Leeds, Jr. For a millionaire who played with airplanes and speed boats like an indulged child with expensive toys, he was unimpressive: a short, slight man with a head shaped like a light bulb. Once he was aware I was no one of consequence, I ceased to exist to him, making the execution of Nadia's insane plan that much easier.

The glimpse I got of the polished oak paneling and plush curved divan was impressive, with the portholes sheathed in heavy velvet and the light provided by shaded lamps, casting everything with a warm, rouge glow. It was here where the honored guests were escorted in, in ones and twos, to meet with the last surviving member of the Royal Family of Russia, the Grand Duchess Anastasia Romanov.

Although I was under strict orders to remain concealed, I confess I peeked.

She was dressed in elegant finery, beaded and bejeweled in a gown of emerald green with a scarlet sash. But the woman herself presented as careworn, with a sadness gathered about her blue eyes, and every so often her voice seemed to fade, not surprising, as Nadia told me the woman had suffered great illness over the years. Seated just behind her and assisting at every turn was Princess Xenia in a matching emerald gown but without the sash.

Throughout the evening, guests were ferried out from the Yacht Club and taken to be presented, and here they held brief, quiet conversations with The Grand Duchess. As time went by, my hopes grew that Nadia was wrong, and that tonight would be free of danger...until I heard a disturbing announcement.

"May I present, Mr. Nicholas Ravenwood and Miss Hella Rhine."

The Devil was just outside my door.

I breathed as quietly as I could as I closed my eyes and strained to hear Nicholas. "Good Evening, your Royal Highness."

"Mr. Ravenwood, how good of you to come."

"I am your servant, your Highness. And in that spirit, I am pleased to announce that all arrangements have been made. I have inside this case the plans and treaties necessary for us to begin, and now only require the small investment to see things through."

"Princess Xenia? Would you be so kind? Mr. Ravenwood, I fear I am fatigued. If the Princess will escort me, I shall return her to you with our treasure."

"By all means, your Majesty."

From the crack in my doorjamb I could see Princess Xenia assist the Grand Duchess in leaving the room, and then return shortly with a black lacquered container that she carried a bit awkwardly in both hands. After she walked out of my sight, I gripped my pistol and kept such a hold on my breathing that I felt a touch lightheaded as I waited for a signal. Then I heard Nicholas say, "Oh, daughter. Really? Don't you remember? I'm the one who first sent you that perfume."

I slammed the door open and saw Nicholas reaching into his suit jacket as the woman before him, now Nadia, dressed like Xenia, tossed the box she'd carried into Nicholas's face while Hella cursed and jammed her hand in her bag, grasping for a weapon.

My gun came up, but before I could settle on a target, Nadia's hands, holding her 'little sisters', that were hidden beneath the box, slashed Nicolas across his arm with her dagger and punched Hella straight in the face with her knuckleduster. Nicholas roared and spun and shoved a screeching Hella into me, who grabbed me and pulled me down as she coughed out her own blood and broken teeth.

"Come on," Nadia cried out.

I wrenched myself free of Hella and raced through the long saloon, past the servants who'd been knocked down in Nicholas and Nadia's wake. Once out on the open deck, I looked to see Nadia at the railing, and when I got to her, I looked down and saw Nicholas Ravenwood clinging to a vessel that protruded out of the dark waters. As the realization hit that I was looking at the half submerged *Fenian Ram*, flashes of muffled gunfire erupted from below.

I grabbed Nadia and pulled her down to the deck as bullets knocked against the hull of the *Moana*.

"He's getting away." She got up and ran.

"Gangway!" William Leeds, in his seagoing Captain's uniform, raced across the deck, holding a Thompson submachinegun. He leaned over the bulwark and let a thunderous stream of fire loose toward the water.

I raised my head up enough to see some of the shots strike sparks off the metal of the little submarine. Eventually, Leeds' toy ran dry, leaving me half blinded from the flashes and deafened from the roar. But in the sliver of moonlight that danced on the river, I could see the dark and sinister submarine slip under the surface.

Just then, Nadia came running out of the saloon, moving as fast as she could to the gunwale, where she hurled something that spun over the water and fell with a splash.

"What was that?"

"Father's briefcase."

"Why did you toss it overboard?"

"It was a bit heavy for paperwork."

I was about to ask what she meant, when a deep-throated boom burst beneath the water, and the ship rocked as a geyser erupted from the river, culminating in a brief rain shower on the deck.

Nadia just stared at me. "Looks like I know my father fairly well, after all."

Chapter Eighty:

I t was Thursday evening, two nights since the wild run-in with Nicholas Ravenwood, and Nadia was playing hostess back at the Palm Gardens of the Waldorf Astoria for her two favorite detectives, McDonough and Broderick. Looking back, it was a miracle things didn't go completely to hell. Nadia's scheme that night was to let Nicholas make his move, then be in a position to spoil his plan, whatever that turned out to be. She'd figured she could hide in the background dressed like Xenia, especially as her father hadn't laid eyes on her in years. But Nicholas saw through the ploy.

After he made his escape, we'd gone after him, of course. Bill Leeds lent us not only a motorboat but his Thompson submachinegun, as well. In my mind's eye, I can still see Nadia as we raced across the water under the moon, dressed in her shimmering gown with her ebony locks flying, looking like a modern-day Pirate Queen. But when we arrived at the boathouse, all we found was the ugly torpedo-shaped miniature submarine that displayed some blood stains within its cramped, malodorous interior.

As we drove home early that morning, Nadia said, "I see it all now. Father was playing two games at once, arranged to make it look like the Communist leaders of Russia had blown up a ship and assassinated the last Royal Russian Heir to the Throne, and at the same time killed a prominent American millionaire, while providing proof to the American authorities that the Russians had an armed group of insurrectionists here in New York, ready to rise up against the government after taking credit for the assassination, never mind the poor dupes were fooled into thinking they were actually secret patriots."

"And he expected this to accomplish what, exactly?"

"Start a war with Russia, of course, fueled by American outrage. You told me he almost beat the Bolsheviks before, looks like he's still trying."

I could only shake my head at the absolute ruthlessness of Ravenwood's conspiracy. "What was the other game?"

"Walk away with one of the world's premier treasures, the Faberge *Angel and Chariot*. His supposed payment for providing an army for the Imperial Russian cause."

I remembered my glimpse of the treasure, a delicate, glistening silver and golden *object d'art*, glittering with diamonds and sapphires. It'd been removed from its lacquered container before Nadia threw the empty box at her father. The treasure was again safely in the care of the Grand Duchess Anastasia Romanov as she returned to exile in Germany.

"Not to mention..." Nadia added, "that if war erupted with Russia, then those armaments stocks held by the so called *Fenris Group* would skyrocket in value."

"But why the little submarine?"

"Simple. To fake his own death. He'd be seen being ferried out to the yacht, then he secretly escapes before the explosive charge in his briefcase sinks the ship."

The day after was one glorious time of doing as much of nothing as I could manage. The next night, I roused myself to dress for our dinner with the detectives. For once, they were both in good, high humor.

McDonough was first to congratulate himself. "I suppose it's no surprise to you that we found a match for the fingerprint on May Scott's murder weapon."

Nadia, radiant in a gown of black silk and beaded gold *fleur de lis* designs, batted her dark eyes. "Do tell?"

"That little blonde woman you had delivered to the police station. She still can't talk much on account of her mouth being a bit busted up, but her fingerprints not only matched the one on the sword cane, but also that shiny revolver that Henry Bowen was supposed to have killed himself with."

"Poor May," Nadia said. "She followed Richard that night, no doubt distraught over their argument, stumbled into the conspirators, and got murdered for her compassion. As for Henry, I think he discovered the plan to sink a yacht, and it was too much like what happened to his own father and step-mother on the Lusitania. He was about to tell Johnny Broderick when Hella caught him and staged his supposed suicide."

Johnny Broderick shook his head. "Using a submarine. I wonder if the bootleggers are going to try something like that."

"I couldn't really see out there in the dark," I said. "But I'd be willing to bet it was that guy Hella once called Captain who was driving the thing. Any bets he piloted German U Boats during the War?"

"No takers here," Broderick said. "I'm just glad my Brooklyn raid on the gun cache went off without a hitch. When we sprung on the saps down there in the tunnel, they all just gave up, except for one character who answers to the name of Baker, who we found upstairs, pumping a dynamite detonator. Turns out that pile of guns was sitting on enough explosives to blow us all to hell. Thank God it didn't go off."

Nadia slipped me a sly, sidelong look. "How fortunate. I believe that was the ultimate plan, with the deaths of the Companions of Tyr, its *dead men tell no tales* plot, and adding the deaths of all the police officers, the tragedy and outrage intensifies, forcing our country into a war."

"You may have something there, Miss Ravenwood. Up in the office of the garage, we found fliers in neat little boxes, all proclaiming this was the start of the *Glorious Revolution*. But all the guys we rounded up kept squawking about how they're not Reds."

"So what's going to happen to them?" I asked.

"Probably nothing. In fact, they're all tripping over each other to tell us the whole scoop behind the Companions, and let me tell you, they're all angry as hell now that it was a con job. They keep pointing to one guy we caught, saying he was the ringleader."

"Was this a man with a white eye patch?"

Detective Broderick grinned. "He was. Before we put the cuffs on him, he took the eye patch off and said, 'I guess I won't be needing this anymore'."

"He had Henry duped," Nadia said. "He was playing the part of the snitch who tips off the police while Richard was destined to look like the dope-addicted, inept ringleader. Poor Mary Bowen lost one brother, but at least we were able to reunite her with Richard, who has promised to sober up and be the head of the family now. With Mary at his side, the Bowen legacy will eventually heal and survive."

I looked to McDonough. "What's happening with our Mr. Chang?"

The detective looked smug. "He's singing quite the opera. Seems he doesn't want out of jail now, so he's confessed to smuggling opium into the country. His problem is that the opium he sold was supposed to buy guns for his people in China, only he gave them to the

Companions of Tyr instead. His people back home won't be happy with him, to say the least, and his life isn't worth a pair of chopsticks. He's desperate to make some kind of deal."

Nadia glanced around the table. "I'm surprised Agent Reynolds isn't here tonight?"

Broderick shrugged. "He was sore that I didn't wait to include him on the raid. I got the impression that his boss back in Washington wanted to get some good newsprint of this. But Mayor Walker and DA Banton sent word down the line to keep a lid on all this. No sense starting another Red Scare."

"Mr. Leeds has agreed to keep quiet, as well," Nadia said. "For his wife's sake. He can keep his crew in line with paying bonus money for their silence."

I knew that William Leeds gave Nadia a very generous monetary honorarium for services rendered on behalf of his wife, the Princess. "But Nicholas Ravenwood gets away with it?"

Detective Broderick nodded. "For now, maybe, however, you know what they say...every dog has his day."

I was sure that didn't apply to Nicholas Ravenwood.

At the conclusion of our meal, Nadia handed out her card to the detectives from her recently recovered Chinese dragon-embossed silver case. "To the next time we work together, Gentlemen."

"May it be never and a day," Detective McDonough said, but with a smile.

I doubted he'd get his wish. For now, I was quite proud to escort Miss Ravenwood to the hotel entrance where we'd get aboard her Duesenberg, in which she would terrorize me all the way back to the Brownstone.

Like I said, it's my job.

Michael Siverling

MICHAEL SIVERLING

Michael Siverling, a detective in real life, brings his experience and expertise to the pages of his many novels, including The Sterling Inheritance (winner of the 2002 Best Private Eye Novel Contest) and The Sorcerer's Circle, both published by St. Martin's Press, plus The Secret War of the Worlds published by Belanger Books, and The Blood of Alexander published by Tor/Forge under the penname Tom Wilde.

Michael Siverling

http://www.twbpress.com

**Science Fiction – Horror – Supernatural – Thriller –
Romance – and More**